JUST THE TICKET

BY

D. S. TERRY

D. S. Terry

14/3/08

Printed by Antony Rowe Ltd, Chippenham, Wiltshire

This book is dedicated to Debbie, Emily and Amy

.......and to anyone who has ever influenced,

encouraged,

annoyed,

and loved me.

If you recognise any of these traits in the book,
it could be you.

* * * * * * * *

Thanks to: Libby for her laptop and for believing in me. To Jack, my inspiration. Mum & Dad for their love. To Debbie who never doubted me. But mainly to Simon Sizer without whose technical know-how, drive and conviction we would never have got this far and thanks to Carol, you can have your husband back now! Also thanks to Stuart Redgewell for his cover design and patience.

Biggest thanks to anyone reading this, because if you've got this far, you've bought the book.

One

Beauty walks a razors edge,
Someday I'll make it mine,
If I could only turn back the time,
To when God in her was born.

(Shelter from the Storm, ©1974, Ram's Horn Music)

Bob Dylan wrote *Beauty walks a razors edge, someday I'll make it mine.* I took this to mean that what one man thinks is beautiful, another might think of as Anne Widdecombe like. That's why I'm standing spellbound by this beautiful red-haired woman in my local shop. While the other people in the shop carry on, oblivious to my infatuation. This includes, the dad to my left, trying to convince his thirteen-year-old that she can't rent *The Texas Chain Saw Massacre*, the three noisy kids choosing sweets and the girl behind the counter, with so many body piercings that her scrap value must be enormous.

The mass of red hair is in front of me in the queue. She first caught my eye as I was trying to find the November issue of *Fighting Fit at Forty*. I'd heard a sudden screech of brakes outside the window. I looked and saw this vision of long red tousled hair, caught by the autumn wind as she got out of her low sports car.

She hands the girl behind the counter her lottery numbers and the girl moves to the machine, her various body piercings clanking as she walks. The machine prints the lottery ticket for the mid-week draw, she turns and hands it to the mass of red hair. As she turns I realise just how close I'm standing, and as I try to move out of the way we do that awkward thing where I move one way, she moves the same way, then I move back and she moves back.

Before she stops and smiles, she's seen the logo on my body warmer "SCREW-IT". I try to cover it with one hand while opening the door with the other. I rejoin the queue but my whole attention is still focused on her, I have no recollection of paying or of the girl now clutching her copy of *The Texas Chain Saw Massacre*.

Just as I was thinking she was about to disappear out of my life forever, good fortune struck, she had dropped her handbag, spilling the contents all over the pavement. As she was crouched down stuffing things back in, her lottery ticket was caught by the wind, just like the start of *Forest Gump*, you know the bit where the feather floats on and on forever. It seemed to have taken on a life of its own, as she gets closer, it flips over and races off again.

I'm outside now and I've joined the chase. I try to intercept it. As it settles on the ground between us, we both bend down together. Suddenly, for a split second I'm looking down the front of her blouse, her top couple of buttons, have come undone. She looks up at me, and with one hand she pulls her blouse together, it's a small movement, but probably one of the sexiest things I've ever seen. The wind catches the ticket and the moment has gone, we're off chasing the ticket again. I dive to the ground, just before her and grab the ticket in triumph. As I come up, CRACK, we clash heads.

"Oh my God, are you all right?"

"Yes, fine, fine," her voice sounding flustered, as she kneels on the ground. To my horror a small trickle of blood runs down her forehead.

"Err...... Do you know you're bleeding?" I say hesitantly.

At this she touches her head, and looks at the blood on the tips of her fingers. I could see she was turning pale. Pointing over my shoulder to my flat. I say,

"I only live over there, would you like to come up and get cleaned up."

"No, no I'll be fine," she says, as I helped her to her feet. She takes a step towards her car, wobbles and grabs my arm again to steady herself.

"I think you may be right," she said, her voice faltering.

I lead her the short distance to my new flat next to the shop situated above the warehouse where I work. I tell her my name – Nathan, she tells me hers – Hazel.

My heart is pounding, I don't know why, I'm just helping a perfect stranger, (emphasis on the perfect). Doing my good Samaritan bit. A feeling tells me this is the start of something, probably a law suit. It's all going very well, I don't think! I could have used a selection of chat lines from an article in *Fighting Fit at Forty*. -

"Do you come here often?"

"How do you like your eggs in the morning?"

"Heaven must be missing an angel."

But that wouldn't be Nathan Peterson's way, I'm sure all these would have failed miserably, but not as bad as scarring her for life.

Inside, I put the kettle on for the all-curing cup of tea. We sit opposite each other waiting for it to boil. By now she has found a tissue and cleaned the blood from her forehead, it has stopped bleeding and it doesn't look as bad as I first thought. Well nothing a good plastic surgeon can't fix! The kettle clicked. I moved to the kitchen area, Hazel has become aware that three walls of the flat are covered, floor to ceiling, with shelves of LPs. On the floor at the bottom of each shelf are large boxes of singles.

My collection consists mainly of early blues, 60's motown, The Stones, The Who, Ska, seventies Punk rock, The Jam, The Police and of course Bob Dylan, (much of which, I inherited from my Dad, including many rare bootlegs).

Hazel stands up and moves towards the nearest shelf, and is running an index finger along the spines of the sleeves, from left to right. I'm nervous like a mother waiting for her child to be picked for the school team. She hates my music taste, she has already finished the first, and is half way along the lower shelf, then suddenly she stops. She pulls out Bob Dylans' *Blood on the Tracks*, looks at the back, and nods, like acknowledging an old friend. I'm visibly relieved. Hazel moves on to the next rack, my blues selection, again she selects another LP, studying the sleeve, a smile of recognition on her face. She is totally engrossed, giving me the opportunity to take a closer look at her.

Her most striking feature is her flame red, tousled hair; every now and again a strand would drop in front of her eyes and she would curl it behind her ear with one finger. She is wearing a white silk blouse, with red spots down the front, no wait that's not spots that's blood!

I come in with the tea, I only possess three mugs, I've selected my best two, I have my football mug, and she has the Simpsons mug. I thought using my novelty mug, shaped like a large breast would have been a bad idea. My mum gave it to me after a pub outing to Bournemouth a couple of years ago.

"Sugar?"

"No thank you," she replies dragging herself away from my collection and sitting down again.

"That's quite a collection," Hazel says while sipping her tea and turning her head to nod at the shelves.

"Yes, it s a bit of an obsession of mine."

As soon as I said this, I think Oh! shit – why did I use the word *obsession*, she'll think, obsessive personality, probable stalker, I can read the headlines now:-

GOOD SAMARITAN, OBSESSIVE DYLAN FAN,
SUBJECTS ME TO FIVE YEARS OF STALKING HELL!

But luckily she ignores it and goes on sipping her tea.

"Have you lived here long?" Hazel inquires.

"No, we've only been here a few weeks."

"We?" Hazel says looking round for any signs of a womens touch.

"Ah... No. When I say WE.... I mean me and my record collection."

I didn't, the *WE* was really my six-year-old son, Bob and me. I wasn't going to mention him just yet. I don't know why, perhaps I was hoping this might be leading somewhere, and saying, 'I'm a forty-year old single parent' may have led to her knocking me down on the way out. It's that whole surrogate mother thing, the thought of having to look after someone else's kid. This lady looked like a smart business women with no wedding ring.

How did I end up, looking after my six-year-old son alone ?

Bob (my son); short for, Bob Dylan Peterson, (how cruel, I hear you say,) but hold on, my dad named me, after Nat King Cole (Nathan King-Cole Peterson), he was a big fan, and it hasn't caused me too many problems. He also became a big Bob Dylan fan, up until he went electric, Dylan - not my Dad, in fact he was at the infamous Manchester Free Trade Hall concert in 1966. It took him two years to accept the shift to electric; he really thought the electric guitar was a passing trend. It wasn't until I started showing an interest in playing guitar that he encouraged me to listen to his Bob Dylan albums again. I remember bugging him to get the *John Wesley Harding* LP. My dad relented and his rift with Dylan was healed. I met Bob's mum, Sasha, at the 1994 WOMAD festival in Reading. We had a mad weekend, and at the end we never went home. I don't mean we lived in a tent by the Thames, I mean she came home with me. Soon after Sasha found out she was pregnant. She was ten years younger than I was, and she wasn't about to settle down or change her wild ways. She would often disappear for days on end, to a concert or festival somewhere. But her wild life style did catch up with her.

Bob was born premature, and was very ill, in hospital.

At the same time my Dad was diagnosed with terminal cancer, and was in the same hospital, losing his fight for life, while Bob was trying to win his. Sasha stayed for the first couple of weeks; she then went missing for about four days, she came back looking hung over, and told me she was leaving.

I must admit it was a relief, one less person to worry about, what with Bob ill, my Dad dying, and trying to keep Mum together. I gave up work for a while and lived in the hospital, only going home to sleep. I was emotionally drained at the end of the day. When Bob was four weeks old, he had a turn for the worse. I had a phone call at 2 am, saying that I had better come in. It was something to do with his breathing. There were three nurses and two doctors dwarfing this tiny bundle, not much bigger than a bag of sugar.

The same night my Mum came to say Dad wasn't going to make it through the night. I didn't know what to do, stay with my son, who I had known for such a short time, or go and say goodbye to my Dad who I had known all my life. My Dad, who had shaped, guided and influenced me so much.

Mum said he would want me to stay with Bob. So I stayed through the longest night of my life praying and fighting for Bob. Around dawn the doctor told me Bob's condition had stabilised. My Dad had his last lucid moment telling Mum someone had to die, so Bob could live, just before the morphine kicked back in and he slipped away.

This helped Mum cope. She had the idea that the only reason Bob was ill, was because someone didn't die when they were called, selfishly hanging onto life, so Bob had to wait for another slot, my Dad had given him his slot. Sure enough, from that night on, Bob's condition improved. Three weeks later he was allowed home. With Sasha gone, we both moved into Mums. We helped each other through those first difficult months.

Hazel finished her tea, and started to stand up,

"Can I use your bathroom?"

"Yes of course," I say pointing at the door, while desperately trying to remember what sort of state I had left it in that morning. Hazel looks round the bathroom for signs of a womens touch, ugh! definitely none at all as she looked at the grime in the bath and the stack of magazines positioned strategically by the toilet. Hazel, even opened the bathroom cabinet looking for tampax boxes. Was she mad. Hazel couldn't understand why she should be checking, why was she hoping this man should be available. There was something strangely attractive about this man, his long blond hair, the fact he was tall, but in that ungainly awkward way making him kind of sensitive. But this was crazy, she was in a happy relationship, wasn't she? She then caught sight of a large bottle of Rugrats bubble bath, funny she thought. Hazel fills the sink and washes her face; with her eyes closed she reaches for the towel patting her face dry before she sees the stains on it. This is madness, get out of here now. Hazel goes back into the lounge,

"I ought to be going now, I'm feeling better." Hazel gathers her things and moves to the door. I make a desperate attempt to stop her leaving by saying,

"Have you got far to go?"

"No, just Thames Wharf, do you know it?"

"Very nice!" I say.

I remember delivering there when they were being built. I work for a firm delivering screws, nails and fixings, hence the "SCREW-IT" logo on my body warmer. Thames Wharf are twelve rather exclusive riverside apartments. With balconies facing the river, at the back is a large gravelled drive with a block of garages and two tennis courts. I seem to remember some talk of a swimming pool in the basement. Seriously expensive property.

Hazel takes hold of the lock. She is going to leave, I need to say something, she could only say no, what's the worse that could happen, apart from total humiliation.

"I can give you my number if you like?" there is a long and painful pause. Hazel then turns as if she's just made a big decision.

"I'll tell you what, take me out for a drink tomorrow night."

"Err... Yes" I say, stunned. She took this hesitation that I was mentally going through my packed social diary to see if I were free.

"... If you're not busy?"

"No, no" I jump in before she's finished, losing my cool and coming across as too keen now!

"That'll be great," I say. A small hint of a smile flashes across her face. As she stands in the open doorway the wind is blowing her red hair around. We arrange to meet at the Red Lion at 8 o'clock. I tell her to be careful on the stairs, and she's gone. I close the door, lean against it, and exhale loudly through my teeth.

"YES....YES....YESSS," I'm shouting.

I run across the room, jump the coffee table in one leap, I pick up her mug, and hold it aloft with both hands, like it's the F A Cup, while making the noise of a roaring crowd. I see the lottery ticket on the work surface by the kettle. I pick it up kissing it before placing it on the fridge with a letter magnet. I need a record -a loud one- I'm going on my first date in years, type of record. The Who - *Live at Leeds*. The reassuring crackles and hisses you can only get from a record comes through the speakers. Then the first few bars of *My Generation* blast out. I'm playing the drums, arms flying everywhere imitating Keith Moon. I switch to air guitar; I do a scissors kick off the coffee table and ram my imaginary guitar into the fridge.

It's safe to say I'm quite pleased with myself.

Two

Close your eyes, close the door,
you don't have to worry any more
I'll be your baby tonight

(I'll Be Your Baby Tonight,© 1968, renewed 1996 Dwarf Music)

It's 6:37 only 83 minutes to go *roughly* that's if I choose to be on time. Let me see, that would be cool, let her wait five minutes, enough time for her to think I'm busy, I do this all the time and I've just remembered our date tonight.

WHAT ROT!

1. I've thought of nothing else for twenty-four hours.

2. Of course I'll be there on time, in fact I plan to be there fifteen minutes early.

3. I'm not out every night and I've only been out with 3 people, in the six years since Bob was born.

I'm sitting in my flat, I've only been here a couple of weeks, I moved out of mums, mainly because of the size of my ever-growing record collection. Mum looks after Bob in the week, it's just easier with me starting work at 8.00, and he's good company for mum. I pop in most evenings for tea, and Bob stays with me at the weekend. I decide to put a record on while I get ready. I have a particular LP in mind, one that always gets me in a good mood. I know roughly where it should be, but I've already been looking for some time. Finally I find it - *London 0 Hull 4* by The Housemartins. I carefully remove the disc from the inside cover, holding it at the edges while gently placing it on the turntable. I lower the stylus onto the edge of the record. I take great care of my records, I consider each one to be an old friend. I step back and press my remote control, the red volume light flashes as I turn the sound up.

I'm standing with nothing on but a pair of baggy pants. God I wish I had some new knickers. What am I thinking of, she probably won't even turn up, and if she does, I reckon she'll be looking at her watch, and after half an hour make her excuses, like having to wash her hair.

No, my baggy pants will definitely not be on view. I select some jeans and a polo shirt; I stand in front of the bathroom mirror. I try the shirt tucked in, and then out, then I tuck it in again, but finally decide it did look better out.

Side one of the LP finishes at 7.03 p.m. I have this habit of playing only one side of an album, before moving onto the next. I select Bob Dylan- *Live at Budokan*, side four.

I use Bob Dylan in much the same way as some people use any self-help programme. I can pick any of his records to change or fit any mood that I happen to be in, happy, sad, excited, depressed, in love, out of love, lonely, bereaved or going on your first date for months with a beautiful red head!

I make myself a cup of coffee, I'm reading the sleeve, as Dylan fights to be heard above his backing singers. LPs give you something substantial to hold. You can cuddle up to a record cover, fall asleep with it. You can't do this with a CD, often the writing is so small and it's too small and sharp to cuddle.

You can make love while one side of an LP is playing, twenty minutes is all the time you need to do everything. Put on a CD with bonus tracks and hidden extra tracks and you could still be at it over an hour later! No good unless you're Sting, with his traumatic sex, or whatever it's called!

To me Singles are like first kisses, LPs are for making love, CDs for long term relationships and marriage.

As the applause fades on *The Times They Are A-changin*, the last track, I'm out the door, it's 7.39.

I arrive at the Red Lion nine minutes later. As I enter the bar there are only six people scattered between the main bar and snug. A couple deep in conversation, two suited men at the bar, mobile phones close at hand, one old boy reading the paper and a woman in the snug on her own, who picks up a book the minute I look at her. She's obviously waiting for someone and uses the book as a defence mechanism to ward off any unwanted attention.

The Red Lion isn't my local, it's a bit posh for me, but I didn't want to say this to Hazel. I order a pint of lager and sit by the door. I think I look too keen here, so I move round the corner to the snug. Now I can't see the door, that's no good, now she'll come in, won't be able to see me and assume I've stood her up. I move again, the woman looks nervously over the top of her book as I walk past her and sit down at the table behind her. I relax, I can see the door from here.

I check my watch, it's 8.07, now she's late. Then the door opens, it's her, my relief is overpowering, I stand up and wave both arms in the air. Playing it cool as usual.

* * * * * * * *

Hazel pulled into the car park of the Red Lion at 8:05. Clive had gone off to rugby training as he did every Wednesday. He manages the local team, which keeps him busy, but also means Hazel has to go to boring club dinners.

She told him she was going out with Joan, her best friend from work. Hazel had come out of a long relationship before meeting Clive. She and John were childhood sweethearts. They had met at school. It was one of those relationship where the parents became great friends, even to the point of going on holiday together. He was a frustrated musician with very bad timing. Just as he formed a Punk band the New Romantics took off. As he chased his latest dream she would end up footing the bill, new amps, guitars and stage outfits. The last thing he did was to apply to be on *Stars in their eyes* .... It was then she knew it was time to go. She had never left before, not wanting to upset her parents, which was ridiculous as she was in her thirties now.

Joan had told her of a job going at Clive's firm. It had meant moving from London, but it gave her the chance of a clean break. Clive was just going through a difficult divorce himself, with his two grown up sons having just left home, suddenly he and his wife had nothing left to talk about. They sold their large country home, split the money and split up. Hazel started going out with Clive from day one. They went to lunch after her first interview, it was so nice to be wined and dined without having to pick up the bill. She started working for Clive and moved into his riverside flat a few weeks later. Clive helped to pay off a lot of her debts. The last thing she did for John was to pay for the Gary Glitter costume for his audition for *Stars in their eyes* (just as Mr. Glitter was taking his computer in for repair) bad timing again.

Her biggest concern was that she was thirty-five, and her biological clock was ticking. Sometimes so loud it would keep her awake in the small hours. John had shown no interest in wanting children, another thing which had caused friction. She had mentioned it a few times to Clive, but he said there was no rush. She knew Clive had had his children and may not want to start again, but she was happy for now, and hoped in time he would change his mind.

So why was she here? I don't know there's something about him. Something she couldn't put her finger on – a kind of inner peace – and he does have an incredible record collection.

She opens the car door, it's pouring with rain, she runs to the door of the pub, bursts in, shaking raindrops from her long red hair. Everyone in the pub turns to look at her (well all six people that is). She searches the pub before becoming aware of a crazy man waving both his arms at her.

Oh! God it's him.

* * * * * * * *

She looks lovelier than I remember. I've already drunk my pint because I'm so nervous. I stand up to greet her and ask her what she would like to drink, she has a gin and tonic, I go to the bar and order the drinks. Hazel removes her coat shaking rain from it, and placing it on the back of her chair. We sit down, there's a short silence. I panic, because I can't think of anything to say. So I ask her what she does for a living. I hate this question but it breaks the ice. She says she works as a trouble-shooter for a computer firm. I ask her how her head is, she says it's fine.

She asks me about my records and music, I tell her that I play guitar. Playing live every Sunday night at a local pub. Now she's got me onto my favourite subject, I feel I'm doing all the talking, but she seems genuinely interested in what I have to say. I've relaxed a bit more now, and the conversation flows more easily. She asks me about my job. I used to have a high-powered sales job. But after having Bob I had to re-evaluate my life, scale down work to be home to look after him. Anyway suddenly it just didn't seem important, all those sales figures, targets and only being as good as your last sale week. I tell her what I do now. My day starts at eight o'clock, I load up, by nine I'm on the road. I have my set route, stick on my cassettes, by four I'm done, back to Mums to have tea with. No late nights or away trips and no stress. I keep my brain active with my music, planning my gigs and reading.

Van Morrison has a brilliant track, *Window Cleaning*. In the song he describes an idyllic day at work but you don't know what he does till right near the end of the song. He builds up this picture of the sun shining, going to have breakfast at a cafe, and going home for lunch playing records. Then in the end it turns out he's a window cleaner. That kind of sums up my view of work now. OK it's an idealistic view, when it's dark and pissing down with rain in the middle of January it loses some of its gloss.

We talk about our past relationships, she talks of John; what went wrong and the Gary Glitter incident, I can't stop laughing when she tells me this. Its all very natural like we have known each other for years. We talk about Clive. Her life, nice house, car, career and foreign holidays. I talk about Sasha briefly, but omit to mention Bob which is a bit like mentioning McCartney without Lennon when talking of the Beatles! I think, what can I offer her, a one bedroom flat, a massive record collection. Still it's been a nice evening if it ends now – so be it.

So at the end of the evening, I'm surprised when she asks if she can see me again. We arranged to meet the same time next week. When we part there was an embarrassing moment when I went to shake hands, she takes my hand, laughs, pulls me close and gives me a gentle peck on the cheek. Hazel disappears through the pub door into the dark rainy night. I sit and ponder for a while. This Hazel must be married to her career, she must be one of these new women who don't want children, who spend all the time telling people how having children is a tie, a stereo-typical move by society.

But Bob is such a big part of my life how can I keep it secret?

Best not get carried away; let's just have a bit of fun, I can keep this separate from my real life. I stand up to leave, the pub has filled up considerably but I was so engrossed with Hazel I hadn't noticed. The lady with the book catches my eye, she is still alone – must have been stood up. She closes her book and smiles at me encouragingly. I walk past and leave.

Three

May you grow up to be righteous,
May you grow up to be true,
May you always know the truth
And see the light surrounding you.
May you always be courageous,
Stand upright and be strong,
May you stay forever young

(Forever Young, © 1973, Ram's Horn Music)

Dads gone out, he never goes out in the week, unless it's for football. He met me from school but didn't stay for tea at Nan's like he normally does, there's something going on.

So I'm sitting at the kitchen table doing colouring in. If I do a good enough picture it will go on the fridge. I have to do some pictures for Dad's small fridge at his new flat. Nan has a tall fridge/freezer so I stand a better chance of getting it put up here. I know when I go to bed Nan must take some of my old pictures away, I know 'cause I've done billions of pictures in the past and you wouldn't be able to get in the kitchen by now!

Also on Nan's fridge are photos of me when I was born. I'm very small 'cause I was born too soon. My Dad says he would have liked to have been born sooner, by about ten years then he would have been a teenager growing up in the sixties.

Nan has just taken my picture to show Grampa: he lives on the telly. Not in the way the Rugrats or Pokemons live on the telly. His photo is on the telly, Nan talks to it all the time. He went to be an angel just after I was born, I don't remember meeting him but Nan says I passed him once but I don't know what she means.

"Here Bill take a look at this one," she says holding up my picture for him to see.

"I'll put it next to the one with all the macaroni stuck on it," the one with macaroni stuck on it that my teacher, Miss Heatherington calls a collage, college or something like that. Nan calls it a pain in the neck, because every time she brushes past it, bits fall off. I go back to start a new picture, I draw my Dad in his van he's waving out the window. Nan's sitting next to him and I'm sat in the middle. I haven't ever seen my mum, but she would have to sit in the back with all the screws so it's just as well.

"Bob bath time," Nan says, as she ruffles my hair. I hate this, most of the time you forget you've got hair, until someone touches it. Now it tickles and it's all in my eyes.

I have the same floppy blond hair as Dad, it's a bit long really.

"I haven't finished my picture yet," I say to Nan, who comes and looks, over my shoulder.

"Is that Dad's new girlfriend in his van?"

"No, that's you!" I say turning to face Nan.

"Has Dad got a new girlfriend then?"

"Well I know he's out with a lady tonight"
So that's why Dad's gone out.

"Well you can ask him all about it on Friday. You have a day off, a Baker Day, so you're helping him in the van all day." Nan says leading me up the stairs for my bath. So I've got a day off, a Baker Day is like a school day for teachers. I'll be with Dad, he gives me the map and I have to show him the way, but I think he knows really. Great I can't wait.

* * * * * * * *

"Humph......... !" Bob says as he shrugs, folding his arms in an exaggerated movement. I've just made a disparaging comment about a large-breasted lady in a tight white top. She has just crossed the road in front of the van. I love these days with Bob, he's navigating with my large Great Britain map book, which is almost as big as he is. At the moment he's tracing the A9 just north of Inverness with his little index finger. Which is strange as we are just going through Wallingford, south of Oxford!

I push in a cassette, '*Come gather round people, wherever you roam, and admit that the waters, around you have grown.*' Dylan sings, during the song there's a mouth organ solo. Bob pretends to play, holding his hands up to his mouth, all skinny arms and elbows, flapping up and down, looking at me with smiling eyes. After a while Bob gets bored with this. He's looking out the window and says nothing for a few miles, but I know he's thinking. I can almost hear him.

"Dad....." Here it comes, I thought something was bothering him.

"Do you think I could have a new mum one day?"

I'm a bit thrown by this, Bob rarely comments on the fact he has never seen his mum. It came up when he started school. I just said because he was very ill when he was born, this made his mum sad, so she had to go away on holiday for a long time. This he accepted and has hardly mentioned it since..... until now!

"How do we go about getting a new mum?" I say, turning the volume control down while looking at Bob.

"Kelly Johnson just got one." I remember something about Kelly Johnson's mum, she ran off with a cable repairman. Mr Johnson should have picked up on the fact that they did have every new cable channel going. As it turned out, just three weeks later Mr Johnson moved his secretary in to the marital home (all a bit convenient). She is twenty years younger than the old Mrs Johnson, very good looking, I recall from the last school fete.

" It would have to be someone I like too." I said.

Bob thinks,

"How about the women from the gardening show, the one who makes all the ponds, you know, wears the big T-shirts." I laugh at this.

"She wouldn't like it, I don't have a garden." A long pause follows, I'm just about to turn the volume up and return to my cassette when he shouts.

"Ahah!" Bob says putting his hand up to make a point,

"Tim's mum," Bob says looking very pleased with himself.

I remember collecting him from Tim's last week, Bob had been invited to tea. She's a twenty-two year old single mum.

"She may be a bit young for me." I say pouring water on Bob's master plan.

"You could be right, 'cause you're really old Dad," says Bob having second thoughts.

"She also shouted BUGGER! What does that mean?" says Bob looking up at me with big innocent eyes.

"Why did she say it?"

"She had dropped my burger and had to give me one from Tim's plate," said Bob.

"Ahh! Well there you go, bugger means having to share." I say – got out of that one, what a brilliant parent I am. I drive on in relative silence except for Bob muttering under his breath,

"Bugger, share, Bugger, share." After a mile or so I pull into a petrol station. On my van the petrol cap is on the passengers side, I have to open the passenger door to release the flap. I go round and do this, I start filling up. I am aware of a blue car pulling up on the other side of the pump. Suddenly I catch a flash of red hair out of the corner of my eye. Oh! God it's her.

"Quick Bob it's the Jehovah's witness." I whisper out of the corner of my mouth. At this Bob throws himself flat on his seat, out of view. Bob knew at Nans if she shouted this, it was a signal to get down out of the way of the window. Living on a large estate we were plagued by Jehovah's witnesses knocking at the door most weekends.

Hazel has got out of the car, selected the green unleaded nozzle from the other side of the pump and is filling up less than four feet away. Bob has spread himself flat on the front seat out of view. Hazel is concentrating on the pump and hasn't seen me yet.

"Hi!" I say. Hazel looks up and smiles, she then looks sideways at the car, raising both eyebrows as some kind of signal. I look over her shoulder and can see someone else is in the car sitting in the passenger seat, it must be Clive. I nod and look down, Hazel finishes first and goes in to pay. By the time I go in she's just signing her credit card slip. I select a bottle of coke from the fridge and grab a bar of chocolate. I go up to the bored looking attendant and pay. I can sense that Hazel is still in the shop as the automatic doors remained closed. What is she playing at, Clive is sitting, facing us in her car. I turn and try to calmly make my way to the door, trying not to look in her direction.

Then something extraordinary happens, as I walk by she grabs my arm, pulls me behind the donut stand and kisses me full on the lips. As we pull apart, she places one finger on my lips, as if to stop me saying anything. Then she's through the automatic doors and gone. I'm left standing stunned. The bored attendant has perked up, and is smiling and shaking his head. As far as he knows this total stranger has just planted the sexiest kiss of my life on me!

By the time I pull myself together Hazel has driven off.
I look up at the van, oh God! There is no sign of Bob. I run to the passenger door, pulling it open, Bob nearly falls out. He's still lying flat resting his head on the door handle.

"Oh sorry son, it's all clear now. Here, I got you a coke." I hand him the bottle. I go round the drivers side and jump in. I pull out, I'm still in a daze. Bob opens his coke, it hisses, spraying all over him. He looks across at me, with an *I'm in big trouble now*, look on his face, I haven't even noticed. I open the chocolate bar, I eat three chunks one after another just staring at the road ahead. Suddenly Bob starts shouting

"BUGGER! BUGGER! BUGGER! SHARE! SHARE! SHARE!"

I'm broken from my daydream. Slowly it dawns on me what Bob is shouting about. I break off a chunk of chocolate and push it in Bobs big smiling mouth.

I laugh out loud, I love him so much it hurts deep inside. I know I've changed since I've had Bob. I know I didn't physically have Bob, but I don't know many Dads who have had to look after a child from such a young age. I'm very sensitive now, I can't see a child in any pain or distress on the telly without my bottom lip going all wobbly and tears welling up in my eyes. For instance I can't watch *Casualty* any more. It always starts with a small child playing. I say oh! he looks just like Bob, how sweet, before it dawns on me this boy is about to meet a terrible fate – why else would he be in the program. Will he be sucked up by an out of control road sweeper or trampled by a runaway circus elephant. The unlucky child is then rushed to hospital. The doctors and nurses will start shouting lots of number and letters. Quick give him a C V with M C C. he's 60 over 10! At this point I've probably switched over, totally distraught and in floods of tears.

I look over at Bob, he has Coke all over his jeans, and chocolate dribbling down his chin. His blond hair flopping down over his eyes, I think he's never looked more beautiful. I've made up my mind. I'm going to tell Hazel all about Bob the very next time I see her. I lean over and ruffle Bob's hair – I know he loves it when I do that.

Four

If I had wings and could fly
I know where I would go.
But right now I'll just sit here so contentedly
And watch the river flow.

(Watching the River Flow ©1971, Big Sky Music)

I open my eyes, the red numbers of the digital clock on the bedside table read 6:38. I try to brace myself, for in two minutes my alarm will go off and I have to get up. Then I bask in the fact that it's Saturday morning no work. I turn over and try to go back to sleep. I always do this, wake up just before the alarm goes off, even in the week, it's an annoying habit. I have a very good mental clock. I normally lie with my finger poised over the alarm-off button trying to catch it just before it bursts into life with its ear splitting beep, beep. A bit like James Bond disabling the nuclear bomb that's counting down and thus saving the world from total devastation.

My mind has woken up and thoughts have started racing through it. Bob is always the first thought to come into my head. But over the last few days, Hazel has been competing to be first .

After yesterday I have lots more questions. I won't have any chance of getting the answers for a few days. To be exact, 4½ days; 108 hours, I start to work out the number of minutes, but I give up. I'm wide awake now. I decide to read, I reach down the side of the bed for the book I'm currently reading; B.B.Kings' autobiography. I grope around on the floor and the first thing I touch is a cereal bowl. It contains a spoon welded to it by dried Weetabix. I lift it up by the spoon – I've discovered a new super glue. The next thing I find is my latest copy of *Fighting Fit at Forty*. I haven't had a chance to look at it, well a lot's been going on. I look at the front cover, it has a picture of an unnaturally muscled man walking out of the sea. Over the picture it lists the articles to be found in this months issue;

EXERCISES TO DO WHILE WAITING FOR YOUR PIZZA TO BE DELIVERED   Page 12
DIET AND HEALTHY EATING BY POP IDOL RICK WALLER   Page 20
HOW TO BE MARRIED FOR EVER BY LES DENNIS   Page 27
FIRST DATE – IS IT GOING TO LAST?   TRY OUR SPECIAL QUIZ   Page 32
TRY NEW FOOTBALL SEX, THERE'S ELEVEN POSITIONS TO CHOOSE FROM   Page 40

The first date quiz catches my eye, but I'll just have a look at this football sex thing first, purely for educational purposes you understand. I turn to page 40, there's a two page colour spread with an attractive naked couple pictured in various positions on a king size bed. Each picture has detailed descriptions of how to get into the positions.

For example, for LEFT BACK, you lie on your side with her back to you, well you get the picture, kind of spoons really.

The CENTRAL DEFENDER position, I'm pretty sure is illegal.

I image myself running up and down the side of the bed naked, doing warm up exercises. I'm waiting for the hunky man in the picture to get a groin strain or something. The linesman would then hold up one of those illuminated boards with my number on it. I could take over and jump into bed. Anyway, I would probably be left in the dug-out forever a substitute, like all those years ago with the school football team. I was always twelfth man, waiting for Simon Harris or Andy Neal to be injured, giving me a chance to play.

Most of the time I would end up having to be linesman. I hated this especially if we were at a rival school. I would have to run the line trying to avoid the kids tripping me up. Often we wouldn't have a linesmans flag and would then have to improvise. I remember one dreadful occasion when the assistant head, Mr Teagal gave me his white handkerchief to wave. I could even see his crusty bogies on it. I held it between two fingers at one corner.

Anyway the last few months has definitely been the closed season as far as sex goes. I think it's time to call full time on the football sex, I turn to page 32. The first date quiz is set out to test your compatibility with a woman, after you've been on your first date. Each question is worth a certain number of points. At the end, you add them up to get your rating, you know the kind of thing.

First question choices;

1. Where did you go on your first date?

A. FISH AND CHIP SHOP   1pt
B. FOOTBALL MATCH   2pts
C. PUB OR WINE BAR   3pts
D. RESTAURANT   4pts
E. FLYING DOWN TO MONACO FOR THE WEEKEND IN YOUR PRIVATE JET   5pts

Damn, I knew last Wednesday was a bad day to have the plane serviced. I carry on working through the quiz until I get to the last question,

20. How did you part at the end of your date?

A. DID SHE SHAKE YOUR HAND AND SAY THIS MEETING HAS BEEN VERY PRODUCTIVE 1pt
B. GIVE YOU TWO AIR KISSES ON EACH CHEEK 2pts
C. INVITE YOU IN FOR COFFEE BEFORE REVEALING SHE HAS BEEN WEARING NOTHING UNDER HER OVERCOAT ALL NIGHT 3pts
D. DID SHE GIVE YOU A PASSIONATE KISS BEFORE SLIPPING YOU A PIECE OF PAPER WITH HER HOME AND MOBILE NUMBERS PLUS FAX, E-MAIL AND HER HOME ADDRESS 4pts
E. DID SHE TAKE YOU STRAIGHT ROUND TO MEET HER PARENTS, WHERE, ON THE TABLE ARE SEVERAL COPIES OF BRIDE AND WEDDING MAGAZINES, YOU ARRANGE TO MEET NEXT SATURDAY, 3 P.M. AT THE REGISTRY OFFICE 5pts

I add up my total score, it's 27, the top score would be between 90 and 100, the synopsis for this is:- you will be married, have 2.2 kids and own a Ford Mondeo within a year. I look down the page, anything 20 to 30, it says you are totally incompatible, in fact it says you are totally incompatible with the whole female race and should change your sexual preference or join a monastery!

Depressed and disillusioned by this I throw the magazine back on the floor and finally find my book. I read for about an hour. Around eight I get up and make some breakfast. I'm due to pick up Bob at ten and take Mum to bingo. I take a shower, get dressed and slip out down the stairs to the shop next door and get a paper. It's very cold, there's been a sharp frost.

Back in the flat I put on the local radio station. It's football today and I'd better check if a pitch inspection is planned. I'm a season ticket holder at my local club along with Bob. I won't tell you the name of my team, because half of you may have little interest in football, so it will mean nothing. The other half will just take the piss out of me. All you need to know is it's nearly Christmas and we are languishing in the lower half of the Nationwide second division. The sports announcer confirms the game is on. I put on my jacket, and head out to the van. I scrape a small hole in the ice on the windscreen about the size of a dinner plate. I start the van and drive the short distance to Mum's house. Mum lives on a council estate in the house I was born in. It's one of those town houses with open plan gardens at the front and a courtyard with a block of garages at the back. After Dad died I took advantage of the right to buy scheme and Mums full discount. So I have a small mortgage and Mum has no financial worries now.

I pull round the back. I can see Bob standing on a chair waiting for me at the window. Round his neck is the football scarf Mum had knitted for him. It goes round his neck about three times and still drags on the floor. I come in, Mum gets me a coffee, Bob returns to watching Saturday morning telly, he is sat on a large cushion in the middle of the front room. Mum and I sit on the sofa behind him. She starts to interrogate me about this new girl in my life. I tell her the minimal facts, I don't mention Hazel is in a relationship. She keeps trying to get more out of me, but I'm distracted by the attractive girl presenter on Saturday morning TV, I'm trying to watch her through Bobs head.

I tell Mum I'm due to see Hazel again on Wednesday. Mum then asks what she thinks of me having a six-year-old son. I lie, to my own mother, well it's a sort of white lie, I say she doesn't t think much about it. This is true in a way, I convince myself, as Hazel knows nothing of Bobs existence, so technically can't think much about it, can she?

My Mum is something of an enigma, although she was a full blown hippie in the sixties, she never got involved in the free love thing. The only man for her was my dad. In some ways she may strike you as quite straight -laced until you get to know her. She still smokes the odd joint, but these days mainly to ease her arthritis. Mum always thinks the best of people, never judging or going on first impressions. She still has long blond hair down to her waist, with a few streaks of silver grey like frost on a cob web, but she normally hides it in a kind of bun thing these days.

Mum gives up trying to push me for any more information about Hazel. I turn back to the telly, the girl has just made a suggestive comment about a banana being used in a cookery section. She then looks into the camera and winks. This goes right over the heads of all the kids, especially Bobs, who is now lying down with his head resting on the cushion. We finish our coffee and get ready to go out.

Bob and I drop Mum off in town. She goes off to the Saturday afternoon bingo session. This all started one Saturday almost a year to the day after dad died. The first year she went out very rarely, she suffered a lot from shock, which manifested itself when she developed a large totally bald patch in her hair. Her beautiful hair, it was so cruel, God took away the biggest influence in her life, the man she loved for as long as she could remember. To me it seemed God then decided how can we kick her a bit more now? I know I'll take away her hair, her confidence, and with that maybe her will to live. Mum had other ideas, on this Saturday I was sat in the lounge with head phones on when she came down from upstairs and stormed through the room saying,

"I've come to a decision I'm going out," I try to talk her out of it and then offer to drive her in, but she insists on catching the bus. I spend a worrying afternoon waiting for her to come back. When she does return she is wearing the most awful grey wig and then tells me she's been to bingo. She wears this wig for months, but within two or three weeks small fine hairs start to grow back. It's like God has given up, saying well you ain't ready yet. Mum said as much as she would love to be with dad, she's got plenty of living to do yet, she has to see her darling Bob is all right. She wants to be around to see him grow, see him ride a bike, be in school plays, maybe even play guitar like his grandad.

Bob and I head off to the supermarket to do the weekly shop. Bob has no inhibitions, something he gets from his gran, and will talk to anyone. Today he approaches an attractive young mum. Bob with his floppy blond hair and blue eyes stares up at her, asking her, where the frozen chips are.

"I have to help Dad with the shopping 'cause mums gone," he says in all innocence. She has a small boy with her, younger than Bob.

"It must be hard bringing up a small boy on your own, what happened?" she says in a sympathetic voice. We start talking, I think we're getting on quite well, people often assume something tragic has happened to my partner. She has started telling me her life story, how tragically her husband was killed in a car crash eighteen months ago. She then remarks it must be hard for me on my own, looking in Bob's direction. I look at Bob, he has a strange look on his face, all coy. Then I realise this is all about Bobs 'get a new mum' master plan. Then Bob totally messes up his plan by piping up with,

"Oh my mums not dead, she's on holiday in Australia."

Bob would ask from time to time where his mum was. So far, I had always told him Sasha was on holiday in Australia, the place she said she was heading.

The woman picks her son up, jams his legs into her trolley and storms off, in the direction of the frozen foods, assuming I was married and this was my usual cheap pick-up line. I think this is quite amusing. I tell Bob to push the trolley and bribe him with a french stick to chew on, this keeps him out of mischief for the rest of the trip. I finish off the shopping and return to Mums to put it away. I call into the flat, to change and drop off my shopping. This includes some essentials for the week, six cans of lager and a half bottle of whisky. As I put the lager in the fridge, one of Bobs pictures falls off, I put it back up rearranging the magnets in each corner.

"Its up-side down" Bob says pointing and jumping up and down. This was news to me, as I was completely unaware that the mass of red, blue and green paint actually had a correct way up. I get changed for football, I don't wear replica football shirts. I think they look naff on anyone who is:

a) Thirty-five or over
b) Someone who has *'eaten all the pies'* and has a large beer gut.
c) Or someone wearing, two t-shirts and a sweatshirt underneath, because it's so cold.

I wear a club sweatshirt a large coat and a club scarf. I wrap Bob's scarf three times round his neck and kneel before him to do his coat up. Then Bob and I go round to pick up Graham, the last member of our football watching clan. He is a sixty-five year old life-long fan who is partially sighted. I met him at our local pub, The Horse and Groom (referred to by the regulars as The House of Gloom). Graham had never missed a home game for fifty years even after going blind, his wife would take him. Sadly his wife had died five years ago and thus making it impossible to carry on. I got talking to him in The House of Gloom about a year ago, at the start of the following season I arranged to get a season ticket for him. As we sit in the disabled section I now get mine at a reduced rate. I commentate through-out the game into his right ear. The arrangement also was to include Graham buying all the beer but this is a little one-sided as he always gets out of buying the beer, but he's a nice old boy. He has an incredible memory, he can rattle off the full team, from the first game he ever saw way back in the 1953-54 season. I couldn't tell you the whole team from last week.

We arrive at the new stadium, it is part of a new out of town development and is situated on the site of a reclaimed rubbish tip. It is between the large local brewery and the sewage works. It's a very cold November day, the wind is blowing from the north bringing a smell of hops from the local brewery, this is far better than the smell if the wind is from the south. We arrive in good time and spend two hours in the club bar watching the early kick off on Sky TV. Around quarter to three we make our way to our seats, as we sit down our team is in the middle of the pitch doing one of those embarrassing group huddles. I lean over Graham and Bob and we have our own group huddle as we always do, its part of our pre-match tradition. I hand out packs of chewing gum, this too is part of our tradition. I always supply each of us with a pack of ten sticks of gum, this is a good guide to how tense a game has been, by counting the number of sticks chewed.

We kick off in clear blue skies.

After the game..... look I don't want to talk about it, or go into any more details than are necessary. All you need to know is we lost and I wish I was partially sighted, or at the very least a partial supporter, so I could only worry about the team on Saturdays and then forget about it the rest of the week.

On the way home we call in the King Wok fish and chip shop. When we get back to the flat I realise Bob's been very quiet and its not till I take his coat off that I realise how cold he is. I make him his favourite hot chocolate with spray cream and topped with grated chocolate. We sit on the sofa, I have fish and chips, Bob has a battered sausage. He doesn't eat the sausage but expertly picks all the batter off with his teeth with the precision of a leading surgeon.

We settle down to Saturday night telly. This is aimed at brainless people with no life - or single dads that can't go out. BBC One has a programme containing groups of friends doing party games against each other, to win an 18-30 holiday. Or on the other side, older people who tell the host about their biggest nightmares. For instance, this bloke tells the host he has an extreme fear of heights, in the next shot, the poor bloke is having to abseil down Canary Wharf in order to win a Saga holiday. All the while his apprehensive wife looks on, clutching his life insurance policy close to her chest.

Bob falls asleep around eight-thirty, I carry him gently to my bedroom and put him to bed, parting his blond locks and kissing him on the forehead. On Saturdays I sleep on a sofa bed in the lounge. I go to the storage rack of records nearest the bedroom and remove a large Bob Marley and the Wailers collectors box set from the shelf. Inside there are no records but a small tin. I place it on the table, open it up, it contains some cigarette papers, a lighter and a small amount of grass. I put on *Another Side of Bob Dylan* gently lowering the needle, the reassuring crackle and hiss you only get from vinyl comes through the speakers, before Dylans angry mid-sixties voice comes through and I roll myself a joint.

I get my guitar out of its case and start to tune it. I'm due to play my normal Sunday night gig at *The House of Gloom*. My Dad taught me to play, my earliest memories are of him playing guitar to me. Our house was always full of music, from dads old wooden music centre to strange people strumming away. Quite often I would wake up and find a band and all their equipment had moved into the lounge. Before they would move on to play their next gig.

We never owned a telly until after I was around twenty and only then because my Dad won a small portable in the Scout Christmas raffle. Having no telly left me a bit of an outcast at School. With most conversations starting; did you see? *Steptoe and Son* or *Monty Python* last night. Most kids musical taste fell into two main camps, those who bought singles, and were into Slade, Wizard and T Rex and those who were into progressive rock, Uriah Heep, Yes, Genesis and Pink Floyd. The progressive rock kids looked down on the kids who brought singles as their bands generally didn't release them. Then there was Nathan Peterson in a camp all on my own being ridiculed for singing the praises of Bob Dylan. Only Andy Davis suffered the same kind of abuse for being a fanatical Beatles and Paul McCartney Fan. The other kids were more understanding of Andy as he was a "David Watts" character – good at sports and able to take his exams and pass the lot.

I pull a silver mouth organ from the top pocket of my shirt. It's one of my most treasured possessions as my Dad left it to me. Originally it was a gift from my Mum given to him after the Isle of Wight festival in 1969. It's engraved with the words *Tonight I'll be staying here with you*. I was there at my first festival, but it was all too much for me as I was only eight, Dylan came on so late I slept through his entire set. I now take my mouth organ with me at all times, when I play it I can almost feel his breath.

I run through two or three numbers, writing them down on the back of an envelope. I carry on until I've got a set of around ten songs. I play only Bob Dylan songs to an audience of around twenty if it's a dry night and there's nothing good on the telly. I don't think Colin the landlord has ever seen my entire set, but he knows I draw a few people in on Sunday nights and his cider consumption increases. I think he just likes the fact that he can put a sign out the front saying LIVE MUSIC.

By the time I've completed my set list its gone eleven o'clock, I put my guitar away and replace my tin to the safe-keeping of the late great Bob Marley. Suddenly it feels very cold. The heating has gone off, I have two options here, to turn the heating back on, or make up my sofa bed. I choose the bed, but decide to make myself a drink. I pour a large whisky into a tall glass. I get the ice tray from the small freezer section of the fridge. As I bend the plastic tray an ice cube skids across the work surface dropping on the floor. I leave it to melt, but as the room is so cold, chances are it won't. I push out another couple of ice cubes into the whisky. I turn off the lights and jump into bed, guided by just the light from the telly. With the remote I flick through the channels, I'm forced to pause at channel five, as a girls impossibly large breasts fill the screen.

I turn over, the premiership is on ITV, it's nearly finished but I'm not worried as I like to watch the Sunday morning repeat, with breakfast in bed and if we've had a good result, the Sunday papers. After today's score I shan't be buying the papers tomorrow.

With only the light of the telly I select a record and put it on, *Blood on the Tracks*. I then switch the telly off plunging the room into darkness, only the various red lights on my stereo shine like red stars. I prop myself up on my elbow and drain my glass, I feel the warmth of the whisky. I close my eyes and concentrate on Dylan's pain, sorrow, passion and bitterness all laid down on vinyl as his marriage failed. I must have drifted off to sleep, I don't remember the record finishing.

*   *   *   *   *   *   *   *

I wake up with the record sleeve over my face. I can see a chink of light through the curtain so I figure it's gone eight o'clock. I get up and make my way to the bathroom; I select a magazine from the pile by the side of the loo. It's the November issue of record collector. I turn to the ads section and check out anything of interest. I'm due to go to a record fair today, I spot an advert for it with reduced admission if you produce this ad, so I tear it out.

When I come out of the bathroom, a small bump has appeared under my duvet. I move nearer the sofa bed and slip the piece of paper in my jeans. I then make a loud exaggerated yawning noise while gently spreading myself on top of the Bob-shaped bump. Bob lets out a small squeal and slides out the side of the duvet on to the floor. He jumps up and makes a high ugh! karate noise while chopping me in the stomach.

I roll around on the bed in fake agony before collapsing and lying dead still. My head is left hanging off the side of the bed in front of Bob. My eyes are shut, Bob slaps both cheeks with his hands. Still no signs of life. Then Bob leans forwards and gives me a gentle kiss on the lips. I spring into life, chasing him round the room. We then have a mad five minutes. Bob shouts and screams as he tries to shoot me with the telly remote control. It's a good job no one lives below me, otherwise social services, the police and the S.A.S. would all be on their way. The premiership is about to start, so I calm it down.

"Come on Bob, breakfast," I say as I move to the kitchen area. I get a bowl out while Bob looks in the cupboard below and he chooses his cereal. He comes out with a large box of Coco Pops and he climbs onto a chair. Bob insists on pouring his own. At first he does quite well as four or five Coco Pops drop into his bowl. Then whoosh the bowl is swamped and disappears under an avalanche of Coco Pops.

"OOPS" says Bob looking at the mess.

"Not to worry, I'll sort it out" I say and get another bowl for me and then slide some into it. I then use my hand to scoop the rest from the work surface back into the box. We settle down to watch the Premiership while eating our breakfast.

As soon as the signature tune heralds the end, we get dressed. Bob into his latest Pokemon T-shirt and me into my Dylan *Time out of Mind* tour shirt. Then we head out to Mums. She's due to take Bob swimming at the local leisure centre, while I spend an hour at the record fair in the hall. Because of the length of her hair, Mum insists on wearing one of those old fashioned bathing hats with pink lilies on it. Which is why she does the swimming and I go to the record fair.

I walk in the hall and hand my torn piece of paper to the man sitting at the entrance table, he looks at it suspiciously and I give him a pound. The hall is divided into two by a net curtain, the half I'm in has tables and tables of CDs, records, books and concert programs with sad people hunched over them. The other half has a step aerobics class, a large group of fit looking young women in tight leotards gyrating about to the latest J'Lo track, I'm quite sorry I haven't brought my leotard.

I recognise one or two of the stall holders. Each stall has a sound system playing a selection of their wares, The Clash, Jam, Rolling Stones and Red Hot Chili Peppers compete to be heard above the grunting ladies and J Lo. Then I see big Dave. We go back a long way right back to school days, Dave was firmly in the progressive rock camp those days. He has a small record shop in town as well as doing these fairs. He's my best mate. Dave has helped me through the three great trials of life: Birth, death and relegation. He's wearing a faded Rolling Stones T-shirt with the big mouth and tongue logo on it. It covers the majority of his stomach, except for the three inches of fat below his belly button. He sees me coming through the crowd.

"How you doing man" he says while bending down under the table and pulling out a stack of records. He always puts aside anything that might be of interest to me,

"I'm OK, it's the others," I say taking the records from him. His table is crowded with people, so I move to the side and start to go through the pile. I discard the first two as I have them, the next is an EP: *All I really want to do/Oxford Town/To Ramona/Spanish Harlem Incident*. It's a French import its got a sticker with £35 on it. I put it to one side. A Rolling Stones bootleg is blasting out on Daves' sound system. He jokes with another punter doing a disturbing impersonation of Mick Jagger. I select two other records from Daves recommendations, they come to £110.

"Here Dave will you take £100 for the three?" I ask optimistically.

"No way, come on, a mans got to eat" Dave says while holding up his T-shirt and wobbling his ample belly with both hands.

"Come on do yourself a favour and miss a meal or two"

"Go on then Nat, as its you. But I'll be at the *House of Gloom* tonight so you can buy me a beer," Dave says as he put the records in an old Asda bag.

I spend another hour looking round, till I catch Mum and Bob waiting by the door. I pull myself away from the records. I walk past Daves stall, on the way out Bruce Springsteen's *Born to Run* is blaring out. He looks up and points at me, like he's shooting a gun and winks.

"Catch you later dude" Dave says just as Clarence Clemons of the E Street Band begins a saxophone solo, prompting him to do the same with a large baguette he's eating.

When we come out it's a cold grey November afternoon, the road has that white look you get before snow.

As soon as we get in I set about the Sunday lunch. Cooking holds no fears for me, although it worries the hell out of those who have to eat it. I'm not a great one for following recipes. I'm not very good at quantities, a tablespoon can be anything from a pinch to a cup full, depending on whether I like the ingredient or not. Soon the chicken and roast potatoes are in the oven, the carrots and swede peeled and chopped and in the various saucepans ready to cook. I sit in the lounge and read Mums paper, she buys the News of the Screws (News of the World). I read who's doing the dirty on who and who's been dumped. This is all very depressing, but not as depressing as when I turn to the sports section to check out our league position.

After dinner we settle down to watch telly, soon I doze off. Then I'm having this incredible dream. I'm sitting in a large armchair with a huge pair of brown checked slippers on. A pipe is in my left hand, I'm stroking a large Labrador with the right hand. Through the patio doors Hazel is pruning a rose bush. Beyond her is Bob in a paddling pool, a small girl is in the pool behind him, I can't see her clearly as Bob is holding a hose pipe and obscuring my view. Then Bob moves out of the way and the girl stands up. She is laughing and giggling as her hair gets wet, her beautiful red hair. It's some kind of idealistic scene, like an advert or an old fifties movie. But all of a sudden, Hazel has turned into my mother. She's standing over me and holding a tea towel.

No hang on, I've woken up, it is my mother, she's telling me the washing up is done and it's my turn to dry. My lovely dream has been shattered. I dry up and put everything away. I then connect Bobs Playstation to Mums telly. We play a motor racing game, I win, but I'm careful not to win by too big a margin, so Bob doesn't get fed up. We then load a football game, Bob wins 3-0, I make a mental note to practice one night when Bobs gone to bed. I load a Rugrats game and leave Bob to play on his own.

"I better make tracks as I'm on at *The House of Gloom* tonight." I say to mum.

"This girl, when are you seeing her again?" Mum inquires.

"On Wednesday, look Mum don't get too excited, I've only seen her once."

"Well, keep me posted oh!, and have a good JIG tonight," she says giving me a hug, I look at my Dads photo on the telly.

"Tell her Dad, it's called a GIG," I say to his photo, shaking my head.

"I'll play, *If not for you,*" I always pick one song to dedicate to him. Bob's concentrating like mad at his game.

"See you son" I say ruffling his hair. It's all fallen in front of his eyes now, frantically he tries to blow it out of the way, without letting go of the control pad.

Five

When I get back to the flat it's freezing cold. I put the heating on, I leave on my coat on and put on *Exodus* by Bob Marley and the Wailers - that should warm me up. I dance around to get warm. As soon as I can feel my fingers and toes I take a shower and get changed. I have about half an hour to kill so I get my guitar out for a bit of a warm up jam.

I muck about trying to write a song. I believe every great musician has one outstanding song that stands out above all the rest. Jagger/Richards: *Jumping Jack Flash*; Lennon/McCartneys *Yesterday*; Eric Claptons *Layla* , Oasis *Wonder Wall* and Chuck Berrys *My Ding a Ling*! Or maybe not.

But with Bob Dylan it's very hard to pick just one song above any other, they all seem relevant at the time, my choice changes with my mood. This is what I come up with, backed by a blues riff,

> *Hazel I'm nuts about you,*
> *Not crushed but whole,*
> *You're hot, you could say roasted,*
> *So I'm ready lets get salted,*
> *don't be a walnut,*
> *Get out on the dance floor,*
> *Shake your coconuts,*
> *'Cause Hazel I'm nuts about you.*

That should get McCartney and Jagger quaking in their boots. It's time to go, I'm not on for an hour, but I like to have three or four pints to lubricate my vocal chords. I put my guitar in its case and put it over my shoulder, I touch my breast pocket with my right hand to check my mouth organ is safe.

When I get outside it's sleeting so I run all the way to the pub. Don't get too excited it's only two hundred yards. I burst through the pub door; Grahams sat in his usual chair with Quinn his blind dog at his feet. Quinn is named after one of our team's old players - everyone in the pub helped raise money to pay for it.

"How you doing Graham?" I say while bending down to stroke Quinn.

"Fine, just fine," he says as he finishes his drink, not his first by the look of him. We talk football for a while, how bad WE played, which player was worse, what WE would do to change things, our league position and if we might get relegated. I don't know why football fans, speak of how WE played, as if a blind sixty-five year old and a tall bloke with little co-ordination would ever play for our team. Anyway its all total doom and despair, but we work out when the next home game is and arrange what time I will pick him up.

Graham leans forward in his chair and grabs my sleeve with his left hand while removing a handful of change from his jacket pocket with his right. He places the coins into my hand and closes my fingers tightly around them.

"There Nat get yourself a drink and I'll have another whisky, oh! and don't forget Quinns half of bitter," he says looking pleased. I make my way to the bar, my guitar still on my back clearing the way. At the bar I open my hand and count Grahams change, its only £1-76p. Graham always does this to me. The worse thing is, when I get back with the drinks he asks for any change back. I don't like to upset him so give him £1-27p back in coins. I get twenty pounds for a Sunday night. I've spent £5.47 on drinks and one of those was for a dog! I go through to the back room and place my guitar on the stage. When I say stage, it's four drinks crates with a sheet of plywood nailed on top. I check the lighting, one angle poise lamp that shines up at me from the floor. The *House of Gloom* is a typical large country pub with low beams and an open fire. The back function room was built on at a later date. It has a small bar at one end and chairs and tables down both sides. Around forty people can fit in it when it's full. The most I have had in is twenty-six and that includes Quinn.

I go back into the main bar. I see one or two of the Sunday night regulars are in. Tom and Sue are real folk people, Tom has a waistcoat and sandals on with dark brown socks. Suddenly from across the bar I hear a voice I dread,

"Hi! Nat," the lady moves through the crowd and gives me a huge rib-crushing hug. She stands back and looks at me,

"Wow, you've got a great aura around you tonight, it's going to be a great gig man."

The lady is called Sky and is lost in the sixties. Between you and me I know for a fact her real name is Barbara and she's actually a reformed Tory. At this point I see what she's wearing. She has stripy rainbow trousers on, and a hand crocheted tank top. With no bra. As I look there's definitely two things poking out, due to the cold weather. It goes straight into the top five most disturbing pieces of knitwear ever:

At 5. The purple and black tank top knitted by Mum for me in 1973.

4. Starsky and Hutches cardigans.

3. My fluffy yellow and black punk jumper, I wore all summer in 1977.

2. The jumpers of Noel Edmonds

A new entry at 1. Sky's tank top with protruding nipples.

I prise myself away, and move to the stage, I take my new pint and great aura with me. On the way someone taps me on the shoulder. It's big Dave.

"You going to be playing any Sex Pistols or Undertones tonight?" He thinks this is absolutely hilarious.

"I don't think so."

"Oh go on it would be like old times," he says while pogoing up and down. Dave and I played in a punk band called Gordon and the Gobblers. Gordon Marsh was the lead singer, he supplied the amplifier and most of the equipment, so he got to choose our name. I played lead guitar and Dave played drums. We did cover versions of the Sex Pistols, Boomtown Rats and The Undertones. We played three dates in our short but illustrious career; one in the school hall, one at the local Scout hut (for George Oggs birthday) and the last at the Nags Head in High Wycombe, supporting the Safety Pins, who went on to make the single *If it ain't Punk it ain't worth a F...!* Which stormed the charts reaching number 49. We really didn't look the part of a punk band, Gordon's mum would only let him go on stage in a shirt and tie, I wore my large yellow and black fluffy jumper, and Dave had national health thick black-rimmed glasses at the time. Which, when he got hot and sweaty slipped down his nose causing him to stop drumming to adjust them. We split up due to musical differences – I was musical they were different!

I make my way to the stage and Dave follows me.

"I could join you on stage for one number on backing vocals," Dave said in all seriousness.

"Look at that stage Dave, its only just strong enough for one. Here get yourself a drink, get me one. Bring it up to me I'm gonna start."

I step on to the stage and turn on the light. It shines up at me throwing shadows behind me, it's quite a cool effect. I adjust my mike stand. Behind me is a poster Bob helped me make, I wrote it in glue and Bob poured glitter on it only some of the glitter has since fallen off, it now reads;

Ap earing to ight
Live
Nat an Pete son

I look up, about twenty people are in. The room is dark. The only light is from over the bar and coming through from the door to the main pub.

I start off with *The Times They Are A-Changin*. Then I start the opening rift of *Mr. Tambourine Man*. Most people are sitting down the sides or standing quietly at the back, around the bar are three lads from the local Rugby club. They're drinking lager and being a bit loud. As I sing the first line someone stands up and starts dancing. I know who it is, it strikes fear into me, it's Sky. She's doing a spaced-out sixties dance with her eyes shut, arms circling in the air above her head.

As I finished the number a few of the regulars shout out requests. One of the boys from the rugby club shout out,

"Play some garage music!" they all roar with laughter. Another joins in the banter with,

"Come on play some house music!" more raucous laughter. I announce the next song.

"OK, now something requested by the boys at the back, some house music."

I sing the first line, *There is a house in New Orleans, they call the*

Rising Sun. The joke goes over their heads through the smoke and up to the oak beams of the roof. Sky has thankfully sat down. I'm aware two women have come through from the other bar. I finish the song, a voice comes through from the darkness at the back.

"If not for you"

My heart beats faster – it can't be! I search through the darkness and smoke. I catch a glimpse of red hair. It's Hazel, what's she doing here? I'm staring into the darkness.

"Get on with it!" The rugby boys at the back shout, I compose my self and start.

> *If not for you,*
> *Babe, I couldn't find the door,*
> *Couldn't even see the floor*
> *I'd be sad and blue,*
> *If not for you.*

Halfway through the song, I get a shock as Dave comes on stage, but it's all right he only put my pint down in front of me. I finished my last song to warm applause, except from Sky who whooped and shouted.... More.... more, while lighting a cigarette lighter and holding it up in the dark. What is she on!

Someone puts the main lights on, people gather their things up and leave. I'm putting my guitar in its case when Hazel comes over.

"Hi! How did you know I was playing here," I say,

"Well it's in the local paper, how many Nathan Petersons can there be," she says. I remember Colin the landlord had put an advert in the live section of the local paper. Behind her is an older lady, she introduces her as Joan a friend from work.

"You were great," Hazel said.

"Well I don't know about that," I said trying to be modest

"Would you like a drink"

"No I really have to go," she says. Joan starts to walk to the door, When she's out of earshot Hazel says,

"Look, would you like to go to the cinema on Wednesday ."

For a second I think, hang on, is there a new Rugrats or Pokemon movie out? Of course, they do make films that are not about kids in nappies or fighting hamsters. But with Bob these are the only ones I get to see.

"Yes, great."

She looks behind her then she leans forward and kisses me on the cheek. On the way out she turns,

"I'll pick you up at seven-thirty."

I put my guitar in its case and swing it on my back, I check my mouth organ is safely in my pocket and move to the main bar. Colin is behind the bar. He fancies himself as a bit of a ladies man, with slicked-back black hair, a silk shirt and his trousers are far too tight.

"Good show tonight, sold a lot of cider," Colin says handing me a twenty from the till. I've spent £18.76 let me see, that makes £1.24 profit. I think to myself – Nat don't give up your day job.

In the main bar Graham is asleep, I wake him and tell Colin I'll make sure he gets home safe as he's one of Colin most valued customers. Graham has had a skin-full and Quinn is not much better having had at least three halves of bitter. I say goodnight to Colin and lead Graham by the arm while taking Quinn by his harness. He only lives four doors down from the pub but in that short distance Quinn manages to walk into a lamp post. He really is the worst guide dog; I need to train up a small Jack Russell to guide him home from the Pub.

When I get back to the flat, it's gone eleven and I make myself a coffee with a dash of whisky. I sit down, take a sip from my breast-shaped mug and sigh to myself contentedly. The weekend is over, work tomorrow. But I think to myself I've succeeded in three of my four great passions.

1. To looked after and spend time with my beautiful son.
2. To support my football team through bad and worse times.
3. To listen to and play my favourite music.
4. To spread peace throughout the world.

I Finish my coffee, put my cup in the sink and walk across the lounge to the bedroom. Just before I turn the light off. I think to myself, that world peace thing, I'll pencil it in for next weekend.

Six

And there's nothing she doesn't see.
She knows where I d like to be
But it doesn't t matter.
I want you, I want you,
I want you so bad,
Honey, I want you.

(I Want You, © 1966 renewed 1994 Dwarf Music)

I hear a familiar screech of brakes, it's dead on seven-thirty, yep it must be her. I go out the front door turn and double lock it, pull my collar up against the cold wind. Go down the metal stairs and slid into Hazels low sports car. She leans across and kisses me on the cheek.

"I thought we would go and see the new Johnny Depp film," Hazel says as she pulls away.

"Sounds great," I'm not up with current films. Shit! If we hadn't lost I'd have bought a Sunday paper, which would have had the current films reviewed, anyway I'm not too sure who this Johnny Depp is. Show me a Pokemon or a Rugrat and I'll tell you his name for sure.

I enjoy the film. It's good to watch a film without kids screaming and talking through it. Only I think it's a shame that I only get to see Hazel once a week, and I'm spending it sat in the dark, not being able to talk to her. I buy a big tub of popcorn; when I say big it's the size of a forty-five gallon drum. We struggle to eat it all, I tell Hazel I'll take it home to finish it (with the view to letting Bob eat it).

When we come out of the cinema, it's snowing, not wet snow, but the kind with large flakes, so large you can almost make out the individual design. We are nearly home when Hazel pulls into the car park of the local park which is opposite the House of Gloom, before I know it, she opens the car door and is running across the grass which is covered in a virginal blanket of white snow. It's a full moon, the light is very strange and the snow is almost glowing.

She stands in the middle of the virgin snow her arms in the air, mouth open catching snowflakes. I open my door and set off after Hazel, when I reach her she slowly lowers her arms around my neck, pulling me to her. I can feel the warmth of her breath before she kisses me on the lips. Large snowflakes glint in her hair like diamonds in the moon light, she laughs shaking her head and shooting stars into the air around her. She breaks away, bends over and grabs a handful of snow, forms it in to a ball and throws it at me. It explodes over the front of my jacket.

"Right that's war where I come from," I say, scooping up a handful of snow and launching a missile at Hazel. She ducks and it sails two feet over her head. After a frantic snowball fight, I stand with my hands on my knees trying to catch my breath.

"You're out of condition, you need to do some jogging like me. Come on lets start," she runs off towards the car, I take a big breath and follow her. At first I'm running alongside her, then she pulls away, I do the male pride thing desperately trying to overtake her. Hazel, I find out, is a regular runner and reaches the car with time to turn and face me, arms folded, mocking me. I try to stop, but skid past the car ending up on my backside. I stand up brushing the snow off my jeans.

Hazel looks at her watch,

"Nat I really have to go, sorry," she gives me a cuddle. I hear a noise from across the road in the direction of the House of Gloom. It's Graham and Quinn on their way home.

"Hold on two seconds, I've just got to check on someone," I say as I cross the road. Hazel follows behind me. I call out,

"You okay mate," Graham looks in my general direction,

"Oh not too bad," Graham says

"Recovered from Sunday night?"

By this time Hazel is standing behind me, I introduce her and Graham puts a hand out, Hazel puts her hand in his and holds it briefly.

"Pleased to meet you," she says.

Quinn sits patiently at Grahams' feet looking every bit a proper blind dog tonight. He must have had a relatively beer free evening. At this point Graham reaches out slowly to touch Hazel's face.

"May I?" Graham says, Hazel looks nervously at me.

"It's Ok, he just wants to make a mental picture of you in his head,"

Graham touches Hazel's hair before tracing the outline of her face, then moving gently over her eyes, cheeks, and lips. Before running both hands down the front of her coat. I have seen Graham do this many times before, when introduced to someone's girlfriend or wife. He always went through this elaborate charade. He told me it actually gives him very little clue as to how someone looks, but it makes an old man very happy. Today I'm shocked to hear him say,

"Nat she's beautiful"

Hazel steps back blushing.

"There, a blind man can't be wrong," I say. Hazel smiles but looks nervously at her watch, she's worried, it's getting late and Clive will get home before her.

"Look Nat I really have to go, nice to have met you Graham." She turns and crosses the road to the car. I tell Graham to mind how he goes. He turns and heads the short distance to his house. Quinn manages to avoid the lamp post tonight, pausing only to cock his leg. I go back to the car and get in. Hazel asks how I know Graham. I explain how we met and about our football arrangement. I think she's suitably impressed.

Hazel drives the short distance to the flat,

"I'll see you next Wednesday," she says as she leans over and kisses me on the lips.

"Yea fine" I say. She must have sensed the disappointment in my voice. She puts her hand on my cheek and makes me look her in the eyes.

"You're alright with this?" I nod, and get out, taking my popcorn from the car. She lowers the electric window on my side and calls through,

"Look, we'll do something special next Wednesday, what with it being your Birthday." I must have told Hazel about my Birthday, but I can't remember when. The car pulls away wheels skidding in the snow. I watch the red tail lights disappear into the swirling snowflakes before climbing the metal staircase to the flat. Once inside I make a drink and switch on the TV. I flick from channel to channel until I come across a film that's just starting.

I start watching, it's about a woman who's married to a wealthy older man but she's having an affair with a much younger man. At one point she's having a conversation with one of her friends in a swanky New York coffee house. She tells her about her affair and how she's in a *love triangle*. It dawns on me, that's it, I'm in my very own love triangle. With Hazel, Clive, and me at each corner. But my triangle does not have equal sides, because I only get to see Hazel one day a week. My corner is very sharp and pointed. So it's not an equilateral triangle, it's a lot messier looking than that, more like an isosceles triangle. I don't know what I'm doing. All I know is that Hazel has given me something to look forward to. I know my son is my whole life, certainly when he was very young, I shut out everything, even to the point of stopping playing music.

All I know is my life B.H. (Before Hazel) was a bit like a closed season when we've been relegated, with no World cup or European championship to get you through a long drawn out summer. Nothing to look forward to, but long trips up north to minor third division clubs. Now my life A.H. (After Hazel) is well, like, we've been promoted, I can't wait for the fixtures to come out to start planning my new season in the first division. My whole week revolves around seeing Hazel on Wednesdays. I count the hours till I will see her again. But I could do with some SEX! My Willy hasn't seen the light of day for so long. It feels a bit like a classic car locked in a garage, jacked-up on bricks and covered by a dust sheet. The engine turns over from time to time, hand cranked of course!

I try not to think about it, I need to add something to my tea. I carry on watching the film. I've finished off the last of the popcorn I had saved for Bob. This reminds me that I still haven't told Hazel about Bob. I've now got the problem that we've been out two or three times and I haven t mentioned it. How could I say, oh, by the way I have a six-year-old son? Maybe I could arrange for Bob to be here next time Hazel comes round. Then she could say,

"Who's that" and I could say,

"Oh him, he's just my six year old son, didn't I mention him?"
Back on the telly the women encourages the young man to assassinate her husband, and so inherit his money, but meanwhile unbeknownst to her, the old man has found out about the wife's affair. – Are you following this? So he hires his own assassin to kill the young man on the very same day. So the woman gets her husband shot dead and thinking she's in the money, races off to find her lover. She arrives at the hotel to wait for him, looking out the window, she sees a suspicious car with blacked out windows. Then her lover arrives in a yellow cab, as he gets out, the window of the car opens and a gun appears, shooting him dead.

That's how the stupid film ends. It's quarter to one, having started I just thought I'd stay up to see the end. Now I wish I hadn't' t bothered. I turn the telly off and I'm just about to go to bed, when I think I'll just check outside. I pull the curtain apart just enough to see out, convinced I'm about to see Clive in a blacked-out car staking out the flat. But the street is deserted, the snow settling on the road now. I can sleep safe in my bed.

* * * * * * * *

I open my eyes, I try to move. I check everything's in working order. Yes, I've made it to my fortieth birthday.

Highlights of the last week:

Thursday: Sid, my boss tells me he's received a speeding ticket for me, possible three points on my license and a £60 fine.

Friday: Parents' evening at Bob's school, Miss Heatherington, Bob's teacher looks only eighteen and is very attractive. Suddenly I take a keen interest in all aspects of Bob's school work asking many questions. My allotted time over runs, causing waiting parents to bang on classroom door. Miss Heatherington tells me that Bob is a musical genius (thanks to my musical tuition), he also has four pictures up on the wall of his classroom. May become singing pavement artist, his grandad would be proud of him.

Saturday: away game, so no football, listen on radio, manage a superb and well-deserved 0-0 draw to small northern club. Take Bob to McDonalds - he has a Happy Meal - only two plastic toys left to collect for full set. May be diagnosed as clinically obese before this is achieved.

Sunday: Buy Sunday papers, small write up in Sunday Express.

Sunday night: Hazel turns up at House of Gloom with Clive. They stand at the back, after one song Clive joins rugby mates back in main bar. Dedicate song to Hazel saying

"This next song is for a special lady who's just come into my life," looking straight at Hazel I sing,

> *Lay, Lady, Lay,*
> *Lay across my big brass bed*

I hope she gets the hint.

As I gaze adoringly in her direction I sing,

> *Why wait any longer for the one you love*
> *When he's standing in front of you*

but someone has comes between us, it's Sky, she has a strange look on her face, she blows me a kiss. Oh surely she doesn't think, Oh my God! Sky is convinced she is the target of my lovesick, sex-starved ranting.

Monday: Get flat tyre in pouring rain on muddy building site. I'm sure the invite to join Ferraris pit team is in the post after taking only 23 minutes to change it.

Tuesday: Have home match, win 3-1. I really think our season could be kick-started by this result.

That brings us to now, how can I be forty. They say thirty is the big one, but I always thought when I reached thirty, hey! It's taken me ages to get to this point, and it's not unreasonable to expect to live up to three times as long, to ninety years of age. But having reached the age of forty its very unlikely you're going to live to one hundred and twenty! My demented thoughts of an early Alzheimer sufferer are broken by a knock at the door, I check my bedside clock it's 6:38. I jump up, I throw on boxer shorts and a T-shirt, and I go to open the door. A cold blast of wind hits me, there's still some snow about from last Wednesday. A small but immaculately wrapped parcel is left on the doorstep. I look out, there is no one about. I go back inside and put the package on the kitchen work surface. I've got a good idea who it's from, I want to savour it. I put the kettle on and make a cup of tea. I sip it while looking at my parcel. I put my Simpson's mug down and I'm just about to open it when it starts to vibrate and play a tune. Shit it's a bomb! Clive's found out about us, I throw myself behind the sofa bed. Then I think hang on, I know that tune, De De De Dar..... it's *Mr Tambourine Man*. Bombs don't play phone tones. I tear open the paper. Sure enough the package contains a brand new mobile. The mobile phone age has somewhat passed me by. In fact the whole phone, Internet techno-logical thing has passed me by, I don't have a phone in the flat. I'm only just beginning to buy CD's. I can never understand who all these people with mobiles strapped to their ears are talking to. I mean twenty years ago when you went past a red payphone, there was never a queue of businessmen waiting to use it. Now payphones are beginning to disappear, because the only people using them are the old and care-in-the community. (Which is why the inevitable smell of stale urine is not a problem anymore).

I tentatively press the button with the green phone on it and hold it to my ear.

"Hello," I say,

"Good morning birthday boy," says Hazel

"Hi" I say lifting the phone away from my ear to speak.

"Well what do you think of it?"

"Oh it's great, I love the case," Hazel must have been to the club shop, as the phone is sporting a new case in our teams colours.

There's also a small handbook, it contains every language under the sun, but only four pages of English.

"Have a great day, I'll pick you up at seven, wear something smart," Hazel pauses.

"You do have something smart?"

"Hey, do I have something smart," I lied

"I can't wait, must dash. I L....." and she was gone, the phone cuts out.

"What did you say? I'm sorry, I missed that," I keep talking to the phone but Hazel has gone. What was she going to say? I LOSE my signal all the time, I LEFT something under the grill, I LIKE you quite a lot, or maybe, I LOVE you, no surely not.

I'm still staring dreamily at the phone when there's a knock at the door again. I go to the door and open it. It's mum and Bob. Bob has a large parcel in his hands. He runs into my arms giving me a big hug, squashing the gift between us.

"Happy birthday Dad," he says into my stomach.

Thanks son," I say, as I lean forward to kiss Mum, squashing Bob in the middle.

"Hey!" says Bob pulling himself out of the sandwich. They come in and I shut the door.

"Open it, open it," Bob shouts as I take the parcel from him. I know what it is because mum had asked me a couple of days before what I would like. It's a fleece jacket from the football club shop, grey with the club badge on it. I open it and fake excitement,

"Wow! that's great," I say pulling it on over my T-shirt. There's a woolly Bronx hat as well. I put it on Bob's head and pull it down over his eyes. He walks around with his hands out in front pretending he can not see.

"Now the card," Bob says removing the bobble hat, and pushing the hair out of his eyes. I open Bob's card it's a comedy card, on the front is a picture of a man with a lot of arrows pointing out the things wrong with him. Inside it', says you're,

FAULTY TODAY

"Lovely, thank you," I say. Mum gives me her parcel, again chosen by me, it's a double CD, Essential Bob Dylan. Yes I know it's a CD, but it's a new collection not released on LP. I've only just got a CD player within the last year. I thank Mum and put it on top of my stereo system. I'll file it away later. I've taken the fleece off and put it on the back of the sofa. Bob picks it up and puts it on, the sleeves drag on the floor. Mum sees the mobile phone.

"That's nice. Is that from her then?" she says.

"If you mean Hazel, then yes"

"So things are getting serious then"

"Depends what you mean by serious," I say

"Do you think we might be introduced to her then? How about asking her to Sunday dinner?" mum asks.

"Oh I don't know, she's very busy, and I don't know if our relationship is ready for one of my roasts," I say, pulling the fleece off Bob.

"I'll try and arrange something in the next few weeks," I say. Bob has to get ready for school. So I say I'll see him tonight, as mum has invited me to a birthday tea. I tell her I'm going out for dinner so not to make too much. Bob pulls at my sleeve,

"You coming to watch the England match tonight dad?" Mum looks at me as I bend my knees to bring me down to Bobs height.

"No son I can't make it tonight," Bob looks disappointed.

"But, we can still do our bit to ensure they win," I sit Bob down next to me on the sofa.

"Right, close your eyes tight," Bob closes his eyes in that exaggerated way children do. I say in a deep resonating voice.

"Let us concentrate on the England team," I gesture with my eyes for mum to sit on the chair opposite. Then we all join hands.

"Let us think of our Owen," I've got my eyes half shut so I can still see out. Bob opens one eye and closes it quickly. I carry on,

"Our Heskey," Bob repeats under his breath,

"Our Heskey,"

"Our Beckham," again Bob repeats reverently,

"Our Beckham," I pause, thinking of another player, then Bob interrupts,

"And let us not forget our Butts," I bite my lip to stop me laughing and look at mum, she has her hand over her mouth trying to stop laughing too. Mum and I say together,

"Our Butts"

"Come on time for school," I say getting up and breaking the circle as remove his bobble hat and ruffle his hair.

I take a shower, collect my cassette box with today's musical selection in and go down stairs to work.

Sid my boss has put 40 TODAY on my van windscreen in large letters with shaving cream. I get the hose and wash it off. I go off on my deliveries. I now have the problem of getting something smart to wear. The only suit I own I bought for Dads funeral, so it's six years old. I decide I need to buy a new suit, so I go to a large out of town Retail Park. I can't park in the car park due to some newly installed height restrictions, after some travellers had set up camp there a few weeks earlier. So I park in a side street. I spend £247 on a new shirt, suit and tie. Plus some sexy new pants just in case. I get back to the van and it's been clamped, an hour and a half and seventy quid later, I'm on my way. This birthday has taken a turn for the worse.

I go to Mums after work. Mum has made a cake, when I say made a cake, no one makes a cake quite like my Mum. She's made a large chocolate cream cake in the shape of a guitar. Bob insists on putting the correct number of candles on the cake. By the time we light the last few, the wax is running onto the cake from the first ones. The heat is intense so I quickly blow them out. I have a piece of cake from the neck of the guitar, as mum has used chocolate buttons on this bit. The cake is superb.

I tell mum I've got to go, she gives me most of the cake to take to work. I set up Bob's Playstation before I leave and say goodnight. I go back to the flat, shower, shave and put on some new after-shave. I put my suit on, look at myself in the bedroom mirror, I scrub up quite well.

At seven o'clock I hear a car toot outside. I look out the curtains, it's Hazel. I'm out the door, down the stairs and sliding into the car.

"Wow! aren't you the smart one," Hazel says. Hazel is wearing a rather boring and formal navy blue business trouser suit. She must have seen me look at her.

"I know, I was delayed in a meeting, but don't worry I'll get ready on the way," Hazel says smiling.

On the new relief road into town there are three sets of lights. We get caught at each one.

1st Lights: Hazel puts lip stick on, mascara, eyeliner and a little blusher.
2nd Lights: Hazel lets hair down, brushes hair, puts it back up with hair

clips leaving a couple of strands dangling down.

3rd Lights: Hazel pulls arms out of jumper lifts to neck revealing sexy black bra, and turns to get the shopping bag from back seat, it's from one of those expensive designer shops. Even the bag looks expensive, with gold writing and a fancy string handle. She starts to pull out what looks like a little black dress. I'm intrigued by how she's going to slip into this dress in the front of a sports car. I turn sideways with my back to the car door, a) to give her more room and, b) to get a better view. Then she turns to me smiling wickedly,

"Ha! only joking, I'll change at the restaurant," she says, pulling down her jumper and tossing the bag on to the back seat. A car toots its horn from behind. We have been stopped for so long the lights have gone full cycle and have just changed from green to red again. The bloke in the lane next to us is looking over open-mouthed. Hazel blows him a kiss, then opens the electric sunroof and waves at the cars behind as she wheel spins away. She's in a funny mood tonight.

We get to the restaurant, I can see by the reaction of the staff that they know her, a small bald and ever so camp waiter leads us to a table for two.

Hazel excuses herself and disappears into the ladies, I'm left to choose the wine. I pick the house red to be on the safe side. After five minutes Hazel makes her entrance, everyone turns to look. The dress is slightly off the shoulder and backless. Hazel sits down, I lean forward to kiss her on the cheek and whisper, "

"you look wonderful tonight,"

Starter: I have King Prawns in garlic butter, Hazel has paté,

Main conversation point:

Hazel was at Bob Dylan's Blackbushe concert

Dad and me had taken time off to follow Dylan around the country on his 1979 tour. Then it was announced that Dylan would play a final concert at Blackbushe airport, ironically less than 10 miles from home! It was amazing that we were actually standing in the same field, all be it with 200,000 other people.

Main Course: I have T-bone steak in pepper sauce, Hazel has the sea bass.

Main conversation point:

Hazel and Clive are not having sex at the moment.

Due to the fact that he has *crotch rot*. Apparently quite common with people who play rugby and wear a jock strap all the time? YUCK!

Dessert: I have profiteroles, Hazel has crème caramel.

Main conversation point:

I tell Hazel about my Dad.

What an amazing person he was, how extraordinary his life was, growing up in our house. I then go on to tell her about how he got ill, how I watched him die, one day at a time. I became emotional, I don't think I've ever relived it verbally with another human being before. But I don't mention Bob, I nearly do, I'm almost going to slip it into the conversation, but I bottle it. Well Hazel's going on about her job and life style, it's obvious children play little part in her life and she has no intention of having any. Besides, the waiter came and interrupted me.

Coffee: I have Irish, Hazel has straight black.

Main conversation point:

Hazel asked if she could stay the night.

Although I totally missed the magnitude of this request. She tells me that Clive would be away as a client had given her two tickets for the England game. That's right two tickets to the World Cup qualifier, the most important game since, since ..... well since the last one. The international that only my big birthday date with Hazel, had stopped me from watching. The game I had left Bob to watch alone, so young to have to cope with the pain and disappointment that will surely follow an England World Cup qualifier.

The game was to be played at Old Trafford and Clive was then staying in a hotel overnight before travelling back down the next morning. I still can t comprehend it, I'm trying to stay calm in this posh and intimate restaurant, thoughts race through my mind. I love football, it's one of the biggest things in my life, after my son (and Dylan). Jesus, I've done my time, I have suffered 30 years of hurt, every England failure, pictures and images flash before me like old Pathé news clips.

1970 World Cup in Mexico. England v. Brazil (Bobby Moore's incredible tackle in the penalty area, then he's swapping shirts with Pele at the end, we've lost 1-0)

1973 England v. Poland at Wembley (The 'clown' Polish goalkeeper stops us scoring and we fail to qualify for the 1974 World Cup)

1986 England v. Argentina, (the notorious 'hand of God' incident)

Clive is a Rugby nut, as far as I know he's never been to watch my local team, let alone England. He'll be drinking and munching prawn sandwiches all sodding night, ignoring the game. So Hazel is telling me that she wants to stay the night, move our relationship on to a higher level and even have sex with me, and I'm giving a brief history of the fall and fall of English football. I start ranting on about England tickets.

"How could you do it? Graham and I could have gone, Clive's never been to a Football game in his life."

"Look forget about the silly Game, do you understand what I'm telling you?" Hazel asks in exasperation. Then almost shouting she says,

"I WANT TO MAKE LOVE TO YOU," a sudden and embarrassing hush descends on the restaurant, everyone turns to look. The husbands and boyfriends are looking Hazel up and down and nodding their approval before being hit and cajoled back to their own conversations.

Then the penny starts to drop, slowly at first, a bit like one of those machines in an amusement arcade, zig-zagging slowly down before dropping onto the other pennies. Until, if you're very lucky it and one or two other coins clatter out into the tray at the bottom.

"Oh! You mean like ..... stay the night," I say hesitantly.

"No I mean have a sleep-over, we could hire a video and stay up really late and have a midnight feast," Hazel say sarcastically. I reach over and take Hazels hand.

"I would love you to stay," I say, then add,

"But after that meal, I think we could skip the midnight feast!"
At this point the waiter comes over to ask us if we require anything else, before he can finish the sentence, I almost shout,

" NO THANK YOU"

Hazel asks for the bill. She pays, its her treat, she says. I don't waste time arguing. I remember how much my suit had cost me. As we leave the restaurant one or two of the male contingent give me a knowing nod and a smile, before returning to their wives while trying to remember the last time she had begged them to make love.

On the way home all the traffic lights are green. It's a sign, we are destined to be together. We pull up outside the flat. I make some excuse about having to put the heating on, and race up the stairs before her. I go to the fridge and take down Bobs' drawings along with a school photograph. As I move them I find the old lottery ticket, Hazel's lottery ticket, I'm holding it dreamily when Hazel comes through the door and quickly shove it in the bread bin with Bob's pictures. I feel bad about doing this, but I wasn't going to get into any discussions about Bob now, nothing was going to get in the way of the possibility of me having sex.

"I'll make coffee," I say nervously.

"Oh! we're actually having coffee" Hazel says with a wicked grin as she moves toward the bathroom. I put the kettle on and take down two of my three mugs from my sad-looking mug tree. I give Hazel my Simpsons mug. And I have the novelty breast shaped one; I'm past caring now.

While I wait for the kettle to boil, I put on my new CD, I load both discs to play consecutively. The kettle clicks off, I return to the kitchen area and make the coffee. As the first track starts, Hazel comes out of the bathroom, she has a small overnight bag that I didn't see before.

"I'll just slip into something a little more comfortable," she says as she moves towards the bedroom.

"Ok," I say, my voice breaking up because my throat has gone dry. I take a big sip of my coffee and burn my mouth. I'm leaning on the sink watching the bedroom door. Should I follow her? I'm just about to move when the door opens.

Hazel is standing there wrapped in my duvet. She turns to go back into the bedroom while dropping the duvet to her waist. Her red hair falling down her bare back, she looks over her shoulder.

"Well come on then," she says giggling as she disappears into the darkened room.

I drop my breast-shaped mug into the sink breaking off the novelty nipple. I follow Hazel towards the bedroom. Something stirs in the trousers of my new suit. I get this mental picture of a creaking garage door and someone pulling the dustsheet off a classic car. I jump into the car and nervously turn the key, the engine fires up first time like it's never been off the road. I push the accelerator to the floor, the engine roars and strains under the bonnet.

I go into the bedroom. I leave the door ajar, just enough for some of the light from the lounge and Dylan's voice can get in. Hazel is in bed propped up on one elbow, she moves over, lifting the duvet, inviting me in. For a split second I think about asking her to move over as she's on my favourite side of the bed - God! I've been alone for too long.

*　*　*　*　*　*　*　*

I shan't bore you with too much detail. But, well, all you need to know is, my willy behaved nothing like a classic car. It was more like the Bat-car crashing out of the Bat-cave on a mission to save Gotham City, certainly no hand cranking needed. The only other thing you need to know is, I lasted to well into the second CD, track five, *I Shall be Released* - quite apt really.

So eat your heart out Sting!

Seven

Yet she's true, like ice, like fire.
People carry roses,
Make promises by the hours,
My love she laughs like the flowers,
Valentines can't buy her.

(Love Minus Zero/No Limit,©1965, renewed 1993 Special Rider Music)

My idealistic domestic bliss is shattered at 7.12 the following morning when Hazels' mobile goes off. I'm cooking breakfast in the kitchen area, showing off by throwing eggs in the air and catching them, before breaking them with one hand into a pan. I've just made a pot of tea, pouring it out into my two remaining mugs. This leaves my mug tree looking positively autumnal.

Hazel is kneeling on the sofa, watching me, and resting her arms on the back. With my duvet snuggled around her, but leaving her red hair cascading down her bare back. Her skin is white and smooth like porcelain, my eyes follow down to the small of her back, where I can just see the start of her bottom, a beautiful proper curvy bottom. It's the most attractive workmans' bottom I've ever seen.

The ringing comes from her handbag; she rummages inside to find her mobile. She looks at the front of the phone and recognises the caller, suddenly she gathers up the duvet around her shoulders, (as if he can see down the phone) and shuffles off to the bedroom. It's obviously Clive.

After about ten minutes Hazel comes out, she's got dressed in a blue skirt and jacket, her hair is up in a tight bun; she is ready for work.

"Clive?" I say,

"Yes, he's just left Manchester," Hazel says as she moves to the bathroom mirror applying lipstick before adding in a slightly distorted voice,

"Oh England won." As if this will make me feel better, anyway I know this because I recorded the highlights, leaving a warm and naked Hazel to watch it at 5am this morning (that's how dedicated I am). But I tell Hazel none of this, only adding,

"I heard."

We sit and eat breakfast in near silence. Alone with our separate thoughts. I think about Bob, I could come right out and tell her now. I then think about England; we could now qualify as group winners, then we could really go on to win the World Cup. I decide to tell Hazel. Not about my views of our World Cup chances. I have to tell her about Bob,

"Hazel I have......," I start, but I don't get time to finish, Hazel gets up and looking at her watch says,

"Look I really have to go, I have an appointment in London at nine." She gathers up her things and moves towards the door. Just as she opens the door she says,

"Look I'll phone you tonight," then pausing in the doorway,

" What were you going to say?" she asks,

"Oh," I say, flustered,

"I..I was just thinking we could win our Group now." Hazel is pushing the buttons on her phone looking for a number, while trying to find her car keys in her handbag. So luckily she doesn't hear properly.

"Yes.... maybe, I'll phone you. Love you," she says as she disappears out the door and down the stairs.

I clear away the breakfast things, I go to put the bread back in the bread bin. I see Bob's pictures, guiltily I arrange them back on the fridge door. Bob has a set of magnetic letters spread over the fridge. In the middle he has spelt out three words, football, van and Bugger. I take some of the unused magnets and fix the pictures back.

I take a shower and get dressed for work. I have a fairly uneventful day at work apart from not concentrating. I leave off part of an order and I'll have to go out of my way to deliver it on Friday.

When I get home I make tea, a jacket potato, beans and cheese, then my phone rings and I smile as the tune plays and press the green button, I know who it is, as I have told no one else the number.

" Hi," I say. Hazel starts talking but there's a lot of echo in her voice.

"Where are you, in a tunnel?"

"I'm in the bath," to prove this she tells me to listen as she raises her leg and with her toe turns the tap on. I can hear running water down the phone. I get this mental picture of one of those massive walk-in baths, it's full of bubbles, which almost covers Hazels body. I'm standing naked, except for a strategically-placed champagne bottle. I step into the bath and slowly lower myself down.

"So what do you think?" Hazel says, but I'm lost in my fantasy and have not been listening.

"Yea great," I say hesitantly.

"So I'll see you just after seven tomorrow. Be ready for action we won't have long," Suddenly Hazel is talking to someone else in a raised voice.

"No I'm singing dear," Clive must have heard her talking and knocked on the bathroom door. Then the phone goes dead.

I don't know what Hazel is up to, but I'm glad that I'm seeing her more than just the one day a week, this is a good sign. I've decided to sit her down and tell her all about my son. I don't know what future we have, if any, but that future has to include Bob.

So it's now seven o'clock on Friday. I'm ready for action whatever that means? I'm nervously pacing up and down the flat, trying to think how to tell Hazel about Bob, why I kept him a secret. *Under the Red Sky* by Dylan is playing on my stereo. Suddenly I hear pounding feet racing up the metal staircase. Then a frantic banging on the door. I open the door. Hazel almost flies through the door. She has on tight Lycra shorts, a baggy sweat-shirt and a personal stereo. The complete jogging kit. Her face is red and flushed, she stands for a few seconds with her hands on her knees getting her breath back.

Hazel then set off across the lounge discarding trainers and clothing as she goes. I follow behind her as a low flying sports bra hits me in the eye.

"Come on we haven't got long, in fact you've got eighteen minutes to make love to me," Hazel says looking at her watch. It turns out that Hazel goes jogging on Mondays and Fridays. She has a set route that she follows. Clive actually keeps a record of her times to check that she's improving. It's his coaching side coming out. Hazel knew how long we had if Clive wasn't to get suspicious. I remove my T-shirt and follow her to the bedroom,

"Oh right well best forget any foreplay then"

*   *   *   *   *   *   *   *

The following weekend is miserable, I take Bob and Graham to football on Saturday. It's freezing cold and wet. We lose 1-0 to a struggling team and lose out on the chance to move into the play-off zone. It's the 1st of December, it's going to be a long hard season. Bob cries. Not noisy crying but quiet sobbing tears stream from his eyes. Should I really be subjecting him to so much pain and suffering, for someone so young? On the way home I buy him an advent calendar to cheer him up, one with chocolates behind each window. He opens the first window and eats a chocolate snowman. We sit watching TV and eat the entire calendar. As he opens the window marked 24, containing an extra large chocolate representation of Jesus in his crib, Bob asks if Santa will come tomorrow now. I tell him no and explain that he'll have to wait. Bob goes to the the cupboard and finds two boxes of Smarties in his sweets box I keep for him. Carefully he places one Smartie behind each window before he shuts them, so that the calendar is as good as new again.

On the Sunday we go round to mums and stay in all day, as it's so cold, wet and windy. I cook a Sunday roast, a small beef joint. I try and make Yorkshire puddings but I burn them and they end up solid as a rock.

In the afternoon one of my favourite movies is on, *Spartacus*. We settle down to watch it. Mums coal fire is roaring and I struggle to stay awake. I watch up to the bit when the Romans have captured most of the rebel slaves but are unable to identify Spartacus. They ask them to give up their leader or they will all be crucified. Just as Spartacus is about to step forward. Someone steps forward before him and says,

"I am Spartacus," then someone else step forwards until they all start calling out. So the road back to Rome is littered with bodies. This is the point I must have fallen asleep. I start a vivid dream, I'm at football, it's half time and the stadium is full. Then this man walks on to the pitch. He stands in the centre circle and addresses the crowd.

"Someone is having an affair with my girlfriend. I know his name is Nathan, would Nathan please step forward, or my rugby team will beat the crap out of all of you," I'm just about to step forward and declare I am Nathan, and so save all my fellow supporters, when someone in the north stand to my right gets there before me. Standing up to declare:

"I am Nathan," then a voice joins in from near the directors' box. Suddenly the whole stadium is full of people standing and calling out,

"I am Nathan," in unison.

Next to me Graham stands up and steps forwards and promptly falls into the lap of the lady in front. The stadium is in uproar, then the club mascot, a seven foot furry lion, runs the full length of the pitch and floors Clive with a flying drop kick.

I wake up, what a weird dream. I wonder how Clive would really take it, if he found out. What would Hazel do? I sometimes feel I'm on the outside looking in. If it all blows up, I'll be devastated at first but soon I'll just go back to life B.H. (before Hazel). In a way it's good, it's all about me, and can't affect Bob.

Mum has made some beef sandwiches and a new pot of tea. I connect up Bob's playstation and we play for about half an hour. Then it's time for me to leave as it's Sunday night (House of Gloom gig night.) I give my mobile phone number to mum. So she can get hold of me in an emergency.

I play a good gig, well I enjoy it. I play *Jokerman* from Infidels. I really like the line that goes:

'I was born with a snake in both my fists, while a hurricane was blowing'
No, I don't know what it means but it's typical Dylan, you can really spit the line out. Sky was acting strange, I don't know how can you tell the difference, but worse than normal anyway.

I'm on the second verse of, *Is your love in vain* from Street Legal, when Sky walks up to the stage, she has a low cut white silk blouse with ruffles on the front, she leans forward to put a new pint in front of me. The blouse hangs open, I can see right down the front, it looks like a large cavern with ancient stalactites hanging down. I try to avoid her for the rest of the night and leave soon after my last number, asking Colin if I can slip out the back way.

In the dark I fall over some old mixer crates but manage to climb over the fence with my guitar still on my back. I jump down the other side, and check my top pocket, for my mouth organ. I make my way home, once inside I check my mobile for messages, there is one:
She has sent me a text message:

CU 2moro
FOR HORIZONTAL JOGGING
ILUVU

After ten minutes of reading the instructions, I reply:

IN TRAINING
FOR RELAY
BATON IN HAND READY£

So Hazel is due to arrive at seven tomorrow for frantic, passionate and quickie sex. Sex is about 90% anticipation and 10% perspiration so they say. Obviously when you think you might have sex it's quite exciting, but when you know you're about to have sex, well the excitement doubles.

It's almost seven o'clock on Monday. Hazel is due in 12 minutes. I think, I know I'll get into bed. I go to the bedroom take off all my clothes and jump into bed. I lie there for 30 seconds then change my mind, get dressed again and go back to the lounge. I try and sit down, put a cushion on my lap, but I'm really ready for action now. I need to calm down. I need to think of something to cool my passion. I know, imagine I'm in bed with someone old and ugly; like say Dot Cotton or Nora Batty; Dot Cotton and Nora Batty together Ugh! That does the trick.

My little sperm troops, (just like tadpoles in tin hats) are in full retreat. Like a black and white film from the History channel showing troops evacuating the beaches of Dunkirk, snaking off into the distance queuing for a boat to take them home.

Suddenly I hear pounding trainers on the metal staircase. My sperm troops return to full action stations, jumping out of amphibian vehicles storming up the beach, and streaming out the back of Hercules aircraft. By the time the door opens I'm ready. We only make it as far as the sofa. Eighteen minutes later that battalion of sperm troops has been wiped out. The next battalion of troops are already in base camp starting basic training.

Eight

"I've met someone," Hazel says.

"What do you mean, you've met someone," Joan says almost spitting the words out. Hazel and Joan are in the photocopy room at work. It's a small glass room at the end of an open plan office. Around twenty people are set out in strict lines, their desks adorned with pot plants, family photographs and cuddly toys. On each computer the owners vie with one another to display the most exotic postcards from around the world. Others have notes with words of wisdom like 'you don't have to be mad to work here but it helps,' and the like. Each person has tried to stamp their individuality on their little island, but in so doing have only ended up all looking the same. As Hazel and Joan continue their animated discussion, one or two people look up from their computer screens, tearing themselves away from opening today's junk emails, about how to get Viagra or telling how you've won a digital camera. Joan moves closer to Hazel, they turn away from prying eyes and face the window. Joan is Hazel's best friend although she's about fifteen years older. She has worked for Clive since the company started, and helped Hazel get her job there.

"Just that, I've met someone and we've been out a few times," Hazel continues.

"Oh so it's not serious then," Joan says

"Well," Hazel says with a wicked grin.

"You're joking, what about Clive, your job, the apartment,"

"I know, I know," Hazel says stopping her.

"It's just that Clive is always out, what with the Rugby and work," Hazel says. Joan can't believe it. She thought Hazel was so happy.

Joan is 49, for twenty years of that she had been married to Keith. Until he did the old trick of running off with a girl half his age who he then married. Joan struggled to hold down her job and raising her daughter,

Carol, alone. It was the same old story, Joan did the everyday things involved in bringing up a child alone. Dealing with the sulky, moody, untidy and argumentative monster that is the *teenage girl*. It was her that set the boundaries, who reined in her daughter, but also was always there for her. All Keith had to do was to arrive on a white charger once a fortnight, take her off to some exotic location for the day, shower his daughter with gifts before disappearing into the sunset. Then Carol got in with the wrong crowd, she started eroding the boundaries set by Joan. If Joan said she should be home at 10.30, Carol would roll in at 11 o'clock. Joan was pretty sure she was drinking and maybe other things. Joan was at her wits end, so she turned to Keith asking him to have a word, it was time for him to play the bad-cop role. So he had a word, well he had five actually, 'come and live with me.' So Carol jumped aboard his white charger and left.

Joan was devastated, suddenly she was portrayed as the big bad witch, an image Keith did little to erode. The only good thing to come out of the mess, was that by moving Carol broke her circle of friends. She even met a nice bloke, not the man Joan would have chosen but that man may not exist. They moved in together just down the street from Keith and in the next few years had two beautiful children. Joan was besotted with her grandchildren, now she had time to enjoy them. Without the worry she had when Carol was young. Carol doesn't know the whole truth, Joan shielded her when she was young. The times she forgave Keith's little indiscretions and the times he was out of work, his drinking and the thing Joan hid best, his violence. Oh, never enough to seek help, he was always careful, preferring to resort to slapping, shouting and evil threats.

Life was so unfair, now he had this new young wife who was best friends with her daughter. A good job and he had even joined a gym. He looked younger now than he did when he left her. Joan couldn't bear to be around Keith, this made visits to her grandchildren awkward, especially at birthdays and Christmas. She had to arrive early, give out her gifts and slip off before Keith arrived, to avoid any trouble. So Joan had grown bitter and hard, no one was going to hurt her again.

These last few years Joan had learnt to be in charge. No man was ever going to rule her emotionally or financially. No she was in charge.

That's how it was with Clive. He thought he came to her when he needed her. But she only let him in on her terms. It had been going on for three years, on and off.

When she got Hazel the job, she had no idea things would work out like they have. Clive had just started making waves saying they should go out more, be seen together. She knew what that meant. The next thing he would want her to move in, or worse marriage. So Hazel was a blessing. Oh at first he had stopped their affair. They were polite and courteous in front of work colleagues. But after a few months he came crawling back. The age gap was beginning to tell, he was finding it hard to keep up with Hazel. So Joan and Clive had returned to their long lunch time meetings, drives in the country or pub lunches out of town and then the afternoon at a hotel.

Oh she was in charge in the bedroom too.

Now Hazel had to rock the boat with talk of someone else. Hazel continues enthusiastically,

"Oh he's so sweet and kind, we have so much in common, music, he plays guitar," Hazel says looking dreamily out the window. Joan followed her gaze to a group of office smokers (21st century lepers) who are forced to stand in the car park to indulge their habit. They huddled in a tight circle to keep warm, their smoke blown about by the fierce December wind. God I could do with a cigarette myself Joan thinks,

Then she realises,

"Oh god it's him, it's that hippie guy you dragged me along to see the other Sunday," Joan says looking round at Hazel.

"Might be" Hazel says with a grin.

"Oh Joan, I don't know what to do, I," she hesitated.

"I...I think I love him"

Joan let out a long breath through her teeth, she turned to face the office and caught the eye of one or two people in the front row. They looked down embarrassed. Joan and Hazel had been in the photocopy room for twenty minutes now. The office could tell it was a somewhat important discussion (they knew about Hazel and Clive) and they knew Hazel would confide in Joan with any problems. Joan tried to smile reassuringly at the office gossips.

"Look Hazel you won't do anything silly, I mean, does he know how you feel,"

"Well he knows I like him, he knows about Clive, but that's as far as it goes"

Joan holds Hazel by her arms,

"Well keep it like that, have a bit of fun, don't make any rash, promises." Just then Jill, a temp, tries to enter the room, but one look from Joan and she recoils like she burnt her hand on the door handle. The temp scuttles away, to the general amusement of the rest of the office.

"Look Joan thanks I really needed to tell someone, I thought I would burst if I didn't,"

"Look you know you can talk to me, but don't go telling anyone else. You know what this lot is like," Joan says gesturing with her head at the office.

"You'll be out on your ear girl," Joan says giving Hazel a hug.

"I know its crazy," Hazel says glancing up at the large clock situated above the photocopier, the clock everyone in the office tried not to constantly watch. Hazel gathered up her handbag and moved towards the door.

"I really must be going, I have an appointment at two." Joan removes her compact mirror from her hand bag and checks her make up.

"Me too, I have one of my long lunch meetings."

*   *   *   *   *   *   *   *

On Wednesday we have a mid-week match. Hazel agrees to come along. Bob doesn't go to mid-week games, not on a school night. I have forgiven Hazel over the England ticket thing – well she did make up for it.

Hazel has never been to a football match before, the funny thing is she's never been to a rugby game either. Strange considering Clive is the coach of our local club side. But she always managed to avoid it. If they had a big important game, Clive would insist that she should go, but Hazel would turn up just at the end of the game. Clive had been so busy barking orders from the touchline that he never noticed.

Hazel was quite good, she didn't ask any really embarrassing questions. The only slight blemish was when the east stand started a song about the dubious parentage of the referee. Hazel flicked through her programme, before asking where she could find the lyrics.

It turned out to be a great game, totally out of character with the rest of our season. We played the leaders of the division and won 4-3. The game had everything, the opposition had a player sent off, while another broke a leg. We also had a streaker for some reason. Not a very professional one, even our streakers are strictly second division. He came racing out from behind the right hand goal, but he had failed to fully remove his trousers, preferring to keep them around his ankles, this meant he fell over four times before he made it to the centre circle and was apprehended by a combination of a policeman, a steward and a seven foot furry lion.

Hazel was a bit quiet, I don't know if she was a bit overawed. I kept asking her if she was all right. When she dropped me off. She didn't come in.

Hazel said she was tired and it was getting late.

I get in side and make myself a coffee. I sit in the lounge illuminated only by the small light from the kitchen area.
I think to myself well if we haven't had sex tonight.
It could be:

[a] We have a relationship that is not solely based on sex.
[b] She can only make love after jogging for 12 minutes before hand.
[c] she has been subjected to my entire repertoire of sexual positions, and has become bored.
[d] She's decided it was all a big mistake, time to cool it.

The thing about our relationship is it doesn't cross over into my normal life. My spare time is covered by say 20% music, 20% football and 60% spent with Bob. So what I'm trying to say is a whole 60% of my life Hazel knows nothing about, but then again look at it the other way round. Hazel; Time spent with Clive 98%. Time spent with Nathan; Mondays 17 minutes, all Wednesday nights and then 17 minutes on Fridays again.
I don't know how serious we are.

I say things with my head (or what I think she wants me to say) like, well we're having a good time, besides I'm not looking for commitment or a long term relationship, I'm not that kind of guy, love them and leave them that's me.

Bollocks, what I want to say, with my heart is, I love you, I never want to leave you, I want to spend the rest of my life with you, I need stability for my son. But I can't say any of this or I would scare her off. I've always been a jump in with both feet, hook, line and sinker, shot through the heart with cupids arrow, kind of guy. I've never been any good at one-night stands, although if I had had more opportunities I may have got used to them.

So it's Friday, jogging day again. I have a long phone call from Hazel on Thursday in the day, I've brought a hands-free kit for my phone, we spent just over an hour chatting and joking. Then this morning I get a text message;

LET'S RUN THE ANCIENT
GREEK WAY NAKED!
JUST AFTER 7

So its 7.10 p.m. I'm standing naked, yes that's right I'm absolutely starkers standing by the door. Waiting for the sound of Hazel's trainers on the metal stairs.
A prelude to our 17 minutes of mad and frantic love making.
Before Hazel gets dressed, puts her personal stereo on and checks her watch and completes her training, returning to Clive with his stop watch in hand. If he only knew the truth.

There it is, the sound of footsteps, a little slow today. I judge when she has reached the top of the stairs. I take a deep breath and pull in my stomach before flinging open the door, and shouting,

"TARRAH!"
My mum steps through the open door

"Mum, I...I was expecting someone else,"

"I hope you were," she says giving one of her special laughs, a sort of female Sid James kind of laugh.

I frantically look for the nearest thing to cover my embarrassment. On the coffee table is a selection of LP's. I grab the first two albums, placing one in front and one behind. I've got Dylan's *Desire* at the front, (but that's obvious!) and *The Basement Tapes* covering my bum.

Mum comes in and shuts the door.
I start to edge across the lounge to the bedroom. Suddenly things go from bad to worse. I can hear trainers pounding up the outside staircase. The door bursts open, Hazel is bent over hopping on one leg while trying to remove a trainer and her crop top at the same time. I desperately try to stop her.

"Hazel," I shout.

"Hazel I'd like to introduce you to my mum," I blurt out. Hazel stands up, her face red and flushed from running.

"Arh nice to meet you," she says looking embarrassed. Standing there with one bare foot and her crop-top half over her head, exposing her left breast.

"I'm sorry Nathan, I really need to talk to you," Mum says, as she makes a tactical retreat to the kitchen area to put the kettle on. I knew it must be serious for mum to come round after dark and to leave Bob with someone. No this certainly was not a social visit.

Hazel adjusts her clothing and pulls on her discarded trainer. I back away to the bedroom still clutching my albums. Although the front LP is hardly needed now as my desire has somewhat cooled down – a cassette would have been quite sufficient.

"Look Hazel I'm sorry about this," I say sticking my head round the bedroom door, while hopping on one leg as I get my tracksuit bottoms on.

"Yes I better be going, I'll ring you later," Hazel says, then turning to my mum she says,

"It was nice to meet you,"

"and you dear, I hope to see more of you," then mum realised she would probably never see so much of Hazel again! – more cheeky laughter. Hazel blushed with embarrassment, covering this by checking her watch before running off into the cold December night.

Mum has made two coffees and is sitting in one of the armchairs. I sit down and apologise, and try to explain what was going on, but end up digging a deeper hole for myself, so I'm glad when mum dismisses it.

"Oh no problem, I was young once," she says, her cheeky laughter trailing off, as she thinks of a long-ago incident, I interrupt her mental picture.

"OK mum what's the problem?"

Nine

I don't care
How many letters they sent
Morning came and morning went
Pick up your money
And pack up your tent

You ain't going nowhere (©1967,renewed 1995 Dwarf Music)

"Here you better read this," Mum says, handing me a postcard. On the front is a picture of Bondi beach with a surfer catching a large wave. I turn it over and read it:

Dear Daisy (my mums Christian name)
Thank you for your last letter, it was good to catch up on all the news. Just dropping you a line to say I'm coming home for Christmas. I thought it might be a good time to meet my son. We will be arriving around the 18th of December. Hope you can arrange things with Nat.
Love to everyone
Sasha.
PS Paul my fiancé will accompany me.

I stare at the postcard trying to digest all I had just read. I ask Mum about the letters. It turns out she had been writing to Sasha for years. I can't believe mum has been writing all these years, I feel betrayed by her. Sasha let me down, like I had never been let down before.

I was losing my Dad, my mentor, my rock, my fountain of knowledge. If this wasn't tragic enough my, no, our, painfully small and fragile son was hanging precariously to life.

Mum was falling apart and I really needed someone, to stand by me, maybe this was too much to ask of Sasha, she was so young.

I sat for a long time staring at the postcard, until the words blurred and merged, I became aware my hands were shaking. I placed the card on the table and went to the kitchen to make a drink. Mum watched me intently, trying to gauge my true feelings, I didn't offer mum a drink, as I only had whisky.

When I sat down mum started talking, in her quiet and gentle way. She told me how writing the letters was one of the hardest things she had ever done. At first it was easy, after all she was a mother, she knew that however screwed up and unable to cope Sasha was, she had to know her son had survived. She didn't expect Sasha to reply, she certainly didn't expect her to carry on writing, urging Mum for more and more news and details of Bob's life. Each time Mum wrote, a colourful postcard would return thanking her and requesting more news, with a new forwarding address. Once or twice a year a more detailed letter would come several sides of A4 detailing Sasha's life. Mum noticed a change over the years, almost as if she was witnessing Sasha growing up through her letters.

I thought I was angry, but I was wrong. I could never be angry with mum. She didn't have a malicious or deceitful bone in her body. I wasn't angry with Sasha, not now, not even back then. When she left I was too emotionally drained to be angry. I was too busy dealing with Bob's needs to waste time with anger. In the hospital, encouraged by the nurses, I fed, changed and just held him for hours. By the time Bob came home many weeks later, I loved him, he was the most beautiful thing I had ever seen. So small and helpless, yet so unique and magical. I was so grateful that he had made it, I could forgive anyone. Bob had an insatiable appetite for life, he crawled early, he pulled himself up on tables and chairs so he could see more of his world and finally he walked much sooner than was expected. It was as if given the chance of life he was going to make the most of it.

Mum stood up and went to the kitchen clicking the kettle back on, before reaching in her handbag. She pulled out a desk diary. She made a coffee and sat back down placing the book on the table on top of the card. I picked it up and started to leaf through it.

Mum explained that she had copied every letter she had written along with Sasha's replies, every few pages was an exotic postcard. I guess she knew that one day it would come out. I started reading, here was Bob's life, month by month it charted Bob's achievements. Through his difficult first year, Bob's first tooth, his first words, the strange piece of rag he took to bed each night, the time he cut his nose on a chest of drawers playing murder in the dark with me and Bob's first attempts to play his guitar. Every little thing written down and dated.

The last letter was dated the first week in December, although most of the letters actually had only the passing mention of me. But this letter did mention a new girlfriend and how Bob was reacting to this, most of which I had no idea about. You always try to shield children by keeping things from them, but all you do is worry them with the unknown. Bob had confided in mum that he was worried whether my girlfriend would like him. He didn't know that his dad didn't have the guts to tell Hazel he even had a son.

I stood up and paced about tapping the card with my fingers, while thinking. I wonder why the sudden interest in making contact with her son now. There had been no mention of this fiancé Paul in Sasha's letters or cards. Surely she had no ambition of obtaining custody after all this time. I had never made any inquiries about the legal side, I had my name put on Bob's birth certificate. I can't really do much about stopping her seeing Bob. Bob had started asking about his mum. I tell mum that there's nothing to worry about, I'm cool about the letters. I ask to hang on to them, as I'd like to read some more.

I ask Mum more about the letters. What has Sasha been up to for six years? It turns out she has her own shop making hand-made jewellry. I take a magnetic letter and fix the postcard to the fridge. Mum seems reassured, she says she better be going as she's left Bob with Tim's mum. I kiss her on the cheek and insist on running her home in the van.

Hazel rings when I get back to the flat. We have a good laugh about the jogging escapade. In future we agree that she will ring me a warning on jogging nights.

The following week is much the same, Monday jogging, Wednesday we go ten-pin bowling and then Friday jogging again. So we are now well into December, as I can tell from the empty windows of Bobs' Advent calendar.

I have a confession, come closer, I don't want everyone to know this, but I love Christmas. Some of my earliest memories are around Christmas time, the build up and traditions. Reassuringly regular things like the wooden manger Dad made when I was around five, Mums paper angels and Santas that she had put on the walls for years, the white of the angels wings yellow with age. Watching of *It's a Wonderful Life* on Christmas eve, my favourite film. The last few years have been excellent as Bobs has really got into Christmas, with all the magic only a child can show. I don't know if he still believes in Father Christmas. It may be that it's to his advantage to humour me. It's a case of here's my list to Santa, but woe betide if I don't get everything on it.

So in the first week of December Bob is writing his letter to Father Christmas. Bob's letter goes like this;

Dear Santa
I hope you are well, I am, I have also been very good this year, but I'm sure you know this. Oh, that swearing thing, using the 'B' word, wasn't my fault.

I know you're very busy, so I won't keep you.
My list,
1 Playstation 2
2 Hear'say CD (don't tell my dad)
3 New football shirt (must be latest, I know the old colours are on special offer)
4 Pokemon or Rugrats video.
5 A scooter or skateboard.
Love Bob XXXXX
P.S. Please deliver to my Nans house, as she has a chimney.

So I'm getting ready for Christmas, planning the Christmas dinner ordering the turkey. I order an organic free-range turkey, it means the turkey gets good food with no added antibiotics to eat. They can also run around in the fresh air. That way the turkeys have a short but ultimately happy life, okay they still don't make too many social entries in their diary for January.

The only bad thing in my diary is the imminent arrival of Sasha. With this in mind I decide to test the waters with Bob, to see what he thinks about meeting his Mum for the first time. So it's our normal Saturday night in watching crap telly. Bob and I have been to football, we won again and things are looking up, we are on a six game unbeaten run, and a play-off place is a remote possibility. Bob and I stopped at the Taj Mahal Indian on the way home, I have a korma and Nan bread, while Bob has a large plate of popadoms with some plain rice.

I decide to opt for the straight forward approach

"Bob how would you like to meet your Mum," I say as I mop up some sauce with some Nan bread. I look at Bob's face for any reaction. After a short pause Bob says, a little understated,

"It would be nice." Still staring at the telly, as Cilla asks us if a short, bald bloke should date or dump the attractive leggy blond model on Blind date (who obviously has come on the show looking for true love, without a thought of furthering her modelling career). Bob attacks another defenceless popadom. I'm a bit taken aback by his general apathy, I thought he would be really excited.

"Aren't you interested in what she's like, or how she looks?"

"I know what she looks like, she's Australian isn't she, I watch Neighbours with Nan all the time," Bob says biting into his second popadom, which explodes showering crumbs down his front.

"Well she's not strictly an Australian, she's just lived there for a long time."

"Hgm!" Bob says pausing to think.

"So are we going to be a proper family now,"

"Well we are a proper family, you me and Nan, and you never miss out on anything or want for anything,"

"I want things, a Playstation 2 for starters,"

"Yes I know, well that's down to Santa we put it in your letter," I said looking through my open bedroom door at the large box under my bed containing Bob's Playstation 2."

"Anyway we were talking about your Mum. So what do you think?"

Some more thinking, while he brushed crumbs off his jumper straight onto the floor, I ignored this.

"So is she going to look after me now?"

"No, no nothing is going to change, Nan and I will still look after you. She just want to meet you, then after Christmas she'll be going back to Australia."

"Yep ok, gotter go," Bob leaps up and dashes to the bathroom. Knocking my can of beer over beside my chair. Bob uses this dashing to go to the loo often as a kind of defence mechanism. It's a signal that he's had enough of a difficult conversation or if he's embarrassed by kissing on the telly.

When Bob comes out he has a white mark on his chin, its toothpaste, he's brushed his teeth. Bob disappears into the bedroom before reappearing in his Pokemon pyjamas. He walks over to me puts his arms round my neck and kisses me on the cheek.

"Good night Dad." Then he runs full pelt to the bedroom and dives on the bed. I grimace as I think of the playstation hidden under there.

* * * * * * * *

Hazel has taken to phoning me in the day, on my travels. We talk for hours about nothing in particular, telly, the weather, music and the political situation in the middle east. I took this as a sign of our relationship moving forward. I don't know forward to what, or forward to where. I mean we're not kids, we both have a certain amount of baggage, (although I wouldn't refer to Bob as baggage). I mean you get to my age you don't expect to meet someone and it be violins and flashing lights, but to be honest I got this with Hazel that first November night.

I decide to get Christmas out of the way before rocking the boat in any way. I had no way of telling the boat was about to get blown out of the water.

Sasha came from Manchester. She has an elderly mother and two sisters there. It was decided that she would stay down here for the first few days to meet Bob, before going up north for Christmas. I thought it would be a bad idea for her to stay with mum and Bob. However well you explained it Bob still might get confused, when his mother who he has never seen moves back in, all be it for a few days. I left it to mum to make all the relevant phone calls, I certainly didn't want to talk to Sasha over the phone, what I wanted to say I would say to her face.

So I arrange for them to stay in the mobile caravan behind *The House of Gloom*. It's not as bad as it sounds. Colin keeps it for staff to live in. Although it had been empty for sometime. The last occupant, a busty blond barmaid was caught in a compromising position (stark naked on top of Colin) by his wife. So on Wednesday morning Mum and I spent two hours cleaning, I also brought a small grocery pack containing the essentials milk, bread, a jar of vegamite and six cans of Fosters lager (See, he who thinks Australian is Australian)

I got a phone call from Mum in the early afternoon. I was on the phone to Hazel at the time, it came through as call waiting... Bleep, bleep, I answered it. Mum said Sasha had arrived at the *House of Gloom*. and had gone to bed exhausted after her long flight. Sasha said she would like to meet at eight in the pub.

Then it struck me, tonight, that's Wednesday night, that's my Hazel night.

I phone her, her phone is on call diverting. Hazel's voice comes through on an answer machine, it sounds official and not like her at all,

"I'm sorry Hazel is in meetings all afternoon, so you know what to do after the beep, please leave a message." That means I can't ring her till after five, she's not going to be happy with me. Just before mum's call she was going on about how much she was looking forward to seeing me. Still this was important and there was no way I could get out of it.

At five I ring Hazel I can hear the radio on she's in her car. She is not happy I didn't really think through my excuse beforehand. I told her we had a rearranged match, but what I hadn't banked on, Hazel was now taking a keen interest in my club and had taken to reading the sports section of the paper. So informed me with some gusto that we weren't due to play until Saturday. I knew I should have gone with; my ex-girlfriend is coming to meet our son. She knew there was another reason. I said desperately trying to placate her,

"Well maybe I could see you tomorrow."

"Arr well... no Clive's in," she said hesitantly,

"So I've got to arrange my life around you, but you can't change things for me." I think if I make her feel guilty maybe she'll forget the total pack of lies I've just told her. I could tell Hazel was getting upset.

"Look you knew what you were getting into, I never lied to you," she said, her voice breaking.

"Well if you had told me the rules where I can only ever get to see you three times a week. I might have had second thoughts," I said lying now, my heart pounding. I was both angry and nervous. I was angry that I was forced into this argument at this time, with my confrontation with Sasha hours away. I was nervous I would push Hazel too far, still not sure of the depth of her true feelings. Hazels shouting through tears now,

"Well I never thought I would break any of my rules. Well not my biggest rule."

I interrupt her.

"Oh yea, What's that," the radio cuts out she's pulled over and stopped,

"I've never broken this rule in my life before," she says in a quiet more controlled voice .

"So what's this big rule then," I say. There's a considerable pause, I'm just about to say her name. When Hazel says,

"Well stupidly I...I fell in love with you."

I start to rant,

"Well if you really love me, why don't you leave Clive? I need to be with you all the time. There so much you don't know about me. For a start I've got a six year old son, I'm sure you'd love him he's so smart and ...hello...hello Hazel are you there," I look at the phone CALL ENDED is on the display. I try her number;

I'm sorry it has not been possible to connect you to this mobile, it may be switched off.

This is all I hear for the next twenty minutes. God I can't deal with this. I'm due to meet Sasha in just over two hours. I may have just broken up with Hazel and it's the eighteenth of December a week to Christmas day.

Ten

I had something to protect
Good and bad, I define these terms
Quite clear, no doubt, somehow.
Ah, but I was so much older then,
I'm younger than that now.

(My Back Pages ©1964, renewed 1992 Special Rider Music)

I get to the *House of Gloom* about half an hour before Sasha's due. I feel the need for a drink. a) to drown my sorrows if I have broken up with Hazel and b), so I can face meeting Sasha. She was always unconventional, having bright pink hair the day we met. I came round the side of a tent at the Womad festival and there she was, sat on a straw bale telling a story to a group of around twenty spellbound children. Sasha was working as a volunteer in the crèche over the weekend. I stood and watched her for twenty minutes, as she held the children's total attention. Sasha was concentrating, unaware of anything going on around her. The Japanese reggae band on the main stage and the large queue for the portable toilets. She animated the story with her hands, while pulling an amazing range of faces. I lent against the canvas and studied her, but I wasn't following her story, she had on a black shirt with slightly too many buttons undone so it fell off one shoulder revealing part of a tattoo, later that night I discover it's a dove carrying an olive branch. She had a short denim skirt, with fishnet tights and black ankle boots which had totally impractical (certainly for an open air festival) stiletto heels. That was Sasha all over, never compromising to suit the situation. She was sexy, but not in a blatant way she was just comfortable with her body. Her attitude was "this is me" if you don't like it, get over it. I wonder if time had mellowed her, back then she was in her early twenties now she would be,what nearly thirty, she could even be thirty I wasn't sure.

Graham was sat in his usual chair with Quinn at his feet. I say hello and offer to buy him a drink.

"No, no let me get these," he says holding out a clenched fist ready to drop some money in my hand. I have no patience to deal with Graham's change games tonight.

"No you're all right mate," I say turning to the bar.

"Oh, very well," Graham says, unfolding a crisp twenty pound note from his fist and returning it to his wallet. My eyes follow the slowly disappearing note,

"Bugger," I mutter under my breath. I order the drinks while asking Colin if Sasha and Paul are happy with the accommodation. He said they were, in fact Paul was overjoyed, as an Australian, living in a pub was his idea of heaven.

I down a couple of pints in quick succession while talking football with Graham. It's good to take my mind off everything, but I keep an eye on the clock above the open fire.

The clock has crept round to twenty past eight by the time Sasha walks in. She is all in black, with a see through blouse, black bra and leather skirt complete with knee length boots. Her most striking feature is her hair now in long black dread locks, tied up at the back, but sticking out horizontally, looking a bit like a tree in Cornwall forced to grow sideways due to the high wind. Three large intricate silver earrings and an eyebrow piercing dominate her face. In a small country pub on a Wednesday night she's quite shocking, and yet, in a way stunning. Paul walks in behind. He's tanned and muscled with shoulder length blond hair. He has made absolutely no compromise to the English winter. He looks like he's walked into a Tardis and been transported straight from Bondi beach. He is wearing a tight T-shirt, denim shorts and open toed sandals. His only small consideration was a shabby cardigan with leather patches on the elbows. I find out later he brought this from the *Help the Aged* shop next to the station.

By now this strange couple transfixes every one in the pub.

"Nat!" Sasha screams running towards me, hugging me round the neck lifting her feet clear off the ground. I manage to prise her arms from around my neck, embarrassed by her attention. I had thought so much over the last few days about how I was going to react, going over and over what I would say to her in my head. This greeting had caught me off guard. Still highly excited and not at all awkward Sasha introduces me to Paul,

"G'day," he says before making his way to the open fire. He stands in front of it warming his blue hands. The pub returns to the business of drinking and putting the world to rights.

On hearing all this commotion Graham has struggled to his feet, and is waiting to be introduced.

"Oh this is my good mate and football buddy Graham," I say. Graham puts his hand out and Sasha takes it while saying,

"Hi Graham, how's it going mate," I notice she has picked up an Australian accent. Graham goes to touch Sasha's face. She looks at me nervously, before glancing down at Quinn in his full blind dog harness. I tell her not to worry he just wants to feel how you look. Sasha steps forward placing her hands on her hips. Graham starts with her face gently following the outline pausing at her piercings and elaborate earrings, almost getting his fingers caught up. He then starts on her hair, Sasha turns sideways so he gets the full effect, clearly enjoying herself now. I feel a little sorry for him, but don't know how to warn him (I then remember the twenty pound note incident from earlier.) Graham gets about 18 inches along the mass of dreadlocks before it all becomes too much. He sits down, totally confused by the mass of hair. I take him by the arm and guide him back to his chair, I help him locate his whisky glass.

I order some drinks and we move to the lounge bar. Paul looks disappointed, as there's no fire in here, but he soon makes himself comfortable by a radiator. I sit opposite Sasha in a booth, made from a reclaimed church pew.

There's a long silence as we drink our pints, Sasha has lost her initial bravado. I start to go through my head all I wanted to say to her, the hours I spent alone in the van this week rehearsing our meeting. Making up a script, she would say this and I would come back with a brilliant and witty riposte. Now I couldn't remember a thing. I want to scream at her, how could you leave me, how could you leave your sick son, how could you march back in to my life after six years, like... like you've just popped out for milk!

But I say none of this. I ask her, how her journey was, about her family, we make small talk. I find out Paul's a full time Surf Instructor. I'm not sure what a surf instructor is, so I make a throwaway comment, I say I thought King Canute tried that. Sasha laughs far louder and for longer than the joke really warranted.

We finish our drinks, Sasha stands up shuffles out of her seat and makes her way to the bar. I'm left alone, I rub my hands together to remove the sweat from my palms. She returns, sits down and takes a deep breath, finally we get down to the nitty, gritty.

"How's Bob?"

I lean across the table at her,

"Oh what, since you last saw him, that would be Mmm....let me see about six years. How long have you got, the pub shuts at eleven." I say sarcastically, but I regret it almost as soon as I've said it, that wasn't in my script.

" I know, I know, it was a terrible thing I did." She pauses, then she quotes Dylan at me,

"But I was so much older then, I'm younger than that now," her mouth breaks into the slightest of smiles.
She's got to me I smile back, I crack., mentally I tear up the script in my head.

"Look Nat it's not like you've done such a bad job. In fact by all accounts you've done a brilliant job. I don't want to change him or take him away. I just want to get to know him." Her voice cracks with emotion as she wipes away tears with the back of her hand, her black mascara smudging. Sasha takes a sip of her drink and composes herself. I stare at my pint making patterns in the condensation with my finger,

"What you were saying about doing a really good job, do you mean that?"

"Look Nat, I kept every letter and every photo your Mum sent me, from when he was a baby…. Its just…well," she pulled out a small black and white photo from her hand bag, a small ghostly image leaps off the print,

"I'm pregnant." I look up at her and over at Paul, Sasha nods,

"When I found out... I just ..I just got to thinking. How can I have another child? When I don't even know my first baby." Sasha reaches into her handbag again and pulls out an Air Quantas flight pack, tears open a wet wipe and dabs her eyes.

I start recounting Bob's life; the first step, his first words, the time he pushed a marmite sandwich in the video, his first day at school, his macaroni pictures that self destruct after a few days, every funny antidote and story. It all pours out.

As do the drinks. Sasha still has little consideration for the tiny life struggling within her. She still smokes (at least three to every one I do), rolling her own, small, thin and perfectly formed cigarettes. By the end of the evening the table is covered in used glasses, the ashtray half full of ash and black smudged wet-wipes. At sometime in the evening Paul must have left to go to bed. I don't know when as I didn't see him go. I'm surprised when Colin shouts last orders, I've lost all track of time.

We finish our drinks, we are the last to leave, even Graham and Quinn have long since gone. Colin walks behind us and bolts the door as we step out into the cold December air. I start to walk towards the mobile home round the back of the pub. Sasha jumps up on the three foot high wall that surrounds the pub car park. She starts walking along balancing with her arms out. Sasha always was an incredible drinker she's had several pints, at least two more than me as I slowed down when I was engrossed in my Bob stories. I have a distant memory of Sasha being a junior gymnast which explains her doing beam exercises, jumping, twisting in mid-air and landing facing the other way. I'm having trouble walking on the ground. She was struggling a little to keep her balance, not due to drink, but the sheer weight of her dreadlocks. Her arms flapped at her side as she steadied herself,

"I'm not going to sleep, my body thinks it's time to get...." To prove this point as she said "UP" she did a complete backward somersault off the wall landing perfectly in her boots. I mime holding up a score card,

"9.5 from the British judge, I'm sorry you lost points due to lack of presentation, your hair was all over the place," I laugh while Sasha squeals, she grabs my arm panting,

"Oh! let's go back to your flat," shit, Mum must have told Sasha where I live.

"Come on we could play singles, dig out all your old 45's, and talk some more". This could take some time, as I had close on 1000 singles and it was already gone 11.30. I had to stop myself and think what day was it. Hang on, do I have work tomorrow? Yes, but I had no deliveries, so no driving (which was just as well.) All the building sites were shutting down for the Christmas break. Sid and I were going to do some tidying in the warehouse. I didn't feel tired, Oh what the hell, what could possibly happen?

"Okay, but you only get to choose ten ," I said while rather bravely jumping the wall and heading off in the direction of the flat with Sasha following fast behind.

* * * * * * * *

Hazel and Joan are in a trendy new wine bar, a converted bank called the Cheque and Overdraft. They were perched on trendy, tall bar stools, not an easy thing to do in short skirts, which is why they had attracted the attention of a group of young lads from the city. There was around half a dozen of them and by the look of the table they had been there a good few hours already. The jackets had gone, top buttons undone, ties loosened. The table awash with glasses in various states of emptiness. They were being far too loud and leery. They could be football hooligans? But no, they're winding down after a hard day selling stock and shares, transfixed by the numbers on the computer screen. Their decisions ultimately affecting thousands of lives with the simple click of a mouse.

Joan and Hazel had ignored the comments of the group as they came in, and chose to sit at the bar,

"So what's up?" Joan said, Hazel had sounded upset when she called around ten saying she really needed to talk. Joan thought she could really do without this, having just finished a row with Carol on the phone. It was the same old problem she had been invited to spend Christmas day, but Keith and that girl would be there. Oh! how she would dearly love to be there, to see her grandchildren's faces as they open their presents. Joan had spent so long tracking down the latest dolls, she'd been on the phone for hours and trawled toy shop after toy shop. How she despised the toy companies for creating this artificial demand every year. She was still a long way from seeing those angelic faces, first she would have to back down, swallow her pride, it was surely too bitter a pill to digest.

Hazel took a sip of her orange juice, Joan thought it strange she had never seen Hazel drink orange before, she was strictly a white wine person, but she let it pass without comment. Hazel put her glass on the bar and spoke,

"It's Nathan I...I think we've split up,"

"What do you mean, you think?"

"Well we had this big row, Nat said he wanted to see me more" Hazel said while removing a lock of red hair from her face.

"Then I, well, I kind of told him I loved him,"

At this point one of the lads made his way over, Joan recognized him as the least good-looking and loudest one of the bunch. Having nasty sweat stains under his arms and thinning hair treated with hair-jell in a desperate attempt to look cool, but he only succeeded in making a multi-legged spider on the top of his head.

"Hello l.l..l..l...ladies," he said dragging the word ladies out for an interminable length of time.

"Would you like to join us, you look like you're in need of cheering up," he said in a slightly slurred voice.

"No thank you, we're just trying to have a quiet drink," Hazel said sounding a little annoyed.

"Oh come on don't be party poopers," the young man said leaning over and putting his sweaty and pudgy hand on Joan's knee.

Joan removed it, as if it was something extremely unpleasant that had fallen in her lap.

"Look just piss off," Joan shouted. The man looked somewhat taken aback by her rebuff. He started to stagger back, but on seeing his younger peers jeering at him, he decided to try a witty and cutting comment,

"Couple of lesbians anyway."

Hazel jumped up, Joan put her arm out in a vain attempt to stop Hazel,

"Leave it, he's not worth it," but Hazel was already at the table, the unwanted suitor dropped onto his chair. The group looked visibly nervous as Hazel stood the other side of the table to the man. She placed a hand on the table and leaned over, the rest of the group fearing trouble, lifted their drinks from the table and pushed their chairs back in perfect unison. From above it would have looked like a synchronised swimming move. Hazel grabbed hold of the bottom of Spider Head's tie twisting it between her fingers, she spoke in a slow and sexy voice,

"Look I may be a lesbian, but every month, I give a man the chance to cure me. Tonight you could be that man," the underarm sweat stain visibly grew, the man swallowed hard before saying,

"I'm your man," laughing nervously and looking round the table for moral support, the group gave him none, they were silent. Clearly he was not liked within the group, most were enjoying his squirming. Then Hazel wrapped the tie around her hand pulling the man towards her, until he was only a couple of inches from her cleavage. Hazel could smell his foul breath, a mixture of smoke, drink and innuendo. Then in one swift movement with her other hand she pushed his full pint from the table into his lap. The man jumped backwards in shock, his chair crashing to the floor. The table erupted in laughter. Hazel walked back to Joan, they collected their drinks from the bar,

"You know this used to be a bank, I think it's still got one or two bankers in it," Hazel said,

This was typical Hazel. Bold and confident with strangers, it made her good meeting clients at work. When it came to matters of the heart, however, Hazel was much more insecure and naïve.

Joan lit up a cigarette and blew smoke up to the roof, Hazel said nothing. She must be in a bad way thought Joan, she always made a passing comment about her smoking by quoting the latest survey on the perils and dangers of smoking. It's a shame men don't come with a similar warning.

Hazel starts to tell Joan about the conversation with Nathan, how he wanted to see more of her. Hazel is clearly upset, she fights back tears as she goes on about how wonderful he is and how with the possible threat of not see him again, she has been forced to evaluate how she truly feels about him and indeed her relationship with Clive. Joan listens with an understanding and caring expression on her face. While mentally trying to assess how this might affect her life style. Hazel pauses like she's lost the track of what she's saying or is she weighing something up, judging whether or not to tell Joan. Something is nagging at the back of Hazel's mind, should she confide in Joan? What was she thinking of, Joan was her best friend. Hazel took a deep breath before dropped her bombshell,

"There's another thing I'm ...I'm late." Joan glanced at her watch inadvertently, before she even registered the time, it dawned on her, the magnitude of what Hazel had actually meant.

Joan took a last suck on her cigarette, she blew smoke out while dispersing it by waving her hand. She stubbed out her cigarette in an exaggerated stabbing movement in the ashtray,

"You're pregnant," Joan said.

"I don't know," Hazel said sweeping back her hair with both hands and exhaling a large breath.

"I know I'm a week late,"

"You need to do a test," Joan said, as she thought.

"Are you sure who the father is?" Joan already knew the answer to this question, but she had to find out if Hazel knew. Clive had told Joan that he had a vasectomy shortly after he left his wife. He had a local anaesthetic and sat up to watch the entire operation, it was his rugby club mentality. Unfortunately it was one of the most painful things he had ever experienced. He still relished in telling Joan the gory details, how they sealed the tubes with a laser, you could actually smell the toasting testis.

He had obviously chosen not to share his amusing story with Hazel.

"I'm sure it's Nathan's," Hazel said getting more upset now,

"Clive and I, well he doesn't seem interested in that anymore." At this Hazel started crying, she covered her face with her hand. Joan lent across the table and touched her other hand,

"Its going to be all right."

"Oh! It's such a mess, I think he's having a affair," Joan let go of Hazel's hand.

"No, I'm sure you're wrong, he thinks the world of you,"

Joan knew this could upset her life, she was happy with her relationship with Clive. She had good exciting sex, while still maintained her independence. Funnily enough her relationship was summed up by a song she had just heard on the radio this very evening, it was a country song played on Radio Two, how did the line go,

I don't want to marry you, just live close, visit often, that'll do for me.

She could also have an influence over company decisions in their pillow talk bedroom /boardroom sessions. There was no glass ceiling as far as Joan was concerned, she got her way staring at the bedroom ceiling. Now Hazel was rocking the boat, with this stupid affair and getting pregnant. She must handle this with care or the excrement could really hit the fan.

"You mustn't mention this pregnancy to Clive. Not yet, I mean, have you ever spoken about starting a family?" Joan said knowing full well Clive's inability to start a family.

"No not really, whenever I mention children, he always changes the subject."

"Well you need to talk to Nathan find out if its over…then we need to talk about other options,"

"What do you mean other options?"

"Well, if Clive is happy about starting a family, which by the sound of it, is doubtful, he's going to be even less keen to bring up someone else's baby. This singing van driver is hardly the family type. Face it Hazel you're in the shit," Joan says lighting another cigarette,

"Do you want another drink?" she asks,

"Just another orange juice, I think I'm going to see Nathan, I need to know where I stand."

Joan moves towards the bar,

"Ok, but don't mention you're pregnant or you won't see him for dust,"

Hazel was left alone at the table. Suddenly she felt very alone, a small tear trickled down her cheek. She wiped it away with a single finger, things were a mess. She always thought she would be married with 2.3 children by now.

Joan arrived back with the drinks. Meanwhile, Hazel had come to a decision, she would go and see Nathan. She knew he was the one, but there was something about him, he just seemed to be holding something back she couldn't put her finger on it.

She left her drink and stood up.

"Look Joan thanks for… for listening as always." She lent forward and kissed her on the cheek. Then in passing she said,

"Have you decided about Christmas?" A couple of days ago Hazel had asked if Joan would like to spend Christmas with them, knowing what a difficult time she found it with the grandchildren and all. She had no idea how difficult Joan would find it spending Christmas at Clive's

"Thanks, it's a lovely idea, but I'm going to talk to Carol," Joan said.

"Oh! that's great I really hope thing work out, life's too short," Hazel said.

Joan had decided to try one more time to mend the bridges, and swallow her pride. If she didn't and things went terribly wrong she could end up alone.

Then Joan said, as Hazel started to walk away,

"I hope things work out," before adding,

"Ring me," and finally, as Hazel was going past the group of 'bankers,' Joan shouted,

"Remember don't mention the pregnancy." Hazel glanced embarrassed at the group but they were too engrossed in two girls who had joined them. She made her way through the bar past the framed Financial Times that adorned the walls and the juke box set in the wall cannily made to look like a cash machine. She came out into the cold December night turned right and walked the short distance to the station and the taxi rank.

The taxi pulled up opposite Nathan's flat, there were no lights visible, only the outside light at the top of the stairs.

"Can you wait awhile," Hazel asked. The man sighed impatiently, before starting a long and agitated conversation on his mobile phone in a foreign tongue. Hazel wiped the condensation off the car window clearing a hole so she could see Nathan's flat. She stared intently at it. After a few minutes two people came into view on the other side of the road. It was too dark to make out who they were, but one started to go up the staircase, she could then see his silhouette, it was Nathan. Hazel opened the car door and was just about to call out, when his name caught in her throat. Suddenly she could make out the other silhouette, it was a women. Well it was certainly female, she had strange-looking long of hair. The couple reached the top of the stairs, she could make out Nathan fumbling for his key. Then the door opened, Nathan stood aside before following the girl in and closing the door. Hazel pulled the car door shut before turning to the driver and interrupting his phone call,

"Take me home, do you know Thames Wharf?" The driver did one of his impatient sighs before pulling away, still deep in conversation the phone tucked under his chin.

Eleven

He woke up, the room was bare
He didn't see her anywhere.
He told himself he didn't care, pushed the window open wide
Felt an emptiness inside to which he just could not relate
Brought on by a simple twist of fate

(Simple Twist of Fate © 1974, Ram's Horn Music)

Sasha and I enter the flat.

"Wow!" Sasha exclaims, as she sees how my record collection has grown. Like a child let loose in a sweet shop she races from shelf to shelf. I direct her to the singles kept at the bottom of each rack of shelves as I busy myself in the kitchen. I open my bottle of whisky, part of my extensive Screw-it Christmas bonus package, which included a twenty five pound M & S voucher. I make the coffee splashing a little in the top of each.

My singles are in four large square boxes beneath the shelving racks, obtained from the last refit from the Screw-it warehouse below. Sasha has pulled out each one and has started making her selection. The boxes have cards with categories marked on them, sixties, seventies, eighties, new wave, soul and R&B etc. Then they are arranged by each group alphabetically. OK, OK, but when you're a single dad you have a lot of free time in the evenings. Sasha sits cross-legged in the middle of the room leafing through the singles with her dark purple nails, occasionally pulling one out for closer inspection. As I watch her engrossed she looks very young, almost child-like. I remember what I loved about her, if it ever was love. It was her initial look of innocence and vulnerability, but when you got to know her she was street-wise and had a forthright opinion on everything.

By the time I place the coffee on the table, she has several singles in her pile. Sasha takes a break to sip her coffee and roll a joint. She takes a couple of intense draws and hands it to me, the sweet acrid smoke fills the room. While she makes her selection we talk some more about her life in Australia, how she met Paul and her jewellry business. I also talk more about Bob, I go and get a large photo album from the shelf and I get my Bob Marley box down.

I stack the first five tracks of Sasha's selection on my stereo. They are:

1   Down in a tube station at midnight /The Jam
2   Teenage Kicks/ Undertones
3   Is your love in vain/Bob Dylan
4   She's so modern/Boomtown Rats
5   Another Girl, Another Plant/ The Only Ones

Her selection is fairly predictable, mainly new wave stuff with the exception of track 3. Which throws me a bit. But I don't say anything, we are both sat on the sofa now, she has her legs tucked up under her and is facing me, with the photo album on her lap. Her first track starts.

"So why this?" I say,

"Ok , Ok , hold on," Sasha says trying to roll another joint but she's a bit stoned now, I'm a bit concerned that's she's dropping bits of grass and tobacco onto innocent early photo's of Bob aged five on Bournemouth beach.

"Well *Down in a Tube Station* paints a picture of inner city life, you can almost smell the breath of the mans attackers 'the smell of pubs, Wormwood Scrubs and too many right wing meetings' as Paul Weller puts it. Best bit, the sound of the tube train coming back in at the end. The second track comes on,

"*Teenage Kicks* comes from a time when the single was king, this was always at number one in John Peel's festive fifty."

The Undertones finish and Dylan starts singing, surely the first time the undertones have supported Bob Dylan.

"so why this?" I ask. Sasha turns to face me and stares deep into my eyes, she's barely six inches from my face.

"This…This was the first song I ever heard you play."
I'm looking into her eyes, they are a deep blue green like a Caribbean sea.

"Your eyes, I don't remember them being that blue before," I say almost whispering.

"Oh! do you like them? Contact lenses, cool hey!" She moves even closer. Oh! God I think she's going to kiss me. Her eyes are drawing me in, do I choose to plunge into these beautiful sea-blue, false eyes.

Then: SHE'S SO TWENTIETH CENTURY
SHE'S SO NINETEEN SEVENTIES
SHE'S A MODERN GIRL.

Sasha's next record blasts out of my speakers breaking the moment and bringing me back to my senses. Most of Africa may have been grateful to Bob Geldof in 1985, but I had never been more grateful for him at that moment. Sir Bob Geldof the patron saint of saving people from disastrous decisions.

I pull away stand up and move to the kitchen, I take deep breaths while pacing up and down the kitchen (not easy to do in my tiny kitchen).

"Look its getting late," another deep breath,"I think you better go," I turn and pace back across the kitchen again,

"I've got work tomorrow,"

"yes you're right I really should go," Sasha says standing and brushing ash from her dress, I'm glad that she seems equally embarrassed by the situation.

I walk her back to the *House of Gloom* in silence. I arrange for her to meet Bob on Friday evening at mums. She kisses me lightly on the cheek and opens the door I can hear Paul snoring way off in the darkness.

I turn and take a deep breath, the cold December wind clears my head. What was I thinking of, or more to the point what was Sasha thinking. At that moment I guess we both grew up a lot. I felt like something had been put to rest. I could move on, our situation had changed, now we could concentrate on Bob. I felt we had never really said goodbye, tonight in a way had done that, I had completed the final chapter turned the page to the big The End. I could move on to new relationships, shame that I didn't have one any more.

* * * * * * * *

It's Friday night I have phoned Hazel every waking hour for two days. I have phoned on my mobile, from work and from mums house, but all to no avail. Each time her phone was either switched off or on its message service. I have left five messages each one more desperate, sad and pathetic than the last;

1. Hi Hazel its me please ring we need to talk.
2. Hi...err look give me a ring, its Nat.
3. Look I really need to talk to you,
   I need to explain why I couldn't see you.
4. Please just pick up the bloody phone, oh its Nat again.

5. Right if you don't ring I'll turn up at the flat, I don't care if I have to ring every door bell at Thames Wharf to talk to you.

I have also bought a small book on text messaging for beginners, from it I constructed these text messages

ILUVY (((H))) Nat, according to the book this should read to anyone up on text talk, I love you 'big hugs,' Nat.

And then the text message to end all messages, from one of Hazel's favourite Dylan songs,

He woke up, the room was bare
He didn't see her anywhere.
He told himself he didn't care, pushed the window open wide
Felt an emptiness inside to which he just could not relate
Brought on by a simple twist of fate

I was proud of this. It cost me 25 minutes of my lunch hour and a terrible case of repetitive text injury.

Right now I have to go and introduce my son to his mother, who he has no recollection of. It's ten past six, normally it would be a jogging night, but I can't see it happening although I plan to be back at the flat by seven just in case Hazel does show up.

I haven't seen her since Monday. Work has been hell. I've been stuck in the warehouse with Sid, my boss. Sid is a small stocky man with far too many tattoos about his arms, almost as if to draw your attention away from his lack of height, but in truth only serving to make you think 'look at the tattoos on that short bloke'. He's one of those annoying people who's always happy and upbeat, don't get me wrong I like Sid, its' just that he's happy and I don't do happy at the moment. I just feel sad and lonely.

So all week we have to listen to the local commercial radio station. It plays only the current top twenty chart hits, it pukes them out in an endless repetitive loop. Believe me, when you start your day at eight o'clock with Sid singing and dancing to the latest pop idol's single. I feel like Bill Murray in *Ground Hog Day* waking up each day to the same song Sonny and Cher's *I got you Babe*. Like him, I just want to smash the radio to bits.

I've got four days to Christmas day. Then I will have to be happy for Bob's sake, but I'm torn apart inside. I need to know where I stand. I can't go on like this.

The worst thing is it's affecting my ability to listen to music. In this situation normally I can seek solace in my record collection, seeking out old friends and memories. The last few days every lyric seams to be aimed at me, pointing out my pain and loneliness. From Dylan, Clapton, B.B. King and Motown comes lines of unrequited, forbidden, tortuous and inevitably, hopeless love. They say that love makes the world go round, I just want to stop it dead, turning back time, that way I could return to the point where it all went wrong. That fork in the road, this time I would take the road to **Happy ever after Town**.

Life's not like that, I've already taken my road and its strictly one way - no turning back. I've already said things, done things, had the reactions to those things and now I'm stuck with the consequences. However sad it makes me feel.

*   *   *   *   *   *   *   *

Blue, blue, blue…shit, shit, shit…Hazel paces her luxury bathroom at Thames Wharf. The pregnancy test has confirmed, what she knew in her heart of heart to be true. She was indeed pregnant.

She had been in the bathroom for half an hour, ever since Clive had given her the air tickets. She had tried to test the water on the subject of children, just casually as you do, saying something like,

"how do you feel about starting a family"

Clive had gone on about freedom, being tied down, having done all that, how his fatherhood days were over. He had then told her to go and look on the Christmas tree, on it was an envelope and inside were two air tickets to the Grand Canaries and a glossy brochure showing a hotel with a golfing complex . She had been upset at first, this was typical of Clive trying to be flash but inadvertently putting a spanner in the works. It was then Hazel had rushed to the bathroom and took the opportunity to do the test. Clive had assumed she was overcome with joy at spending Christmas on a golf course.

Having had half an hour to calm down Hazel was adjusting to the idea, well a week in the sun wouldn't be so bad. Clive would be off playing golf all day. She could think what she was going to do. In a way she was happy not having to do Christmas at home.

She washed her face, looked in the mirror, took a deep breath and opened the door. She told Clive how happy she was, kissed him on the forehead and went off to pack. Clive smiled, not taking his eyes from the

Sky sports channel, certainly he failed to notice Hazel's red tear-stained eyes. They were due to leave that night, staying in a hotel near Gatwick before catching their flight the following morning.

Twelve

The lover who just walked out the door
Has taken all his blankets from the floor
The carpets, too, is moving under you
And it's all over now, Baby Blue

(It's all over now, Baby Blue © 1965 renewed 1993 Special Rider Music)

I'm going to meet my Mum tonight. She left when I was very tiny, you see I was very sick. Mum left because she was sad and went to live in Australia.

Since Dad told me about Mum coming I have been trying to learn about Australia. At school we have learnt that it has lot of strange animals with pockets in them to keep babies in, they did a lot of paintings on a large rock, Australia's very big, if you're sick you have to go to hospital by airplanes and a long time ago if you did anything bad, the police sent you there.

I Have also been watching T V, all the Australian soaps from these I have learned; The sun always shines, so they have Barbies all the time. Most of them have blond hair, they wear T-shirts with no sleeves, most afternoons they go to the beach and they say g'day all the time. I have just finished watching *Neighbours*, they had a pool party, all the girls were wearing bikinis. They all looked very brown. I can't wait to see Mum, I think it will make Dad happy to be a family again. Dad has put on my Playstation, I'm playing, but I'm still thinking a lot about Mum, she will be here soon. I also wonder if Santa got my letter asking for my Playstation 2.

* * * * * * * *

I have just burnt my tongue on my coffee, I guess I'm nervous. Mum and I are standing in the kitchen while Bob is in the lounge, playing his Playstation. I thought it was best to try and make it as normal as possible, and not have him sitting waiting around. There's a gentle knock on the back door, I open it, and let Sasha and Paul in. I'm glad to see Sasha has toned her look down for tonight. Her hair is tied behind her head, and she is wearing less make up. She has a rather conservative jumper and jeans on. Paul is still in his Bondi beach stuff, shorts, open toed sandals and T-shirt.

On the T-shirt are the words of Paul's surf school in a circle around a surfer. Mum gives Sasha a hug and they start to make small talk while I make some drinks. Sasha has a black tea while Paul has a can of Fosters from the fridge. I can hear the sound of the Playstation in the lounge, Bob has made no attempt to come through to the kitchen. The talk dries up, its time, I can't put it off anymore.

I tell Sasha to wait, and go through to see Bob. I tell Bob to save his game, he's a little annoyed having reached a crucial point. I find this quite reassuring, here he is about to meet his Mum for the first time and he's worried about completing this level.

I lead him, holding him in front of me, my hands resting reassuringly on his shoulders. As he comes round the corner I say,

"Err...this is Sasha, your mum," I can feel Bob's shoulders stiffen.

"No, No, this is not right," Bob says, he slips from my grip, turning and running back through the lounge, before disappearing up the stairs.

"I'm sorry, wait here I'll go and talk to him," I leave them with Mum, she's just getting out the cake she baked earlier. It's another 'Mum special' in the shape of Ayers rock and almost to scale.

When I get upstairs, Bob is lying face down in his Harry Potter duvet. I stroke the back of his head.

"Look son, I know it's hard but you must give your mum a chance," he turns, his tears sticking his blond hair to his face.

"But Dad it's all wrong, she looks nothing like someone in *Neighbours.*"

Then it dawned on me, its obvious Bob has painted a picture of this blond and tanned beauty coming back into his life. This was partly my fault, I should have seen the signs, paved the way a bit better. I was preoccupied what with Hazel .

"ah.. Look Bob, Sasha is not an Australian. She's just lived there for a few years." Then I think of something, "now Paul, her friend, he looks like he's come straight off the *Neighbours* set."

Bob pushes himself up, and swings round, dropping his legs off the side of the bed.

"Come on then," Bob sets off down the stairs with me close behind. Sasha, Paul and Nan have all moved to the lounge now. The cake is on the coffee table, missing two large slices.

As Bob comes round the corner, he catches sight of Paul, in his shorts and T-shirt. He turns to look at me giving me a knowing smile. Sasha shuffles along the sofa making room for Bob.

"Hello Bob, pleased to meet you," she says, holding out a hand, as he sits down next to her. He's staring at her hair. Sasha is aware of this.

"Do you like my hair?"

"It's very strange," Bob says.

She pulls out the hair toggle, and shakes her head. This mass of dreadlock hair has taken on a life of it own. Giving her the look of Medusa. Bob reaches across, takes a handful and scrunches it.

"Wow …cool," Bob says, in total awe.

After the somewhat rocky start, the night goes really well. Bob calms down and relaxes. Sasha has brought some photographs of her house, Bondi beach and her shop. Bob attacks a large piece of cake, we have now eaten half of the aborigines' most sacred place. Bob gets on well with Paul, he's fascinated with his surfing stories, especially his story about a near miss with a shark. By the end of the night Paul has Bob standing on Nans ironing board instructing him on how to ride the big one. Bob is lying face down paddling like mad, he then jumps up balancing, looking over his shoulder as this imaginary wave comes crashing down on him.

We're all having a good time, I'm laughing too. It feels good, I think, I haven't done this much in the last few days. This brings me back to Hazel. I check my watch, it's five past seven, I stand up and say,

"Would anyone mind if I make a move?"

"Oh! Dad do you have to," Bob says. Nan cuts in with,

"Bob its nearly your bedtime, let your dad go. I'll tell you what, how would you like Sasha to read you a bedtime story."

"oh yeah, come on, I'll show you my bedroom," he says running up the stairs, he gets about half way up.

"Bob haven't you forgotten something," I say, Bob comes back down, he fakes thinking hard, holding a finger to his chin in an exaggerated pose.

"Oh right," he says, giving me a big hug.

"Good night Dad."

"Good night son, up the stairs to Bedfordshire, sleep tight, don't let the bed bugs bite," I look over Bobs head and smile at Sasha. I say good-night to Mum and Paul. I make my way to the back door, tripping over the ironing board while trying to avoid the sharks. Sasha follows me to the back door

"Look, Nat about the other night ....I.."

"Hey! forget it," I say heading off down the path and so avoiding any embarrassment.

I jump in the van, the windscreen is already frosted up, I can hardly see out. I jump out again and clear a small hole, as I haven't got far to go. I park the van and run up the stairs, struggle with my key and I go in, there's no sign of Hazel, no discarded jogging gear.

I decided to take a run out to Thames Wharf.
I clear the windscreen and mirrors properly of frost. Within ten minutes I'm sitting outside Thames Wharf. I keep the engine running with the heater on full to keep the window clear. I look up at each window and try to work out which flat is Hazel's.

*   *   *   *   *   *   *   *

Joan stares at the phone. She just needed to make a phone call. As simple as that. Only this would be the hardest call ever. She wanted to phone her daughter Carol, to see if the invite for Christmas was still open. All she had to do was pick up the phone, it was logged in the memory on number one. What could be more easy.
Suddenly it rings. Joan jumps with fright. Before composing herself, picking up the receiver.

"Hello"

"Hi Joan its Hazel"

"You ok"

"Well no, not really"

"Have you had a chance to speak to Clive yet?"

"No, but you'll never guess what he's come up with now. We're off to Grand Canaries for Christmas," Hazel tried to sound excited. Joan knew all too well about this, as it was her who had thought of the idea, prompting Clive and even booking the tickets herself.

"So you haven't mentioned to Clive about the other thing," Joan says.

"Well no, I brought up the subject of starting a family. But he just doesn't want to talk about it. Oh Joan, I don't know what to do. I don't think I could bring up a baby on my own. I've never been on my own. I couldn't cope," Hazel says, her voice breaking.

Joan knew Clive wasn't able to change his mind. He had mentioned to Joan about Hazel dropping hints about starting a family. He had said he had done with all that, if she kept on, well, he would have to tell her how it was. If she didn't like it well. He didn't finish. But she knew what he meant. Joan had to help her friend, it was time to sort her life out. She wasn't going to say it now, but she knew Hazel had to get rid of the problem. It wasn't that bad, Joan had …had dealt with her own problem. It was just after she found out about Keith and his indiscretion. Joan had to go through an abortion on her own she never told a soul. Joan couldn't mention the 'A' word to Hazel now.

"Look, don't worry about it now go away, relax have a good time. Ring me when you get back, I'll help you get through it, whatever we have to do,"

"I'll try, you have a good Christmas," Hazel said, not sure what Joan meant by, *whatever we have to do.*

"Promise me you'll ring Carol"

"I will, I was just about to ring, honest," Joan says.

"Look I've gotta go"

"You take care, I'm thinking of you," Joan said, as the phone cut out leaving her alone with the dialling tone. She stayed holding on to the phone suspended in the air. She knew, she would have to make that call. After what seemed like a lifetime she pushed memory button one and started to build some bridges.

* * * * * * * *

I've narrowed it down to one of two flats now, I'm fairly sure it's the one on the top left hand corner, then a big ugly naked guy is standing at a window. The fat man looks straight down at me, before pulling the curtains shut. I decide to try plan 'B', I turn off the van engine and make my way to the front door. By the large glass door with two imposing pillars either side is an intercom panel set in the wall. Then I remember I have no idea what Clive's surname is. I run my finger down the names in the list, but none looks familiar. I'm just about to start a random ring of each one when suddenly I can see someone coming down the impressive stairs carrying two suitcases. I slip behind the right hand pillar. The door swings open a man puts the cases down, and calls to someone through the open door.

"You coming love," he calls, a voice from up the stairs answers, it's Hazel, I can't hear what she says, then I can hear heels over the tiled foyer. She comes through the door. She's that close I can smell her perfume. Hazel looks across the car park and recognises my van. Obviously petrified that I'm about to try and win her back, by re-enacting the naked rose up the arse scene from *Cold Feet*. She thinks on her feet,

"Oh Clive, I've left my phone upstairs, be a love and get it for me," Hazel says.

"You trying to wear me out before we get there." Clive says, disappearing back through the door. As soon as he's out of ear shot she calls into the darkness.

"Nathan are you out there?"

"psst...." I call from behind my pillar.

"Jesus" Hazel says, clutching her chest, not expecting me to be quite as close to her. I move out from behind my hiding place.

"What the hell are you doing here?"

"I've come to see you"

"Well I don't want to see you"

"Look I don't know what I've done, but what ever it is, I need to talk to you," I say sounding a little desperate. Hazel looks back up the stairs anxiously, she breathes out, her breath visible in the frosty air. Passing over her red inviting lips, I want to bottle it up and save it.

"Look I'm going away for Christmas, but I'll give you one last chance to explain, or it's ov..." She stops half way through her sentence as she can hear Clive coming back..

"Red Lion next Thursday lunch time," I say quickly as Clive comes through the door,

"No...No, you're totally lost mate, you need to go back out and turn right,"

"Oh right ... err thanks," I say not very convincingly, I turn and walk towards my van.

"What's his problem?" Clive asks.

"Lost," Hazel says trying to sound bored. Clive looks over at the logo on the side of the van.

"Funny time to be delivering screws."

Back at the van I open the back doors and make out I'm adjusting my imaginary delivery. While fixing my gaze on Hazel, trying to store her image to my mental hard drive for future reference over the next week. Just then a taxi pulls into the drive, it swings round and parks in front of the building. Seeing the bags, the driver jumps out, runs round and opens the side door for Hazel, he's being extra attentive thinking it's a few days before Christmas plus wealthy neighbourhood equals big tip. He then makes a fuss of helping Hazel into the car. Clive has moved over to one of the garages, set out in a row opposite the main door. He pulls the door open and removes a set of golf clubs from the Mercedes car boot. He staggers over to the taxi and stands them by the boot, before getting in the front seat. The driver is struggling to get them in the boot then the bags zip comes undone spilling clubs and balls all over the ground. Clive jumps out of the car and starts ranting and raving at the driver. I'm too far away to make out exactly what he's saying, I can only hear odd words; fool, incompetent, £1000 worth, and kiss your tip goodbye.

I wonder where Hazel's off to, well at least I got to talk to her. I can see her looking at me through the side window. I can concentrate on Christmas now, then I'll see Hazel, come clean, tell her everything about Bob and if she doesn't like it, well I'd lost her anyway. So I'll just have to get back to B H time. 'Before Hazel time.'

I go round and get in the front of the van. I take a last glance in the direction of the taxi, Clive's still chasing golf balls round the drive, while the taxi driver is gathering up expensive golf clubs in his arms. I smile as I start the engine, wheel spin away, overtake the taxi, running over a golf club, on the way past, a five iron I think.

"Oi," I hear Clive shout while in my rear view mirror I can see him angrily shaking the distorted club at me, as I disappear into the frosty night.

I drop the van back to the flat. I decide to pop into the *House of Gloom* for a quick pint or two, as I feel slightly more confident over the Hazel situation and I've finished work for the Christmas holidays. On the short walk I phone Mum to find out how the rest of Sasha's reunion with Bob went. Mum tells me all went well, Sasha and Paul have arranged to take Bob to Mcdonalds tomorrow. I finish my call as I push the pub door open. The pub is packed full of smoke, overloud, sweaty and drunk people all dressed in Santa hats. I fight my way to the bar, Graham is sat in his chair waving a twenty-pound note in the vain hope someone might see it from the bar. I take pity on him and make a grab for it, I can't hear what he's saying, above the loud karaoke coming through from the back room. Through the open door I can see it, Sky singing *I will Survive* (which is more than could be said for the tune).

I guess Graham wants his usual whisky and half a pint of bitter for Quinn. Colin looks hot and harassed, he has taken on a new busty blonde barmaid who may be good looking (in his eyes) but is painfully slow and unable to add up. Luckily I'm served by Colin, he takes the twenty, looks at it, and informs me it's a dud. I can't hear him and don't understand. He leans across the bar and shouts in my ear hole,

"Its fucking dodgy mate," holding up Grahams twenty against a poster delivered by the local constabulary that very afternoon. The poster kindly explained exactly how to spot a forged note. He goes to hand it back, but I tell him to keep it, he slips it in the beer mug marked 'meat raffle'. I open my wallet and hand over my own hard-earned crisp and genuine twenty. I decide not to mention it to Graham, the poor chap probably got it in his pension. So reluctantly I hand him the change from my twenty.

Big Dave waves from the other side of the pub and makes his way over to me, he has a red Santa hat with a white bobble hanging in front of his face, each time he takes a swig of his pint the white bobble dips in his beer. Dave is hot and sweaty, his face almost matching his hat. The pub is packed with people most of whom I've never seen, Colin has rented the back room to one of the large offices in the new development near the football stadium. Lots of sad people, who don't normally go out all year are going mad, drinking too much and doing things they will no doubt regret, by the New Year. He leans over to talk to me, his wet beer-drenched bobble hitting me in the eye,

"Compliments of the seasons Nat," he says in a slurred voice.

"Well thanks mate, busy in here," I say as a large lady bumps into me, spilling a good deal of my pint down her ample cleavage. She has a red -spangled boob tube with white fur edging matching mini and a joke base ball cap with a large reindeer antler on.

"Oops! Sorry darling," she says producing a battered and well-used sprig of mistletoe from behind her back.

"Hi, I'm Gail, let me make it up to you," she says leaning towards me, her large bright red lips seem to fill my entire vision, they're big enough to remove my head at the shoulders. Dave jumps in front of me intercepting the kiss and saving me. He turns to face me, a big lipstick smudge on his lips and cheek, exhaling in an exaggerated fashion he fans his face with his hand. She moves on to find another victim.

"Here, follow me," Dave says, leading me by the sleeve to the back room. A disco and karaoke is set up on my stage. In front of the unit three women are doing a rendition of the Shoop, shoop song; *It's in his Kiss*. Several people are dancing, some really quite badly, it's a bit like your worse nightmare wedding party full of dancing dads. One man in particular is paying no regard to the tune or rhythm, or indeed style, he has a brown corduroy jacket with fetching leather elbow patches which he draws attention to by pointing madly in the air. The typing pool, secretaries and personal assistants all unite cheering on the singers from the sideline, each table awash with empty glasses. The room is thick with smoke, a couple of young men puff inexpertly on large cigars, looking nervously at the ends after each puff as if expecting them to explode. The small bar at the back is packed with people queuing for drinks, I can see Sid at the back of the queue in tight leather trousers and a sparkly waistcoat. I ought to go and apologize for my behaviour the last few days, but I decide to leave it. Dave leads me to the stage he takes a list from the DJ and moves to a vacant table.

"Right come on lets choose something to sing," Dave shouts, above the noise.

"Oh I don't know," I say, as Dave has reached the page marked **Punk classics**.

"I'll need a lot more drink,"

"No problem," Dave says pulling a wedge of money from his back pocket and waving it in the air.

"I gave myself a Christmas bonus." We take the list and move through to the main bar to get another drink. I check on Graham, he asks what the terrible noise is. I explain that it's a Karaoke night.

"Oh great I'll have a go at that," he says struggling to his feet.

"*It's not unusual*," he sings while clutching his crotch in true Tom Jones style.

"It's OK sit tight," I say, helping Graham back to his seat and trying to settle Quinn down, who had become quite disturbed and agitated. Dave returns with the drinks.

"Graham's up for it!"

"How about something by Ray Charles or Stevie Wonder?" Dave says with typical non-PC verve.

"Oi behave yourself," I say

I scan the list and find Grahams song. Dave is looking over my shoulder trying to pick a song. Just then Sasha and Paul arrive. Paul is dispatched to the bar while Sasha joins us and asks whats going on before taking the list off me and organizing everybody. I'm not worried and go along with her, it's one of those nights when I feel I can drink anything. It could be because of the large piece of mum's Ayers Rock cake absorbing all the liquid sponge-like in my stomach.

The atmosphere is really good and everyone's having a great time. I've finished work and I now have a chance of working things out with Hazel. Well at least I have a little hope now, I'll clean the slate, I can tell her all about Bob and we can go from there. I can concentrate on Christmas now.

We all choose our songs and make our way to the back room. We manage to find a table, relying heavily on Graham's disability, a party of six make way for us, (the season of good will and all) I make a big display of helping him to a chair and settling Quinn down. Big Dave takes our list up to the DJ and on the way back he is intercepted by Gail and her ample cleavage. She then attaches herself to our group, or to be more accurately to Dave. We settle down to serious drinking, cheering and taking the piss out of the singers while waiting for our turn.

After three more songs; a team version of *We are the Champions* apparently by the accounts department, *My Way,* performed by the managing director, who received far too much respect from the room, with the exception of our table. So much so that several people came up to us informing us that it was a really bad career move, until we informed them that strictly speaking we were gate crashers and didn't work for the company. Then Sid did his Steps version of *Tragedy*, with full dance routine, a tragedy it certainly was. It was at this point Dave informed me that Sid was gay, something that naively had never occurred to me. As Sid completes his routine with an over theatrical bow the DJ switches on the mike,

"Next up is Dave and Gail to sing a *Groovy Kind of Love*," it turns out Gail is Dave's new lady. They go down a storm. People will be talking about it for years, for all the wrong reasons. When Gail sings the line 'I quiver deep inside,' she puts her hands on her hips to quiver her entire body, this proves too much of a strain for her boob tube. It splits dramatically down one side sending her breasts flying in both directions. A great cheer comes up, Gail pulls her baseball cap off her head and covers one breast, while Big Dave rushes to her aid with his Santa hat for the other. They make a strategic retreat to the ladies, after far too long they return red faced and embarrassed. Gail, with a number of strategically placed safety pins not unlike the famous Liz Hurley dress.

Other highlights include Paul and Sasha singing the Beach Boys *Surfing USA* but changing the chorus to *Surfing Aussie*

Then it's my turn, I do a solo number. Only by the time I'm called I've had so much to drink I make a complete mess of my spot. I've chosen *The Tears of a Clown* by Smokey Robinson, I actually, (trying to be cocky and ignoring the screen) sing *The Tracks of my Tears* to this tune. Although Dave points this small mistake out to me, the sad thing is nobody else in the room notices.

Graham's turn goes really well, he can sing, Ok not the right words in the right order, but it sounded all right. He sung *It's Not Unusual* and it certainly was. Quinn sits at his feet throughout his performance paws over his ears howling along.

As Colin rings his last orders bell its gone twelve, our group says how nice it was of me to invite everyone back to my flat. I don't remember doing this, I glance over at Dave, guiltily he looks away from my gaze. Getting back to the flat is all a bit of a blank. The last thing I remember putting some music on and opening my Christmas bottle of whisky.

Thirteen

Well ask me why I'm drunk alla time,
It levels my head and eases my mind.
I just walk along and stroll and sing,
I see better days and I do better things.

(I Shell be Free © 1963 renewed 1993 Special Rider Music)

I open my eyes, there's a small amount of weak winter light coming through the curtains. I have no idea quite what I'm focusing on, then slowly, very slowly my brain starts to interpret. It's my stereo system upside down well, not upside down, my head is upside down and someone has put a can of beer on the deck lid. I'm on the sofa my head hanging off the side. My brain is killing me, due to the blood rushing to my head and the copious amounts of alcohol I've drunk. I'm torn between the urge to check out the possible damage to my beloved stereo and keeping the pain to a bare minimal by limiting my movement. I decide on a gentle slide off the sofa landing on all fours. I really need a glass of water before I can check anything, still on all-fours I make my way to the kitchen area, keeping my eyes shut.

Almost immediately I come across a body on the floor. I've no idea if it's male or female, I attempt to crawl round it, whoever it is has horrendous bad breath. I'm in the kitchen I can feel the cold tiles on my palms. The next bit could be a bit tricky, I reach up to the sink and pull myself up. I find a half full glass on the draining board I empty the contents down the sink, the stink of whisky from the glass makes me retch. I take a moment to regain my composure by taking depth breaths. I turn on the tap, let the water run for a while till its cold, then I drink three glasses straight down. I can feel the water lubricating my body parts I can almost feel the coldness hit my brain.

I switch on the small strip-light under the wall kitchen unit, I survey the room. Beer cans and bottles litter the floor. A selection of records are stacked on the coffee table, quite neatly. It seemed even in their drunken state my friends understood how I felt about my records. Sasha and Paul are asleep under the window, wrapped in a duvet. Graham is asleep in one of the armchairs. The body on the floor with halitosis, I had taken such trouble not to disturb is Quinn. He has got up and is scratching on the front door while whining. I move across to the door, open it, and let Quinn out. I stand at the top of the metal staircase watching him. The cold wind starts to sober me up, I'm worried my bare feet are going to stick to the frozen metal. Quinn does what he had to do and makes his way painfully slowly back up the stairs. He pushed past me and settled down at his masters' feet. My bedroom door opens and to my surprise Gail comes out. She is wearing nothing but one of my favourite T-shirts.

"Morning" she says on the way to the bathroom. Big Dave comes to the bedroom door, in only his boxer shorts. He leans against the door frame tilting his head back and looking at me a bit sheepishly.

"Ah... Morning Nat, I ..."

Gail comes back out of the bathroom and squeezes provocatively through the small gap in the doorway left by Dave, then oblivious to our gaze, she removes my T-shirt leaving it in a crumpled heap on the floor before slipping back under the duvet. I resist the urge to reclaim my shirt and hang it safely up in the wardrobe.

Big Dave points at the bathroom

"OK if I," he says, moving towards the door.

"Hey go ahead mate, you've used everything else of mine."

Graham is talking and mumbling from his chair, his leg twitches.

"It's not unusual," he mutters in his sleep.

"Hey Graham time to go home, the parties over," he opens his eyes and rubs his head. I pick up Quinn's harness from the floor and rattle it, he immediately jumps up ready for work.

"Hey that you Nat? Where am I?" Grahams says, a bit confused, I explain how he stayed at my flat, I reassure him that Quinn is all right. Sasha groans as she props herself up on an elbow, I could say she is having a 'bad hair day,' but it's difficult to tell the difference, I would certainly say it's a 'a bad to worse hair day.'

I decide to make a pot of tea. I start to get my head together remembering I've got a busy day, Bob is due to go to McDonalds with Sasha and I have to get the Christmas tree so Bob can decorate it later. This morning I'm due to do the big Christmas food shop with mum. I check the time, shit I'm due to pick Mum up in under twenty minutes. After the tea, people begin to wake up and start to get ready to go.

The bedroom door opens Gail is standing there with a change of clothes on, in her hand is a small holdall, I can see the red glitter of last nights outfit sticking out. Strange I think to myself that someone should go to a party with an overnight bag. Perhaps she planned a one night stand. There's an animated conversation between Big Dave and Gail. She then storms through the lounge to leave, as she gets half way Dave calls from the bedroom

"I really like you, that's all I said, I'd just like to see you again," he's still talking as he reaches the bedroom door, he then becomes aware that the room is silent, everyone is looking at him.

"Yeah... So I'll ring you sometime," he says in a some what desperate attempt to regain his cool. Sasha and Paul offer to help Graham home, I tell him I'll see him Christmas morning, as curiously Mum had insisted I invite him to join us for Christmas dinner. Big Dave mopes about, before getting dressed and shuffling off down the stairs, muttering something about women and how he'll never understand them, as he goes. Welcome to the club mate.

I open the curtains, as the light fills the room, I can see the flat is in a real mess, but I haven't anytime now. I put everything in the sink, all the cups, glasses, tins and bottles. I take my bed sheet and duvet cover off to wash at mums. I'm staying at mums over Christmas.

I drive to Mums, pick her and Bob up, and drive to the out of town leisure park. I don't know why they call it that, I know it has an eight screen cinema, a bowling alley and ice rink as well as the large super store, but there is precious little leisure going on to day. It's packed with mums and dads gritting their teeth, trying not to lose their Christmas spirit, both the emotional and liquid kind, with their over-loaded trolleys. They shepherd children in front of them in a state of excitement. Around the entrance are three Father Christmas's shaking charity buckets while carols are piped from their sleigh, which looks very much like a new Range Rover with a hardboard reindeer strapped to the front. It's Saturday, still two days to Christmas, people are going mad its like there's an E.E.C directive that food and drink are due to be discontinued. Bob starts off enthusiastically throwing a pound coin into the nearest Santa's bucket and getting a lolly-pop for his trouble. By the end of the shop he's fed up and tired, the twenty minute wait to get through the check out didn't help, Mum and I look wearily at each other and I make a mental note to try and make sure he is early to bed tonight, otherwise he'll be exhausted by Christmas day.

He's due to go to McDonalds with Sasha and Paul, but before that we have to choose the tree on the way home. I pull in to the local garden centre. Mum slips off to the café for a cup of tea. While I check out the large selection of Christmas trees set out in a large compound, these include, your normal standard Christmas tree that self-destruct by Boxing Day showering needles on the carpet that you're still hoovering up in March. Going steadily up in price they have non-drop needle trees, soft needle trees, trees with roots, trees cut off big trees and trees growing in buckets. I try and get Bob to choose, I run about from tree to tree holding it up for Bob to see, like an excited kid. He starts giggling and keeps deliberately changing his mind. Eventually we agree on one of the planted in a tub types, its about five foot high and quite wide and bushy. I hope that maybe after Christmas I could plant it in mums garden to dig up the following year. The top has a big kink in it, which I point out to Bob, but he's made up his mind. I pay and stand it in the back of the van strapping it to the side to stop it falling over. By the time we get home Bob has fallen asleep against Mums arm in the middle of the van. I carry him in and put him on the sofa. While Mum and I put the shopping away. I carry the tree in, and place it in the corner of the lounge. Mum puts the kettle on while I get the step ladder to get into the loft, I have to get the Christmas box down.

I don't plan to do the tree until Bob comes back this afternoon. I get a torch from the kitchen drawer and reach the top of the ladder. I balance on the top step and pull myself up into the loft, just as I reach the top I hear Sasha arrive. Typical, I drop back down. Precariously lowering my feet onto the wobbling ladder. Mum is gently trying to wake Bob up, he comes to and is crotchety at first before he remembers where he's off to. His Nan gets him to comb his hair and change his T-shirt.

"Don't do the tree while I'm away," Bob says, pointing a small accusing finger at me.

"I know, I know," I say as he goes out the door.

I return to the steps, climb to the top and pull myself up again. I sit with my legs dangling, switch on the torch and the beam lights up the loft. There are a number of boxes, an old ironing board, an old tent in a bag and a coat stand with my dads old Afghan coat. I shine the torch on each box in turn, finally I find the one with "Xmas decs" written on it in black pen. As I go past the old coat I get a whiff of musty Afghan which immediately reminds me of dad. I decide it's time to get rid of it, I pull it off and drop it through the gap, it lands on the floor by the foot of the ladder.

I then drag the Christmas box to the gap and using the coat as a cushion drop it to the landing. I climb carefully down again shutting the hatch. I carry the box into the lounge and place it by the tree. I then go back to get the coat. Mum has come in with a tray of tea.

"I think it's about time we got shot of this," I say, shaking it towards Mum, creating a cloud of dust. Mum looks at the coat with dreamy affectionate eyes, imagining my Dad wearing it at some long ago rock festival. As she reaches for it something falls from the pocket onto the floor. It's a small brown parcel done up with thin string. She picks it up, written on the front is 'Daisy' in my Dads elaborate handwriting. She looks at me and sits down, placing her hand over her mouth in shock. Slowly she slips her finger round the string and pulls the parcel open. A large bundle of money drops into my Mum's lap, along with a small tightly-folded note. Mum holds the delicate note between her thumb and forefinger for what seems an eternity, she knows this is a bridge to the past, a bridge my dad had crossed six years ago over the river of life leaving my mum alone and stranded on the other side. For a long time she had stood waiting for him to return, even contemplating following him over the bridge, but in time she had moved away and rebuilt her life. Slowly and very gently she opened the note.

The note reads:

Dear Daisy,

This is money from gigs I saved. I hope you find this useful

Remember Love minus zero... no limits.

Bill xxx

My Dad must have put the money in the pocket in the weeks before he died, not knowing Mum would wait several years before finding the parcel. He knew she wouldn't throw it out with all the sentimental history attached to it, I can smell the history from here! I try to swallow but there's a lump in my throat I'm blinking back stinging tears. I miss him so much, he had such an influence on my life, still has, every time I put on a record, I can hear him telling me an interesting fact or story concerning the recording. Or when I play my guitar, I can hear him saying, 'play it like that son or try holding the fret this way'. He was such a quiet tranquil man, but powerful in his own way. In a crowded room he could always get his point across without the need to raise his voice.

Mum has her head bowed, I don't know what to say, slowly she counts the money, meticulously peeling each note off the bundle and placing it on the table. As she does this, I can see teardrops splashing on the Queens smiling face.

I sit down and hold her tight.

"Oh Mum, I miss him so much," I say, we're both in tears now.

"I know son... he knows too."

It's always worse this time of year thinking of our Christmases past, the house full of strange and colourful characters my dad had invited. It's the same on his birthday, and of course Bob's birthday because at that time dad had just discovered the lump, the ticking time bomb that would ultimately kill him in just twelve weeks, just as Bob was on the road to recovery.

What my Mum and Dad had was so special, a total contented love, I wonder if I'll ever find anything close to it. Mum has finished counting the completed pile of money sat on the table in front of her, I have tried not to watch her, embarrassed, like I'm witnessing an intimate moment between my parents. I break the silence,

"Come on, Mum, drink your tea," I say, handing her the cup.
She takes a sip .

"Ugh its gone cold," she carries on drinking.

"Just like your dad liked it." My Dad always liked cold tea especially in the summer. I laugh and drink my tea, its cold and horrible, but it's a sort of toast to my Dad as he disappears over the bridge forever.

I never ask her how much money was there, then again, it was nothing to do with the amount was it?

Fourteen

While the world is asleep
You can look at it and weep
Few things you find are worthwhile
And though I don't ask much
No material things to touch
Lord; protect my child

(Lord Protect my Child © 1983 Special Rider Music)

I don't feel I can throw the coat away now. So I return it to the loft, after checking all the pockets in the last one I find a plectrum, I slip it in the small pocket in my jeans. When I come back down, a sense of equanimity has returned to the house mum is busy in the kitchen putting more mince pies in the oven. She has poured herself a large glass of sherry. She is now high, happy and over jolly in her manner. It's her defence mechanism, a way of telling me she doesn't want to talk about the money anymore today. I don't mention it, in fact I never remember us talking of it again.

She asks me to do some jobs around the house, putting wool across the chimney breast to hang some of our Christmas cards on and also put up some streamers across the lounge. We then have another cup of tea, with hot mince pies and Mum's special secret recipe brandy butter. Now I know Christmas is really here.

I then hear the back door open and running footsteps

"Dad, Dad look its Squrtal," Bob runs in holding up a small plastic figure.

"Ah that's… good," I say confused while ruffling his hair. Then it dawns on me the significance of this, a Squrtal, the missing Pokemon, the last in the collection from Mcdonald's Happy Meals. Thank god, I can relax now, no more burgers, I've been saved from cholesterol overload. Bob puts the green Squrtal carefully on the mantlepiece with the completed Pokemon collection. He then looks up at my Christmas card display and the streamers across the ceiling.

"Wow cool"

Sasha and Paul appear from the kitchen.

"Hi, how did it go?"

"Oh fine, he's no trouble," Sasha says looking at Bob as he discovers the box of Christmas decorations tearing open the dusty sticky tape and pulling out coloured tinsel, baubles and china tree decorations, spreading them all over the lounge carpet.

"Ahar," he says, pulling out a rather bent star. It is cut out from card and has glitter stuck on it, he made it in his nursery class. It looks a bit battered and has lost most of the glitter, certainly it was not up to guiding any wise men or shepherds anywhere.

"Dad lift me up," he says, putting his arms up trying to stretch to the top of the tree. I come behind him and lift him under his arms and help him fit the star to the top of the tree, just above the kink. Mum brings in a tray with more tea and hot mince pies. I return to the box and find the Christmas lights. I plug them in they don't work. I sit in a chair and begin to systematically tighten each bulb.

"Err...Nat can I have a word in the kitchen," Sasha says.

"Sure," I say disentangling myself from the lights and get up. Paul offers to take over, I tell him it's a difficult job, but undeterred he sits down and starts waggling each bulb, I shake my head dismissively as I go into the kitchen with Sasha.

"Is there a problem?" I say,

"No, not at all, it's just that we've bought Bob a present, and its just that, I'd really like to see him open it."

"Well?"

"I know its not Christmas till Tuesday," she said flashing her blue eyes at me, Sasha and Paul are due to travel to Manchester tonight to spend the rest of Christmas at Sasha mum's.

"Go on then,"

"Oh thanks, Nat," she said reaching up taking my face in her hands and kissing me on the cheek.

"I'll go and get it." She disappeared out the back door to the hire car. As she did this a big cheer came from the lounge. I go back to the lounge to see what the commotion is, much to my amazement Paul has succeeded in getting the lights to work. Together we start to arrange them around tree. Sasha comes back in with a large box. It's two foot long and six inches tall and wrapped with jolly Father Christmases and all tied together with a big blue bow. Bob looks round.

"Wow!" He says, looking at me with wide eyes, waiting to get the go ahead.

I nod at him and he moves towards the present,

"Now Bob, because Sasha and Paul aren't here on Christmas day, as a special treat you can open their's now," Sasha places the box in the middle of the mass of tinsel still on the carpet. Bob claws at the bow, Sasha tries to help, leaning forward her hair covering the box.

"I can do it, I can do it," Bob says. After a struggle the bow comes off, Bob tears at the paper. The box is plain and offers no clue to the contents. He pulls off the lid. In the box is a skate board. It's blue with large white wheels and has an Australian flag on the front. It is almost as big as Bob. He fights to pull it out of the box, it takes all his strength. Sasha looks at me, with a slightly worried look on her face. I smile at her, with my best reassuring look, trying to look like I think it's a good idea.

"Can I have a go Dad?" Bob says, now just about holding the board upright, and looking over the top. I look out of the window it's just getting dark.

"Ok, but just ten minutes… and put your coat on," I turn to Paul.

"Paul you better go supervise this," Bob rushes back from the hall with his coat on and stands on the skate board.

"I have an announcement, everyone must come to watch."
We all get our coats on and assemble outside. Mums house is in a row of five town houses. Out the back is a large parking area, in front of a line of ten garages. Mum, Sasha and I stand in a group, while Paul and Bob move to the middle.

"Do you think its all right?" Sasha says, cuddling herself with her arms to keep warm.

"It was Paul's idea, you know after the other night, the ironing board," Sasha says, putting her arms out as if on a surf board.

"Well, I'll have to get all the safety gear, a helmet and stuff,"

"Well it could have been worse, Paul wanted to get a surf board at first,"

"But we're fifty miles from the sea," I say,

"I know, I explained that to him," Bob shouts for us to look.

Paul's holding Bob as he glides across the car park. We all cheer and clap, but as they move further away we lose interest and carry on talking. Mum is standing next to me while Sasha has moved around in front obscuring my view of Bob. I carry on the conversation, trying desperately to keep a wary eye on the fledgling skateboarder. Every now and then I lose him behind Sasha's hair.

We talk about her going to Manchester, how long it's been since she's seen her Mum and when she's going back to Australia. Sasha then says how Bob and I must come and visit, but I'm not paying attention. Bob is growing in confidence, I know how he is, I remember teaching him to ride his bike, how he forced me to let go of the seat, prizing my fingers off. I could see his growing annoyance, Paul was insisting on holding tight to his coat while running along side.

Suddenly I can see events unfolding before me, as if in slow motion, but all too tragically this is real time. Otherwise I would have pushed Sasha aside, cleared the fifty feet separating me from my beloved son, then diving full-length to cradle his head, his beautiful head covered in blond hair with those oh so wise eyes, cushioning his skull gently and safely, and thus preventing it from smashing into the curb.

We heard the siren first then the blue flashing lights lit up the late December sky.

* * * * * * * *

Hazel stretched out on the sun bed, she had just got out of the pool. Her skin dripping wet, she liked the sensation of letting the sun dry her. The villa was lovely, set in a private complex only two hundred yards from the sea, but also sadly only two hundred yards from a golf course. Clive was in the shower getting ready to meet his mates for dinner. The talk would be mainly of golf and rugby, she wasn't looking forward to it. She really needed to confront Clive about the children thing.

Hazel heard something behind her Clive placed his hand on her shoulder.

"Come on Babe, you getting ready," he said, sitting on the lounger beside her. He had changed into a lightweight suit, with a shirt with far too many buttons undone for her liking. Hazel sat up and pulled her towel round her as she drew her knees up. She took a big breath.

"Clive, you know what you said about starting a family?"

"Oh not this again," he said lighting a large cigar.

"Yes, this again, it happens to be important to me," Clive sucked on his cigar and blew smoke over Hazel's head.

"Okay, well I guess I'll have to tell you." Clive said putting his cigar in the ashtray, he then leaned forward and looked Hazel in the eye. He began to rub his hands together, the way he did when he was nervous or trying to ask for something, it's funny how these little habits were really beginning to annoy Hazel recently.

"The thing is, I couldn't have children if I wanted to,"

"What do you mean?"

"Well, just before I got divorced, it was a difficult time, Betty was going through the change and we didn't want any accidents so..."

"So what?" Hazel pressed him,

"Well, I had the operation,"

"What operation?" Hazel said, still confused,

"That one," he said, glancing down at his crotch, smiling. "The snip."

Hazel swung round and placed her feet on the ground.

"Why the hell didn't you tell me!" She said angrily.

"Things just moved so quickly, I kept wanting to, believe me, but it never seemed like the right time. I guess, I just hoped the longer we stayed together, it would become less of an issue" Clive said, reaching across to take Hazel's hand, she pulled it away and stood up. Hazel was incensed now,

"I can never forgive you for this," she said, as she grabbed the still burning cigar and threw it at Clive. It hit the large lapel of his jacket showering his bare chest with sparks, before dropping into his open shirt. Clive stood up in panic, pulling at his shirt desperately trying to free it from his tight trousers, but it was no good. The cigar began to burn. As Hazel stormed through the patio door she looked back once only to see Clive jumping into the pool in an effort to extinguish his shirt. She slammed the door of the bedroom and ran to the bed flinging herself on it and burying her face in the pillow.

After ten minutes she could hear Clive in the bathroom next door, then she could hear a banging in the wardrobe, he was getting changed. A few minutes later there was a tentative knock on the door,

"Haze love," God! Hazel hated when he called her that, another thing about him she wouldn't miss.

"I'm off now, you sure you won't come?" Hazel was silent.

"Look Haze, I'm sure you'll get over this. I'll tell you what, how about we go look at that new car, I promise, first thing, when we get back, I'm sure I could stretch to the convertible."

Hazel sobbed into her pillow, whatever had she seen in him. How could buying a new car make everything all right, well that was Clive's answer to all problems, then she realized that's what had attracted her to him. Hazel felt physically sick, disgusted with herself, had she really been so shallow?

After she was sure Clive had gone she got up clawed off the designer bikini Clive had brought her before throwing it across the room. She walked to the door, slipped on the robe hanging on the back of the door. She went down stairs to the villa's phone. Hazel phoned the reps number and proceeded to have a frustrating call. Hazel was saying how she needed to go home but the rep kept saying in broken English, but you just got here. Why you go home? After a frustrating ten minutes she had managed to confirm that all flights to the UK were fully booked until after Christmas Day. Hazel had to face it, she would be spending Christmas Day in the Grand Canaries but harder to take was she would be spending it with Clive.

She made herself a drink, finding a tall glass filling it half full with whisky before topping it up with coke. She made her way out to the pool and sat on a sun bed. She took a long swig of her drink and came to the decision that her and Clive were over. She would keep her distance to get through the week. Then when she got home she would move out, maybe she could stay with Joan, till she sorted herself out.

Oh, but what about the baby, it was definitely Nathan's but did they have any future together, would he be interested in a child, he was so set in his single ways. I don't suppose he's ever thought about children. Well she would see him on Thursday. Maybe things would work out, maybe not, but she knew she was going to have this baby.

Hazel stood up and flexed her back, she felt a release as she walked to the pool steps. She undid the tie around her waist and flipped her robe off her shoulders, letting it fall to the ground. Slowly she walked down the steps, enjoying the cool water slowly creeping up her naked body. She stood in the pool, the water up to her neck still holding her glass. She put the remaining whisky glass on the edge of the pool, neither of them needed it now, she closed her eyes and let her head tip back, her red hair fanning out in the water around her head. She opened her eyes and stared up at the clear night sky. Suddenly something caught her eye just above the tall palm tree at the back of the garden, a bright light tracked across the sky in an arc disappearing behind the villa. Hazel smiled to herself a shooting star, a genuine shooting star that must be a lucky sign. Hazel closed her eyes briefly and made a wish.

What Hazel didn't know was she was wishing on a satellite.

* * * * * * * *

I went in the ambulance, Mum, Sasha and Paul followed in the car. I sat on the opposite stretcher, while the paramedic worked on Bob, taking readings and barking orders to the driver. Bob's hair was soaked in blood, his body unconscious and unresponsive. Every now and then the driver sent out a blast of siren as he swerved to overtake traffic. Cars on their way to restaurants, clubs, Pubs, to office do's and family celebrations enjoying Christmas, oblivious to the drama going on a few feet away from them.. I'm frantic with worry, there'll be no celebrating tonight.

I can't cry, I bite my lip, I needed to hold myself together. My mouth was dry, deep down inside I had a physical pain an actual hard lump cut me open and you could take it out put it under a microscope, look closely and you would find anxiety, worry, anguish, distress and fear. Look in my heart you would find a large amount of hope.

When we arrived at the hospital things moved very fast, they push Bob along on his trolley, it's my worse *Casualty* nightmare, four people shouting indecipherable words and numbers. They crash through double doors where I'm stopped by a nurse with a clip board,

"I need to take some details," she takes me to a side room, it was a long room with a table of old magazines in the middle and half a dozen chairs at each end. A doctor is deep in conversation with a young couple at the other end of the room, suddenly the women cried out,

"Oh my God, no," she says as she buries her head in her husbands chest. I turned back to the nurse, but she is staring past me at the forlorn scene with large brown eyes. The nurse looks very young with dusky brown skin and jet black hair. Reluctantly I glance back at the women she is sobbing uncontrollably now. I turned away embarrassed to witness such a private moment.

I wasn't about to ask the nurse about their story. I didn't need to know about some other family's tragedy, not at this time. I wanted to know about recovery, fight-backs, medical breakthroughs and miracles. The Nurse ran through the standard list of questions. I answered them as quickly and as accurately as I could. She makes me sign a consent form just in case they need to operate and just as I finish, Sasha, Paul and Mum come in and gather round the nurse eager for news. The nurse stands up tucking the clipboard under her arm,

"Right, you need to wait here, as soon as I know anything, I'll come and see you. There is a tea and coffee machine down the hall on the left," she went to leave, I grabbed her arm,

"Please, I need to know if he'll be alright,"

"I'm sure they'll doing all they can," she said patting my hand before taking a last look at the devastated couple, as she went out the door. I can't sit down, I pace around the room. Sasha and mum sit and hold each other sobbing. Paul is standing looking a little awkward. I walk past him three or four times before he reaches out and catches my arm stopping me. He leads me slightly away from the others,

"look Nat…I'm really sorry, I would never have bought the bloody thing if…" I interrupt him.

"It's not your fault, it's not anyone's fault, it's Bob, he just has to push," I say taking hold of Paul by the shoulders and looking him in the face.

"Thanks man," Paul says giving me a hug, the double doors open and we break apart, expecting or hoping for the nurse, but it's a small man in a black shirt and dog collar, I guess it's the hospital chaplain, he nods an acknowledgment to us, before moving to the couple. He talks to them briefly and inaudibly to us before they gather themselves up and slowly go to leave. As the woman goes through the door I hear her say,

"My poor brave baby boy."

No one says anything for a long time, alone with our thoughts, I know what everyone's thinking, that could be us in an hour or so, the three of us going home alone.

Paul says in an effort to break the awful silence,

"Coffee, who wants a coffee," Sasha pulls herself away from Mum it's the first time I've seen her face, it's red and tear-stained, her eyes are now an ordinary brown, no longer Caribbean blue (she must have removed her contact lenses)

"Yes, I'll help you," she says in a croaking, broken voice. Paul and Sasha disappear down the hall. Mum looks up, I'm taken aback by how suddenly she looks very old and tired.

"You all right son," she said holding out a hand. I take it and sit down beside her.

"Oh! Mum," I say, crying into her shoulder.

"He's going to be all right," she says, cupping my face in her hands, so forcing me to listen,

"No one who fought so hard for life is going to give it up lightly." I hear Sasha and Paul on the other side of the doors. Sasha backs through the doors and puts the coffee on the table. She give me a hug, I let out a long breath puffing through my cheeks. We settle down to wait.

Time drags by. The hands on the standard large white hospital clock creep round the face. A couple of times I open the door and look down the corridor to see if I can see anything, before letting it swing closed again. It's just less than two hours when the door opens. The dark-haired nurse comes in, she is followed by a doctor in his white coat, he has a mass of black curly hair with small tuffs of grey bits. He is rough-shaven, more to do with the hours he's just put in rather than making any fashion statement.

"Mr. Peterson," he says shaking my hand, its wet and clammy like it's just been washed. He looks at the other people in the room. I quickly introduce everyone to him. Sasha comes and stands next to me without looking at me. She searches out my hand and holds it tight. The doctor puts his hands together as if he's going to pray then he overlaps the fingers, before he begins.

"Well, Bob has had a serious blow to the head, he has a fractured skull. There has been some internal bleeding in the brain causing a haematoma, we had to operate, to alleviate this"

"So he'll be alright,"

"He's doing very well," the doctor says, pausing, I think to myself, don't say it, don't say BUT, please, please no BUTS.
Then he said it.

"But, its too early to tell what damage has been done, until the swelling goes and things settle down."

"Well how long?"

"Well Bob hasn't come round yet, now this is quite normal, and

114

nothing to be too alarmed about." Immediately I'm alarmed.

"Are you saying he's in some kind of coma?"

"Well yes, but he could come round at anytime, we need to do more tests and a scan, its really too early to say. Look, I have to go, but nurse Sinnatamby will take you to see Bob." I hadn't seen the nurse come through the doors, the doctor patted me on the arm in an effort to reassure me, it failed. The nurse said that it was best if only I could see Bob at this stage. I followed her down the corridor round the corner, she stopped at a double door and punched a code into a box on the wall and pushed the door open. A nurse is sat at a desk doing paperwork by the light of a small lamp, she looks up briefly as we go by. I can see into the room through a glass panel. I was shocked at first, I don't know why, it was almost how I had imagined it. It was just like your normal Saturday night *Casualty*, except this time I can't turn over.

Bob looks very small and fragile in the bed, a tube is coming out of his mouth helping him breath, various wires are attached to his body, machines bleep and lights flash. I stand and stare at first.

"Do sit down," the nurse says directing me to a hospital armchair by the bed.

"Hold his hand, talk to him, try and reassure him," I take hold of his hand it feels cold.

"I'll be back in ten minutes," I lean forward, and start talking trying to be upbeat

"Son …it's me, Dad...you gave us a bit of a fright...you had a run in an ambulance, you would have loved it, we went really fast with the blue lights flashing, horn and everything." I'm trying to be strong.

"You've got to get better son, do hear me," I kiss his hand, I carry on talking, afraid to stop, frightened of the silence, I start to ramble, I describe what I've got planned for Christmas, what's on telly and my dinner menu, anything I can think of. The doctor comes in, checks some readings on the machines and writes some numbers on the clip board .

"Right Mr. Peterson, we need to do some more tests, we do have facilities for you to sleep here."

"Right, yes I'll do that," I say slowly as I push myself up, releasing Bob's hand.

"Can you arrange that nurse?" The nurse nodded, I look at my watch its ten to nine. I go out of the room, I briefly look back through the glass at Bob one last time.

When I get in the waiting room, everyone gathers round. I give a detailed description of all I have seen, trying to be upbeat, but failing woefully. Then we all do, a group hug thing, initiated by Sasha.

Sasha drives us all home, we are very quite on the way home. It has started snowing, but no one chooses to mention it. She drops me off at the flat, I grab all I need to stay the night, I throw a few articles of clothing into a large holdall, I then get my personal stereo and agonize over the choice of CDs to take, but I realize the futility of this and end up grabbing half a dozen from the end of one rack. I then have a sudden thought, I go to the bedroom reach under the bed and pull out Bob's presents. I put the bag on the bed and put all Bob's presents in the bag. I lock up and go down to the van, I open the back, put in the gifts, covering them with an old dust sheet. I jump in the front throwing the bag on the passenger seat. I drive round to Mums, Sasha has phoned her Mum and will stay down here for the time being I'm glad Mum won't be on her own. Mum insists on making me a cup of coffee. I go into the lounge, the Christmas tree looks sad and depressing in its half finished state, Sasha sees the look on my face.

"Don't worry Paul and I will finish the tree," Sasha says enthusiastically, before adding a little hesitantly,

"So it's all ready for Bob when he comes home." I try to smile but don't quite pull it off, I don't want to hang around any longer so I only drink half my coffee throwing the rest down the sink,

"Right I think I'll make tracks," I say.

"You ring us, any news ring us," Mum says holding my arms at the elbows and looking me straight in the face to emphasize the point.

"Try and get some sleep," Sasha says hugging me, Paul shakes my hand, goes to say something but changes his mind. Just as I'm about to leave, I go to the lounge collect all Bob's Pokemon figures from the mantlepiece stuffing them one at a time into my pockets.

I go down the path, I get in the van, as I clear the inside of the windscreen I can see Mum and Sasha holding each other, crying in the kitchen. I get back to the hospital and immediately get lost. I realize I've got no idea where intensive care is. I go back to reception and explain to the nurse on duty. She explains the system, each ward has a different colour code, pink for maternity, red for accident and emergency and blue for intensive care. This is foolproof but not as good as having signs saying, *down this corridor Nathan* or *Hey! Nat turn left here* and finally *Nathan you are now entering intensive care.*

The nurse at the desk has gone off duty, and been replaced by a different nurse. Her voice seems too loud and a bit out of place. But then I think, maybe being loud and positive isn't such a bad thing. I go into see Bob, I keep talking for a while, but find it hard as my words echo around the empty room. I hold his hand and tickle his palm with one finger, going round and round in a never-ending circle.

The next thing I remember is the nurse gentle waking me up. I'm slumped forward head on the bed, I look at my watch with blurred eyes its 3.14 am.

"Why don't you go to bed for a while, I promise I'll come and get you if there's any change." Slowly I get to my feet, I look at Bob, he looks very peaceful, but no different to when I first saw him. The nurse explains where the parents room is. I pick up my bag and somewhat reluctantly leave Bob to find the room. It's a small room with a single bed in, a small bedside unit with a digital alarm clock on it. I'm exhausted I slip my jeans off and get in to bed. But my head is buzzing, I get out my personal stereo select a CD and slip it in. Its Travis *The Man Who,* I'm hoping the sound will stop me thinking so I turn the volume up high. After three or four tracks I drift off to sleep, but I'm woken by the hidden track at the end of the CD. I lie in the darkness my mind racing. Eventually I sleep, a fitful nightmare sleep, full of flashing blue lights and machines flat-lining.

Fifteen

Bob could remember getting the skateboard, opening the box and seeing the Australian flag. He knew that because they had a poster at school called 'Flags of the world'. He remembered going outside, and Paul holding him. He wanted to have a go on his own, but Paul kept holding him. He wanted to break free, then the skateboard was running away from him. Then it's black, a total blackness, not like in bed at night, he could always see light from the crack under the door. No this was true black .

After a while it feels funny, like once when he was swimming, Bob had opened his eyes and looked up through the water at the sky. He remembered seeing strange shapes of people around the pool edge. That's what it feels like, lying at the bottom of a pool and looking up. He can see faces but it's difficult to make them out, just blurred outlines. Sometimes the surface choppy, which made viewing everything difficult. Sometimes the blackness returns, along with total silence. He feels trapped, he can not communicate, he's entombed in a glass cell. His throat hurt like a burning sensation after you've been sick, there is something stuck in his throat.

* * * * * * * *

I wake up, the clock on the bedside table reads 8.18 am. There's no luxury of wondering what day it is or where I am, its all too painfully realistic. I'm straight back into my living nightmare from which sleep has given me no respite. I pull on my jeans, sniff my T-shirt. I decide to put on my football club fleece I got for my birthday and I pull it out of my bag. I feel my face and chin, its rough and unshaven. I leave it for now, I need to know how Bob is. I go down the corridor, the original nurse is back on.

"Morning," I say while standing looking through the glass window at Bob. The doctor is inside holding Bob's charts, making notes.

The nurse looks up from her paper work, which appears to be the *News of the World*.

"Morning"

"Any change"

"Well I've only just come on duty, but nurse Cox said he had a good night. The doctor will see you when he's finished." At that the doctor looks up and acknowledges me through the glass. He makes one last note and adjusts one of the machines, before coming out. The nurse quickly hides her paper.

"How is he doctor?" I ask.

"Well the results of the scan were encouraging, it showed very little internal damage and there has been no further bleeding overnight."

"So what happens now?"

"Later today we'll try too see if he can breathe on his own."

"Right," I say nodding slightly nervously. The doctor leans across and holds my arm.

"Look its going to be a slow process, but we've got to stay positive, the human body is a remarkable thing, it has amazing powers of recovery especially in a child so young." He turns to the nurse and gives out some information, then writes some notes on the pad in front of the nurse.

"Can I see him now?"

"Yes," the doctor said, not looking up from his writing.

"Keep talking to him, keep it as natural as possible, and I'll see you later this afternoon." With that he slipped his pen in his top pocket and marched off down the corridor. I go in and lean across Bob and kiss him on the forehead, then I gently ruffle his hair before sitting in the chair.

"Hi, Bob, err... how are you, I stayed here last night, I've got a little room down the corridor, it's quite nice, but there's no room service. It's Sunday morning do you know what tomorrow is. Yes, Christmas Eve." I stop, bite my lip and turn away, my eyes stinging with tears I take a breath and try to compose myself. Positive...I must stay positive.

"Oh, look what I've got," I start to pull the Pokemon figures from my pocket one at a time, its then I realize how uncomfortable its been with half a dozen Pokemon stuffed in my pockets. I arrange them on the bedside table. I pull the last one out its the Squrtal, I remember his happy, excited face when he was showing me, barely an hour before the accident. I hold it tight in my fist and close my eyes. I wonder if I wish hard enough I could turn back time and stop him going out on the skate board. I open my eyes, but nothing has changed. The door opens, the nurse sticks her head round the door.

"Mr. Peterson," I get up and go through the door, Mum,Sasha and Paul are standing there.

"I'm sorry I can only permit two at a time."

"That's fine I understand, you and Sasha can go in for a while," I say to Mum.

"Any news," Sasha and Mum say in unison.

"Well, no change, only the doctor said they would try to take him off the respirator this afternoon,"

"Well that's got to be good news, hasn't it?" Sasha said looking to the nurse for confirmation.

"Oh yes, yes it is," the nurse said trying to sound convincing before returning to the latest scandal in her Sunday paper.

"And how are you son?" Mum says giving me a peck on the cheek.

"Not too bad," I say sighing.

Mum and Sasha go through the door leaving Paul and I standing feeling slightly awkward and embarrassed.

"Er.. do you fancy getting some air?" I say.

"Yep, OK," he said, pulling his shabby cardigan together, we head off down the corridor, I'm beginning to know my way around now, I only make two wrong turns. We eventually arrive at my destination a small courtyard set aside for smokers. We go outside and stand by the pond in the middle, its black and very neglected with several dog-ends deposited on the frozen surface. Around the edge are several wooden benches, each one has a brass plaque dedicated to a departed patient. The only other person to brave the elements is a pale, thin and extremely ill looking man in one corner smoking a clandestine roll up, he has a drip on one of those wheeled stand. He looks around nervously each time he draws on his cigarette. Perhaps sadly he's sorting out a good location for his bench.

I take a deep breath and the sharp frosty air clears my head, I've been breathing recycled stale hospital air for what seems an eternity. I breathe a long white breath out. I pull out my tobacco tin, select a pre-rolled cigarette and light up a joint drawing in the sweet acrid smoke deep into my lungs.

"That feels better," I say, Paul smiles and nods, I hand him the joint, he takes a puff and goes to speak, the smoke catching in his throat.

"Look I'm finding this very hard, not having a kids,"

"Its hard for us all," I say, Paul hesitates as he hands the joint back to me and releases his smoke up to the sky.

"Cause you know we're having a baby," Paul says obviously not entirely sure if I've been told.

"Yes I heard, I hope thing work out...I mean everything goes...," Paul interrupts,

"That's alright, I know what you mean." Our attention is drawn to a nurse frantically banging on the window behind us, I point at my chest, but she wags her finger dismissively and indicates that the thin man behind us is her target. We turn to look, the man flicks his cigarette into the pond and scuttles away in the opposite direction as fast as his drip will let him.

"Come on, best be getting back," I say, adding my butt to the pond.

The rest of the day drags, we take it in turns to sit with Bob. Mum has brought in some of his favourite stories to read to him. We drink coffee, buy the Sunday papers, eat dry tired sandwiches and better home made cake from the volunteer shop. In the afternoon the doctor came to remove the tube helping Bob to breathe. We look on nervously our faces pressed against the glass panel. Trying to see how thing are going, but the doctor and two nurses in the room obscure our view. After an anxious fifteen minutes the doctor comes out. We all stand around him expectantly.

"Well it went very well, he is breathing unassisted now and all his vital signs are good... But..," I close my eyes, there's that bloody word again.

"There's been no real change in his overall condition, it's still a question of waiting," the doctor looked at his watch, his black curly hair hanging in front of his eyes his face clean shaven now.

"I'll come back and check on him before I go off duty, okay well if there's nothing else, I'll see you later," I feel I should be asking lots of questions, when will he get better? how long will it take? and will there be any long term damage? But some questions the doctor doesn't have answers to and some answers I don't want to know.

I spend the rest of the afternoon with Bob, sometimes with Mum sometimes with Sasha. I read more stories, I also get an old story tape from the van which was stuck at the back of the glove box behind the first aid box and the radio/cassette instructions book. Although he's not so keen on them now, at one time you couldn't go anywhere without having to play them. As soon as he was strapped in his car seat the shout of "story" "story" would start. Paul had a personal tape player, I gentle place the head phones round Bob's head and on to his ears. I hoped it would trigger something in his memory cause some deep stirring.

Around five I leave Mum and Sasha with Bob while I race home to have a shower and get some clean cloths. When I return Sasha offers to drive Mum home, it's been a long day and she looks tired, but before they go I try to point out how it's been a more positive day, at least Bob's breathing on his own, surely a step in the right direction, I'm not sure who I'm trying to convince.

I stay with Bob till around nine, before leaving him and wandering down the corridor. I stop off in the TV room. A large telly is on a bracket fixed to the wall, the room has old yellow coloured straight-backed armchairs all round the edge. It's deserted. The TV remote is secured to the bracket by a six foot length of chain. I take the remote and attempt to sit in the nearest chair but the chain comes up short. I let it drop to the floor, sit in the chair and shuffle to the remote control. I flick through the channels, but can't really find anything to watch. I still don't watch a lot of telly. The main things I watch are US shows. Strangely I noticed recently (maybe lying awake in the small hours) all the shows I like involve just letters in the titles, N.Y.P.D. Blue, ER and CSI. I'm sure a psychologist would make a lot out of this.

I'm still flicking through the channels when a small boy comes through the door, he's completely bald. He has red Liverpool pyjamas with matching slippers. He must be about Bob's age, but it's difficult to tell. He sits down next to me. He tutts when I stop at the snooker on BBC Two. I switch to another side for a while, then switch back, he tutts again. It becomes a game. I keep changing channels but always coming back to the dreaded snooker. This provokes ever louder tutts, now accompanied by small giggles.

The news comes on, I stop the game, but I'm aware he is still staring at me.

"I've got Lineker," he says in a matter of fact way, I think for a while.

"You've got Lineker, what's that then?" I say turning to face him.

"You know, my blood's all bad, they gave me this medicine and my hair all fell out,"

He said rather proudly dipping his head down just in case I hadn't noticed.

"I think you mean …leukemia," I said hesitantly as if it was a swear word.

"That's it Leukemia," in an almost joyous way. In that way kids do when they're very sick and love to tell you all the gory details.

I then get the link, someone had told him about Gary Lineker's son having leukemia, that's where the confusion came from. He nodded gently while stroking his shiny head. I turned back to the telly, the sports news had come on, we both watch intently. The clip shows Liverpool's game this afternoon, they won 2-0.

"Yes" the boy says punching the air with his tiny fist.

"Liverpool supporter eh?" I says stating the obvious.

"Yep all my life," if this was supposed to impress me, I had underpants older than him.

"My Dad says when I get well, I'm going to be a mascot, do you know what that is?" I humoured him switching off the telly and turning in my chair to face him.

"No ,what's it all about then?"

"Well," he says, his eyes lighting up in their dark sunken sockets.

"First" he said counting off with his fingers and holding it up.

"You get a Liverpool football kit. Second, you get a signed football. Third, you get to run out with the team, that's Michael Owen and everybody right, and fourth, err.." the small boy hesitated clutching his tiny finger before dismissing it.

"I don't think there is a fourth but that's still brill, yes"

"Yep, that certainly is brill," at this point a lady comes through the door. She has short bleached spiky hair her face is pained and old beyond her years. She looks across at me.

"Sam have you been bothering this man?"

"No mum, honest, I was just telling him about me being a mascot"

"That's right, he's been no trouble" I say. I recognise her as the lady I had seen the first night, crying with her husband in the waiting room.

I think at this point she recognizes me, she becomes anxious and flustered, worried that I may start asking awkward questions,

"Oh,well its time for bed, say goodnight to the nice man," she said holding out her hand, keeping her distance while waiting for Sam to take it.

"Goodnight Mr" Sam said on the way to the door. I pull myself up.

"Goodnight Sam, Hey! do me a favour, make sure you get Michael Owens autograph for me," he shouts as he disappears out the door.

"Sure will." His Mum puts a hand on his shoulder, looks back at me, she is biting her lip. I nod my head with my lips tightly closed, it's my best reassuring, I know your son is dying, I'm terribly sorry, I wish I could do something, nod.

I put my hands behind my neck and stretch up, letting my hands go up towards the ceiling. I waggle my fingers trying to shake out all the horrific things I had seen in the past few days. I breathed out long and hard. I feel depressed and low now. Tired, but not ready for sleep, my mind was too troubled. I go out into the corridor and turn the opposite way, I'm getting to know my way around now, and decide to explore. I walk down to the end of the corridor. The first door I come to is the hospital chapel. It has a large imposing pine door with a brass handle. I stand outside, my hand hovering over the handle. Then I decide to go in, the door creaks open. The room is empty and dimly lit with small sidelights along the wall. It has ten modern pews divided by a central aisle, at the far end is a large table with a plain white cloth hanging down to the floor. Behind the table is a simple wooden cross fix to the whitewashed wall, it's lit by a single spotlight.

To the left of this is a small door. I wander up the aisle to the second pew from the front. I move half way along and sit down. I've never been very religious, certainly not in the going to church way. But the chapel is peaceful and very quiet and it doesn't have that hospital smell. I bow my head and close my eyes, I'm there about five minutes when I'm aware of the small door opening. With one eye I squint at an old man in a black shirt and a dog collar who comes through the door, it's the chaplain I saw that first night, when he was consoling Sam's Mum and Dad. He is a small man, balding with a small grey edging of hair. Perched on his nose is a small pair of gold-rimmed glasses. He stands in front of the table and bows gentle to the cross on the wall.

He then goes to the back of the room and sits behind me, I'm aware of him but I don't turn round. After some time I sit up and open my eyes, I'm just about to leave when he says,

"Can I help you son?" his voice is deep and hushed, it reminds me of my Dad's. So much so, I find it quite disturbing.

"Ah no," I say turning slightly to face him.

"I didn't interrupt you earlier, when you were talking," he said smiling at me, I thought, hang on, I wasn't talking, then I got it, he assumed I was talking to... God.

"No, you're fine, I wasn't really...I was just looking for somewhere quiet to sit, I don't follow any faith," the man moves and sits down next to me.

"But you do have faith,"

"I do?" I said, wishing I had gone when I had the chance.

"You support our local team, you must have faith in them"
How did he know I support our local team? I think that's spooky perhaps there's more to this religion thing after all. Of course I had completely forgotten I had my football club fleece on!

"How long have you been a supporter?" he said, I began to relax a bit as I was on a subject I knew more about.

"Well my Dad took me when I was around six to see my first game, let me see, over thirty years."

"So you've faced relegation, let me think at least three times," I think to myself, bloody hell, (Oops sorry I remember where I am) that's right, this bloke knows what he's on about.

"That's right," I say recollecting the three miserable seasons.

"So you still kept going, through all the bad times when a lot of people would have fallen by the wayside, given up on them, I would consider that an unquestionable faith,"

"I suppose you're right,"

"Would you like to pray for someone in particular." The chaplain said putting a gentle hand on my shoulder.

"Well, I don't know. I kind of find it funny to pray to someone, I mean that bearded bloke sitting on a cloud," I put my hands on the pew in front and try to stand up.

"No, wait" he says in his calm voice, reluctantly I sit back down.

"Would it help if you picture him as someone you admire?"

"I suppose," I said grudgingly.

"Tell me who's your real hero? he said in a cheerful voice looking on me as a real challenge now. I think well, we do have this player in our team, who's a Christian but in truth he's a frustrating player, being brilliant one match and having an off day the next. No I can't pray to him, might catch him on an off day. So I suppose that just leaves Bob Dylan. He did go through his born again phase so I say,

"I guess that would be Bob Dylan." This threw the Chaplain for a second, I think he was expecting me to name a famous football player.

"He played on the wing didn't he?" he says,

"No the sing..." I break off, as he is chuckling at his own joke.

"No seriously, you could pray to him, that's it, look on him as God's messenger; a face for you to focus on," he said looking pleased with himself as he stood up.

"I have to go now, I have an even bigger boss to answer to, the wife," laughing he held out a hand to me I stood up and shook it, his hand was warm, but not in a sweaty way, it just had a natural warmth to it.

"Look, anytime you need a talk, I'm always home," he said spreading his arms out and looking round his Chapel before patting me on the shoulder as I sat back down. He turned, bowed again at the cross and disappeared back through the small door.

I was left alone in the silence and tranquility of the chapel. It was funny how he never asked me who was ill or why I was in hospital. I was glad in a way, not having to explain everything about Bob. He was a nice old boy. It must be good to have a belief, something to turn to. But then I suppose I turn to my music, especially Dylan, in times of strife, like when I though it was all over with Hazel, I think of the nights I stayed up playing my records into the small hours. I rest my head on the pew in front. I hadn't thought much about Hazel in the past few days. I wish I had someone to talk to, not like Mum and Sasha, someone not so emotionally involved. I've been so stupid, I wish that I'd told Hazel about Bob, then maybe we would still be together, maybe, but if we were, we could be facing this together.

I feel very sorry for myself. I start to cry slow tears run down my cheeks. The door at the back opened. Someone comes in and sits in the pew just across the aisle to me. I sit for a little longer resting my head on my hands. If I were to pray to Dylan, it would have to be the Dylan of 1966, all dark, mean and moody and at the height of his power. Then I slowly lean back and glance to my left through watery, blurry eyes I see Dylan looking straight at me, through dark glasses and a mass of black unkempt hair. He is slumped in his pew with his arms crossed across the front of his long black leather coat.

"What do you want from me, man?" he barks at me in his American accent, making me jump. I shuffle to the end of the pew and turn to face him.

"I just need to know if my son is going to be all right," Dylan uncrossed his arms and leaned across at me.

"Have I ever let you down before, hey?" Dylan said at the same time removing a large industrial light bulb from under his coat, he held it in front of his face and was staring at it intently. Nathan remembered how in 1965 at Dylan's first official news conference in the VIP lounge of London Airport, he had arrived carrying a large industrial light bulb. When asked what his main message was, he responded with the quick-witted reply, 'keep a good head and always carry a light bulb'. Dylan turned and spoke through the bulb, his dark brooding face distorted by the glass.

"All through your life I've been there. Hey man, like when your father died, who helped you through," I nodded more tears now.

"You did, you did," I shout.

"But you must know something," I say leaning across and wiping my tears with the back of my sleeve. Dylan looked left and right as if someone might be listening, he then leans forward across the aisle.

"All I can say is, take the rag away from your face, for now ain't the time for your tears." [1] With that he stood up, glanced nervously up at the cross on the wall and crossed himself. He then turned and handed me the light bulb, before slowly walking back to the main door. I call after him,

"So he'll be all right?" Dylan opens the door letting in the offensive neon light from the corridor, he turned in the door way and mumbling

"As the curtain is drawn and somebody's eyes must meet the dawn, and if I see the day I'd only have to stay, so I'll bid farewell in the night and be gone." [2] The door slammed shut with such force the lights flickered and the cross on the wall shook.

I return my head to my hands and close my eyes. I drift off into my thought. How long have I been here? I look at my watch, I've been here for two hours, I say to myself under my breath,

"Now ain't the time for your tears, as the curtain is drawn and somebody's eyes must meet the dawn." That's it, Bob's going to be all right.

I stand up walk to the front of the church, I acknowledge the

[1] From the Lonesome Death of Hattie Carroll (1963)   [2] From Restless Farewell (1963)

cross with the slightest of bows before gently placing the light bulb in the middle of the clean white cloth. Then I turn and march down the aisle, go through the door carefully closing it behind me.

The bulb glows with a brilliant yellow light that fills the empty church.

* * * * * * * *

Bob can make out a bright light (like a curtain being opened at the dawn of a summers day) the light shining down and cutting through the dark, deep water. Guided by the warm light Bob slowly, very slowly starts to work his way to the surface.

Sixteen

God don't make no promises that he don't keep.
You got some big dreams, baby, but in order to
dream you gotta still be asleep.
When you gonna wake up, when you gonna wake up
When you gonna wake up and strengthen the things that remain?

(When You Gonna Wake Up © 1979 Special Rider Music)

Its Christmas Eve, but I don't think oh wow! Its Christmas Eve. I think how's Bob, its just another day to get through. I get dressed and go and see Bob. No change. No change is worse now. No change before meant that he was stable. Now no change means Bob getting no better. I stay with Bob for an hour or so, reading stories and playing cassettes. Mum and Sasha arrived. Mum goes to the window and looks at Bob,

"How is he?"

"Just the same, really," my voice sounding a little depressed.

"We need to talk," Mum says, as she goes through to Bob. She gently flicks his hair from his forehead before she plants a kiss there. Mum then comes out,

"Right, in the telly room now," she says marching off down the corridor. Sasha and I look at each other and fall in line behind her. The telly room is empty but the TV is still on, Mum reaches up and switches it off. Sasha and I sit down.

"Right, we need to talk about Christmas," I let out a sigh and shake my head.

"Well son it's going to happen whatever, I've spoken to Sasha and told her she must go home for Christmas as planned." I look at Sasha, she leans across and puts a hand on my knee.

"Look Nat there's nothing I can do here, the doctor says he's out of any immediate danger. I'll go home for a few days then I can be back at the weekend." I stood up and paced up and down the room.

"Oh I suppose you're right."

"Well that's settled then," said Mum.

"Now we just have to sort out what we're doing." I turn to face Mum.

"Oh I can't."

"Look son, we can't just ignore it"

"Oh I wish we could," I sat back down.

"Look would everyone like a coffee," Sasha says, standing up, Mum and I nod, and she disappears out of the door. Mum comes and sits next to me.

"I know how you feel, I don't expect you to carry on as normal, but we can have Christmas dinner, Graham can still come round. You only need to come home for, what two hours."

I resign myself to the fact that Christmas was going to happen, even if I choose to ignore it. I was kind of hoping if I didn't think about it, it would go away. I still hoped that Bob would wake up and everything would be fine, but time was running out for that. Sasha came back with the coffee. She was due to drive up to Manchester this afternoon. I knew it made sense, it was just difficult not to think of her leaving, just as the going got tough again. Mum told me more of the arrangements for our Christmas, We would visit Bob in the morning. Then she would go back to cook dinner. I would stay until around twelve then shoot home to have my Christmas dinner. We would leave exchanging gifts until the evening. I would have to sleep at home now, as I was told they need the parents room back.

Paul turned up and went with Sasha to say goodbye to Bob. I'm waiting in the corridor when they come out,

"Err, we're going to make a move now," Sasha said slightly embarrassed before giving me a hug. She pulled away and spoke to me staring into my face.

"You take care now, ring me the minute there's any news"

"I will don't worry," I said squeezing her arms. I turned to Paul, put out my hand for him to shake, then embarrassed I gave him a hug.

"You look after her," I say, looking at Sasha.

"I will," he said, putting a protective arm around her.

"Right," Sasha said taking a big breath.

"We'll be back at the weekend," she said turning and walking away down corridor, I never remember watching her walk away six years ago I just remember her suddenly not being there anymore. As she reached the very end of the corridor she looked back once, well at least she looked back. This time I knew she would be back. She was back in Bob's life, forever.

The rest of the day dragged, once more I spent most of it avoiding anything to do with Christmas. At one time I walked down to the café area, a Carol concert was in full swing. I turn round. I seek sanctuary in the telly room, but the film *A Wonderful Life* is on, this is part of my normal Christmas Eve schedule. I always settle down to watch it when all the jobs and preparation are done, with my first Christmas drink. I then know Christmas has truly began, but not this year. I go back out again past the large Christmas tree surrounded by presents left for the children's ward. I return to the sanctuary of Bob's room which is all functionality and medical, nothing in the room is at all seasonal.

I read the same stories to Bob again, then tired and a little disillusioned I sit in the chair and read my book. I'm still reading B.B. Kings autobiography. I guess it's taken me almost as long to read it, as it took B.B. King to live it.

The doctor comes round late afternoon, I go out while he takes some readings, does some checks and writes some notes. As he comes out I stop him.

"Any change?" I say, the doctor moves to the chair by the desk and sits down, he writes in the book on the desk as he did so he spoke.

"Well no, it's really a matter of wait and see. After Christmas we might think of moving him to another ward,"

"Oh!" I say, sounding concerned

"Don't worry that's a good thing, it means he needs less nursing" He smiled, giving me one of his much practised reassuring looks. Then he looked at his watch,

"Right, I'm off duty now," he said removing his stethoscope and wrapping it around his hand he turned to leave saying,

"Happy Christmas!"

"Hap...," I couldn't bring myself to say it so I just mumble,

"And you," to the doctor's back as he scurries off down the corridor to begin his Christmas festivities. Leaving me alone, I sit with Bob for a few more hours until around eight I head home.

There's a light sprinkling of snow. I jump into the van and glancing over my shoulder into the back I can see Bob's present sticking out from under the sheet. On the way home every window has a Christmas

tree with lights burning bright. I try and focus straight ahead on the wind-screen wipers, as they clean the snow from the screen. Even the weather is seasonal, its like the whole world is mocking me and screaming...
CHRISTMAS IS HERE!

I call in the flat, throw some more clothes into my bag and change some of my CDs. I get to Mums, deposit my dirty washing in a pile by the washing machine in the kitchen. Mum comes round the corner from the lounge as I do this. She glances briefly at the pile but says nothing, things must be bad.

I wander into the lounge,

"Wow!" I say, as I see the tree, Mum has followed me,

"Yes, Sasha and Paul made a good job of it," I'm standing in front of the tree holding a china rocking horse decoration.

"Do you remember this?" Nan looks over my shoulder.

"We brought it for Bob's first Christmas from Harrods,"

"That's right I remember now."

I find it hard to relax, I wander about then try to watch a bit of telly, but I can't settle. I think about going down to the *House of Gloom*, but I can't face all that festive cheer and jolly people. I also don't want to explain how Bob is, to a dozen well-meaning people. In the end I make Mum and I a drink, she has a sherry and I have a whisky. I end up on Bob's bed wrapped in his Harry Potter duvet listening to CDs and reading my book. I feel close to Bob here surrounded by Pokemon wallpaper and books on dinosaurs. In a few hours it will be Christmas Day and there's nothing I can do about it. Eventually sleep comes, as a welcome relief.

"Nat! Nat!" I wake with a jolt. Mum is standing over me with a mug of tea. I'm still dressed, I prop myself up on my elbow.

"Thanks Mum," I say taking my tea.

"The water's hot, if you want a shower," Mum says on her way out. I'm grateful she doesn't wish me Happy Christmas or anything. I swing my legs down and sit holding my tea. I get myself together, shower, and eat two slices of toast for breakfast. The kitchen is warm and a cooking smell is emanating from the oven. I guess the turkey is no longer free range. Mum and I set off to visit Bob, the roads are deserted, the only traffic being one or two kids on shiny new bikes.

The hospital itself is very quiet, anyone who can walk has been sent home for the Christmas period. We make our way to Bob's ward.

Nurse Sinnatamby is sat outside at the desk, a small piece of tinsel in her hair as a concession to the day. She smiles and tells us to go through.

Mum and I sit on chairs either side of the bed. I look at Bob, something looks different about him. I can't put my finger on it just something about him has changed. We spend the morning reading stories. Neither of us mentions Christmas to him. A lot of the time we sit in silence. Around eleven Mum stands up,

"Well if that turkey is not going to be cremated, we need to go and have our Christmas dinner now,"

I wave my arms in a panic,

"Shush," I say looking at Bob, worried that deep in his sleep he will hear its Christmas day.

"Oh sorry," Mum says kissing Bob on the forehead.

"Right, yes you're right, lets go," I say reluctantly gently ruffling his hair. I start to walk to the door, something catches my eye, and I pause and look back studying Bob intently. I could have sworn, there was a flicker across his face. I watch his body for the slightest of movement, but nothing.

"What is it?" mum asks,

"Err...nothing," I say opening the door for Mum, and stand in the doorway to let her pass as I take a last look at Bob's motionless body. At the desk nurse Sinnatamby looks up,

"We're off for dinner now," I say almost embarrassed, as I was leaving my son alone on Christmas day, I find out nurse Sinnatamby would be having no Christmas dinner for the foreseeable future as she was on a twelve hour shift.

"I'll be back this afternoon," I nearly go to say something to her, but change my mind.

Dinner was good, I mean, I could appreciate the trouble mum and Graham had gone too. Even laying out the table in the lounge, with a big holly centerpiece, which Graham kept pricking himself on every time he reached for his drink. It's just I felt so guilty about enjoying myself. I wanted to get back to Bob. I couldn't finish all my meat so I gave it to Quinn. I went into the kitchen to load the dishwasher. I could hear Mum and Graham giggling. I stop the banging and clanking the plates to listen. They sound like a couple of teenagers. Was it my imagination, or merely the drink or were they getting on rather well. As soon as I've set the dishwasher going I pop my head round the corner,

"I'm off now," I say,

"Oh, OK, I'll see you tonight, love to Bob," Mum says as she pours Graham another brandy.

"Yes tell him we need him at football. Ah! that reminds me, Graham said pulling out a bent Christmas card from his jacket pocket. I take it and open it and read it. It says 'Hope you get well soon, Happy Christmas,' but the biggest thing is its signed by our centre forward, Bob's favourite player.

"Wow! how did you manage that?" I say genuinely impressed with Graham's gift.

"Ah well, it pays to have friends in high places," Graham said looking rather pleased with himself.

"I'll put it on Bob's bedside table," I then had an idea. I remember Nurse Sinnatamby's twelve hour shift. I collected all the left over crackers, two boxes of mince pies, a little brandy butter and the spare set of Christmas lights from the decoration box in the hall. As I leave the house Mum's loud endearing laughter follows me up the path.

When I get back to the hospital I offer nurse Sinnatamby one of my mince pies, she smiles and gratefully accepts.

"When are you off home then?" I ask. She studies her watch briefly before saying,

"Three hours and twenty three, no twenty four minutes, roughly."

"Here," I say holding out one of my crackers. Nurse Sinnatamby looks around before taking a firm grip. The cracker bangs sending the contents flying across the floor. She pushes her chair back and scrambles on all fours to retrieve it.

"Here you better have this, I won't be needing it," she said handing me a large orange plastic ring.

"It's lovely. I'll treasure it for ever," I say putting it in my fleece pocket. I glance through the window at Bob. The mood changes. I stand and look through the window Nurse Sinnatamby comes and stands behind me.

"You must have seen kids like this before, will he get better?"

"I've seen children much worse then Bob make a full recovery, I'm sure it's just a question of time," she says. I sigh.

"I hope you're right," I push the door and go in determined to be upbeat.

I pull another cracker with myself and put on the green hat, which immediately slips down over my eyes. I get out the card and place it open on the bedside table. I position the lights around a picture on the wall and plug them in. I then get another cracker from the box,

"Here Bob, your turn," I say I put the end of another cracker in his limp hand. I put my hand around his and squeeze it tight to hold it. We pull the cracker,

BANG! The gift falls on to the floor and goes under the bed, I bend down to pick it up. As I come up my eyes are level with the bed. I can see the torn piece of cracker held tight in Bob's tiny hand. My eyes move up his arm to his face, an unmistakable small grin is on Bob's face. I jump up go halfway to the door, then I'm stuck in limbo not sure which way to turn, if I leave him he might fall back to sleep.

I try to speak but only gibberish will come out I finally scream,

"Nur... Nur... Nurse."

Seventeen

Three angels up above the street,
Each one playing a horn,
Dressed in green robes with wings that stick out,
They've been there since Christmas morn.

(Three Angels © 1970 Big Sky Music)

Hazel sat on the balcony of the villa in the midday sun, her shoulders were sun burnt Hazel always suffered no matter how careful she was. It was the red hair and pale complexion. In the last few days she had spoken barely a dozen words to Clive. She had moved into the spare bedroom. At least she could suffer morning sickness without Clive getting suspicious. They were living separate lives, when Clive had turned up with his mates. Hazel had made her self scarce and stayed in her room reading and playing CDs. She had treated herself to a personal CD player along with several CDs from one of the high street chains at the airport. Most duplicates of old records she had hidden away in a cupboard at Clive's house. She was listening to Dylan's *Blood on the Tracks,* tears running down her cheeks, she was thinking of Nathan. She had never felt so lonely, never in her life.

In her hand she held a small parcel, Clive had knocked on the door about twenty minutes ago, when she opened the door the parcel was on the tiled floor. She still hadn't opened it, slowly she pulled the small red ribbon. The paper fell open revealing an exclusive jeweller's ring box. She clicked open the box revealing the biggest most offensively large diamond ring she'd ever seen, sparkling in the setting sun. She hated it, she wondered if Clive knew her at all, had he learned nothing about her in the last six months? She felt she had wasted the time, she also felt used and a little soiled, but in truth Hazel had been blinded by the high life. Now she was disgusted with herself, true love had opened her eyes. Hazel stood up and looked over the balcony. Someone walked across the lawn and through a gap in the fence to the connecting villa. Hazel recognized her as the holiday rep, funny that's the fourth time she had been round in two days. Then Clive came into view, drink in hand. Hazel called out,

"Oh! Clive," he looked up at first with a small smile on his face, which quickly vanished to horror as Hazel flung the small box out over the pool. He dropped his drink and ran to the long-handled net used for cleaning the pool which was hung on the wall. He ran to the pool making a desperate lunge just as the box was sucked into the pool cleaning system. Hazel went back inside leaving him to it. She took the opportunity to go down stairs and get a bottle of champagne from the fridge. In the kitchen Hazel paused over the fresh bottle of gin Clive had just started, before dropping the ring in the clear liquid.

Hazel went to the bathroom, she filled the deep round bath. Collected her personal CD player and opened the bottle. She dropped her sarong on the floor. Testing the temperature with her toe she slid under the bubbles, right under the surface. The water washed away her tears and cut out all sound. Hazel stayed under for as long as she could then she came to the surface, back to reality. She dabbed her eyes with a towel. She took a large sip of champagne, in an effort to block out everything. She switched on the CD player, Dylan sings, *'Twas then he felt alone and wished that he'd gone straight and watched out for a simple twist of fate.'* More tears. Hazel refilled her glass. Stretched out and accidentally knocked the bottle over. She made no attempt to pick it up, only watching as the chilled contents ran slowly into the bath soothing her red shoulders. Only one more day to endure, then she would be free, free of Clive. She would move out, get another job, Joan and her had even talked of starting on their own. She had clients who would come with her, but that would be a lot to take on now, what with the bab…baby. Well she had said it, admitted the reality that she was going to be a mother and probably a single one at that.

* * * * * * * *

In the end I sort of open the door and shout while still almost holding Bob's hand. Nurse Sinnatamby made a frantic phone call before rushing in and doing a few minor medical checks. She asks Bob a few simple questions which he nods replies to. While I'm a bit over excited and keep interrupting and pre-empt his answers much to her annoyance. Then the doctor arrives, he does a more rigorous series of tests, checking all Bob's reflexes, sense of touch and shining lights in his eyes. Bob's voice was very weak, the doctor allowed him a few sips of water and it becomes a little stronger and more audible. After twenty minutes the doctor pronounced him remarkably fit under the circumstances. He said they would still keep a close eye on him, but he said in a few weeks he would be back to his old self. I was torn between phoning Mum or staying with Bob. In the end I got Nurse Sinnatamby to make the call. I leaned in close so Bob doesn't have to talk too loud.

"What day is it?" he said in a husky voice.

"It's Tuesday," I say (completely missing the point) a short pause then Bob says,

"No what day of Christmas is it?"

"Oh! it's Christmas Day." I say moving back and gesturing with my arm at my pathetic display of Christmas lights. Bob closes his eyes just, a tear runs from the corner of his eye nearest to me. I follow it across his cheek into his ear.

"What's the matter, what's the matter?" I say in a panic,

"Its too late he's gone now," Bob said, turning his head away from me,

"Who's gone?"

"Father Christmas"

"No... No he hasn't I..." I was thinking on my feet now.

"I spoke to him earlier, on the mobile. Err... all dads get his number when they have kids," I said pulling my phone out of my pocket.

"Really" Bob said his eyes getting some of their old sparkle back.

"Well ring him then and ask when he's coming back"

"Ah...what now"

"Yes now"

"Ok I will but only I can talk to him, if he finds out I've told you about the number thing, I'll be in big trouble and he won't come" I start going through my phone book from my menu, and ring a number. I hear it ring, completely flouting the NO MOBILE rule.

"Father Christmas please" I put my hand over the phone, and talk to Bob.

"One of Santa's elves on reception"

I hear 'You've reached SCREW IT for all your fixtures and fittings, unfortunately we are closed for Christmas so please leave a message after the tone.'

"Is that Santa Clause" I say, and pause for realism,

"How are you" I pause again like I'm listening to his reply.

"Yes, you must be knackered after delivering all those presents," I wink at Bob.

"I'll get to the point, I spoke to you earlier about my son Bob needing a late delivery," I pause again and throw in a few "Mmm" and "Errs". Bob appears to be totally taken in now, he listens intently waiting for an answer.

"You can, that's great, so where are you now?" Bob excitedly claps his hands.

"Err... right that's very good of you, thanks very much"

"What's that, he'll have to be extra good next year," I look at Bob who nods his head.

"Oh I'm sure he will. Bye for now," I press the off button just as I hear the message full signal from the work's answerphone.

"He said he's just over Slough, so he'll be about half an hour."

Just then Mum comes bursting through the door, she runs over to Bob and gives him a big hug. Then pulls away worried she might be hurting him. Looking at me.

"It's fine, Mum he's fine," she sits and strokes his blond hair gently. I beckon Mum away from Bob and whisper.

"Look Mum, I need to pop out for about half an hour, it's really important."

Mum looks a bit confused as to why I would want to desert my son who had just come out of a coma. But I explain everything will become clear, I've just got to make Christmas right.

"Very well son if you must" she says as I kiss her on the cheek.

"I'll see you later Bob"

"You'll be back before Santa gets here"

"Oh! sure" Mum looks at me confused, she leans closer to me and says in a concerned voice,

"You're not going to do anything stupid are you?" I stick my head back round the door.

"I'm not sure yet."

Outside the door I take a big breath and collect my thoughts. It's Christmas Day, I look at my watch 3.45 p.m., and I've got to find a Santa Clause outfit and deliver Bob's presents in the next half-hour, what could be easier. I set off down the corridor and turn left. There in front of me is Santa Clause going into the toilet. I don't believe it, I look heavenwards and say,

"Thank you God!"

I follow him in, he's gone in a stall. I pace about biting my lip trying to think of a plan. Then someone else comes in and embarrassed not to be doing anything, I move to a urinal and open my fly. I look across at the other guy, and smile. He gives me a nervous look and finishes quickly. The chain flushes in the stall and Santa comes out. He has removed his coat and beard. He sees me,

"Hot work this Santa job, why are hospitals so sodding warm?" he moves to the sink and runs the cold tap, sloshing the water on his face. I look him up and down. I can now inform you that Father Christmas is in fact around forty years old, a skinhead with nipple piercings and a tattoo on his right arm showing a lion with the accompanying words '*I'm Chelsea till I die*' ...I ignore his appearance,

"Well paid I guess" I say

"No, I'm a volunteer, I does a lot of work for charity," I move closer and place a hand on his shoulder,

"Well how would you like to earn yourself twenty quid?" This was probably not the wisest question to ask a skinhead in a public toilet.

"What would I have to do?" he asks suspiciously,

"All I want to do is borrow your costume for about twenty minutes," I had thought about asking him to deliver Bob's presents, but I didn't trust him and besides it was something I felt I needed to do.

"Oh! I couldn't let down all those kids, just imagine their little faces," I open my wallet and peel off two more notes.

"Forty quid," I say

"Make it fifty and you've got a deal," he said, spitting on his hand and offering it to me. So there you have it, it's a sad world we live in when Father Christmas can be bought for a mere fifty quid.

I explain what I have to do, a little about the Bob situation and this Father Christmas has a small pang of guilt and drops the price by ten quid. He removes his outfit and hands it to me to put on. This leaves him just in black socks, rather soiled boxer shorts and an old Chelsea shirt, he goes back in the stall to wait. Its crosses my mind to offer him a joint while he's waiting, but I decide against it, I don't want to totally shatter my view of Santa altogether. Once I'm dressed I look in the mirror,

"Ho! Ho! Ho!" I say. The disrobed Santa shouts from behind his stall.

"Stop pissing about, I can't stay in here forever!"

"OK I'll be as quick as I can," I open the door and stick my head out, look left and right, all clear. I set off down the corridor in the direction of the car park. First I need to get Bob's presents out of the van. I open the back up and try to gather them up, but there's too many. So I make a sack out of the blanket and go back inside and head to Bob's room. When I get there thankfully there is no sign of the doctor. Nurse Sinnatamby rather disappointingly recognizes me immediately saying,

"Mr. Peterson what are you up to now?" I can see Mum leaning close to Bob deep in conversation.

"I just wanted to give Bob a Christmas"

"Well go ahead, but if the doctor comes back I know nothing about it"

"Fine I won't be long" I take a big breath and push the door open.

"Yo! Ho! Ho!" Bob gasps in excitement and struggles to sit up. Mum almost shouts my name, nearly giving the game away. I place my makeshift sack gently on the floor, arrange the gifts on the bed so Bob ends up encircled by an array of different size parcels. His eyes getting larger as each new present comes into view. I'm sweating like mad in the thick red coat and long white beard. I'm beginning to feel a bit faint but I manage to hang on to see Bob undo his Playstation two then I give another,

"Yo! Ho! Ho!" before disappearing out the door gasping for air. I run straight into the doctor,

"What the hell!"

"Shoosh, it's me," I say quickly closing the door and pulling my beard down,

"That's all very well but your son has been seriously ill. I don't want him getting over excited." With that he squeezed past me,

"Right Bob you can open one more present for now, then I want you to get some rest." I hear the doctor say, as I make my way down the corridor with my beard down below my neck and my coat opened, a very sorry looking Santa.

I'm nearly at the toilet, when a voice cuts me dead in my tracks. It's nurse Cox,

"Excuse me Santa, but the children have been waiting for twenty minutes," I've got my back to her, I adjust my beard and pull my hat down.

"Well come on, follow me, chop, chop." With that she marches off in the direction of the telly room. I follow a few feet behind, we stop at the

Christmas tree. Under it is a large plastic sack, she pauses while I sling it on to my shoulder. When we get outside the telly room, she tells me to wait outside. I stand in front of the door for a split second I contemplate making a run for it, but then I hear from the other side of the door,

"Children we have a very special guest today, who do you think it could be?"

As one I hear all the children cry out 'Father Christmas.' I think to myself oh! that's really lovely, then it dawns on me: shit that's me! I push the door and a loud cheer greets me. In the end I quite enjoy my newly-found celebrity status. I pull out each present and read the name on the label, some of the children wait patiently sitting on the floor, a couple are in wheelchairs, one is sitting in a chair and attended by a nurse who gets up and helps the small girl open her parcel. It's all going well, until I pull out the last present I read the name Sam. I can't remember seeing him, I look out over the sea of heads for any flash of Liverpool red. The nurses look at themselves, nurse Cox gets up quickly,

"Sorry, Sam couldn't make it today." She stands clapping her hands getting the children's attention.

"Right children, I want you to thank Father Christmas, he has to go now he's very busy." A big cheer goes up, I stand and wave as I make my way out. Nurse Cox follows me out,

"Thanks for doing that"

"No problem, err... tell me the last present, for Sam."

"He's very ill," I say nothing, I just nod in silence. Nurse Cox goes back inside. I run down the corridor until I reach the toilet and burst through the door. I've half removed the coat, and the trousers are around my knees. A man in a suit is poised at the urinal, he looks at me nervously,

"You want to try flying round the world in a sleigh without a toilet," I say as I stand next to him at the urinals, strange noises are coming from one of the cubicles. The man finishes as fast as he can and leaves, I push open the stall door. Father Christmas is the worse for drink, on the floor is a large hip flask. I remove the outfit and drape it over him. Put my trainers back on and I try to wake Santa, but he's well out of it. So I leave him and head back to see Bob.

When I get back Bob is fast asleep, so is Mum. I stand and watch them, it's strange how you can start a day with so much apprehension and fear for the future. Now I can start to think of, well me. I can worry about other things like Hazel and me. Let me think, two days and she'll be back. Time has stood still for the last few days now I can't wait for it to get moving again.

I remove the presents carefully from the bed and put them in the bedside cabinet for safekeeping. I decide to take the Playstation home, well it's going to need extensive testing to ensure it's in tip top condition for when Bob comes home. I gently shake Mum's arm, she stirs and opens her eyes and looks at me and then at Bob, smiles before pushing herself up. We stand and look at Bob, he's cuddling his new football strip like a security blanket.

"He's going to be all right now isn't it Mum?"

"Oh yes, Son, now take me home, we need to make some phone calls," I take her arm, outside a different nurse is sat at the desk, (nurse Sinnatamby must have gone to start her Christmas). I haven't seen this nurse before.

"We're off now," the nurse looks at her watch,

"I should think he'll go through the night now," she says.

"I've got all your details here if I need to contact you," she adds.
Mum and I walk off down the corridor, arm in arm. It's six o'clock on Christmas day. Who would of thought this morning, that it would end my best Christmas ever.

On the way home I phone Sasha, I hand the phone to mum so she can talk as I'm driving. More tears from Mum and I guess Sasha, but tears of joy now. She tells Mum, Paul and her will be back at the weekend, before flying back to Australia the following Wednesday.

* * * * * * * *

Joan draws hard on her cigarette as she pulls away from her daughter's house. A broad smile on her face, all in all it had been good day, a great Christmas. Certainly the news that Keith had separated from that girl helped. Joan couldn't believe it, two weeks before Christmas she packs up and moves in with someone else, and get this, she's only been having an affair with Keith's personal trainer. The strange thing is Joan actually enjoyed talking to Keith again. The last few years they had mainly shouted. It helped that he doesn't drink, not even a glass of wine with Christmas Dinner.

Oh! It was so great to see the children open their gifts Joan thought. Even when Carol was young Christmas would be ruined by Keith. He would always be half cut and normally asleep by present-opening time. The biggest thing was after dinner, they were just having an Irish coffee (Keith was just having coffee, decaffeinated of course.) When Carol announces that her and Stuart are getting married, nothing too big, a Registry Office, but with a big reception in the evening. Joan was still old fashioned, she believed in marriage, especially when children were involved. It was truly a super day.

Then to top it all Keith goes and asks Joan out. He just stopped her half way up the garden path as Joan was leaving and said they should go out for a drink sometime. Joan's head was telling her she was busy but her heart was telling her all sorts of strange things. It was good to lead him on for even a few minutes before telling him to go to hell!

Eighteen

When we get back Graham is asleep in the chair, my empty Christmas brandy on the table. The telly is on with some big blockbuster film fighting it out with the *Only Fools and Horses* Christmas special on the other side to win the Christmas night ratings war. I let Quinn out in the garden while I then pour Mum and me a drink. Mum carves some turkey and makes some sandwiches. We sit in the lounge watching telly (*Only Fools and Horses*), I finish and put my plate on the table, at this Mum stands up,

"Well I suppose you want your present now?"

"Oh go on then," Mum goes into the hall and starts to drag a large box through the door, I jump up and help because it looks so big and heavy I'm worried she going to injure herself. I get it into the middle of the room. The box is about four foot long by two foot wide.

"Bloody hell mum what is it?" Always a stupid question, as if she was about to ruin the surprise having spent so long to wrap it.

"Well open it," she says impatiently, by now all the noise and excitement has woken Graham.

"Is that you Daisy" I think to myself how long has Graham been using my Mums first name.

"We're both here Graham mate," I say slowly pulling at the ribbon on the parcel.

"How's Bob?"

"He's fine," I say as I remove the first ribbon, I go on to explain everything that has happened.

"That's great, I so pleased," Graham says while patting Quinn who has come back in from the garden, Mum gets up to shut the back door.

"What's going on?" Graham asks

"Nat's opening his present"

"That's exciting Quinnie boy isn't it?" Graham says as he pulls his ears.

I return to drawing out the opening of my large present as long as possible. Both ribbons are removed now and I'm slowly sliding my finger along the edge of the paper. I remove two sheets of paper intact. Revealing a slightly battered black case with two catches on the side. My heart's beating fast, I know what the case contains my mouth is dry. I take a deep breath before I snap the catches and slowly open the lid. I recoil back in shock sitting back in the chair.

In the case is a red electric guitar. Not any red guitar but a Fender Stratocaster hot rod red maple.

"What is it?" Graham says, but both Mum and I ignore him.

"Do you like it Nat?"

"It's the most beautiful thing I've ever seen," I say as I lean forward touching it reverently with just with the tip of one finger.

"Pick it up then," I lift it out nervously as if it's a fragile new born baby. I hold it up keeping it at arms length a bit like when I was thirteen at the end of school disco having my first slow dance. It was with Julia Chapman, she was the first girl in our year to get breasts. I was so afraid I would accidentally rub against them or touch them if I held her too close. I slowly rest the beautiful polished body of the instrument on my knee, I form a chord with my left hand and strum.

"Oh it's a guitar," says Graham.

I have two main questions going through my head, one I can't ask, like where did she got the money from (it must be dads money?) So I ask the other question,

"Why electric Mum?"

"Because the times they are a-changin'," she said with a smile, a smile that I hadn't seen for a while, suddenly she was young again. Mum looked so pleased with herself,

"I'm sure Dad would have wanted it." With that she stood up ,

"Cup of tea anyone?" I knew that meant, end of discussion, no more awkward questions.

"Oh I'm gasping, thanks Daisy," said Graham. As Mum went to the kitchen she added,

"I've got some money for an amplifier, I thought it was best for you to sort that out," I carry on playing, holding it close to my ear to hear the cords. I then prop it up against a chair so I can just look at it. I go in the kitchen to help Mum, every now and then I stick my head round the corner to check it's still there. I haven't had an electric guitar since my punk band days of the late seventies. I think to myself, Mum's right it's time to move on, make a new start, what with the Bob thing and all. I could play some new numbers, more up to date. I'd still play some Dylan, I couldn't drop him completely. I feel euphoric like a load has been lifted from me, my palms are actually sweating.

I'm standing next to Mum in the kitchen, I lean across and kiss her on the cheek.,

"What's that for?"

"Well it's for being the best Mum ever!"

"Arh if I was the best Mum ever, I would have had my present by now"

"Oh! God I forgot, it's under the tree," we go through to the lounge with the tea on a tray. I give her my present, she opens it. (It's a bread maker, boring I know but what do you get the Mum that's got everything for Christmas.) I'm just that sort of person I'm better at receiving than giving. I give Graham his, a beanie hat in our clubs colours and a matching mug, (the only cup our team's likely to get this year). I did think of buying him a hat in our biggest rivals colours. So he would be sitting in the home stand with this hat on, attracting the wrath of all our fans, but I decided it would be too cruel. I must be getting soft in my new age.

I insist that Graham stays the night, so we walk with Quinn round to his place to get an overnight bag and some dog food. Graham spends the whole time talking about and asking questions about Mum. I sleep on Bob's bed, but just out of necessity as Graham is in my old room, I sleep better than I have for days.

I wake up feeling like I've had an incredibly deep sleep. Its Boxing Day and I can't wait to see Bob, just because I miss him and want to see him. Not like the previous days in panic or concern that he might have deteriorated over night, or worse. I make a vow never to take him for granted and certainly never to deny his existence again. Tomorrow I will see Hazel again, tomorrow I start the rest of my life. Even if things don't work out, I know things will never be quite the same again.

When I get to the hospital Bob is sat up in bed with his new football shirt on. He looks different again, better, more colour in his cheeks, more sparkle in his eyes. He smiles excitedly when I come in.

Around lunch time the doctor comes round. The decision is made to move Bob to a children's ward. I go with him to help settle him in. Soon the other kids are gathering round swapping gruesome stories trying to out do each other with the severity or their illness or injury. Suddenly the single small bandage on the back of Bob's head looks strangely insignificant against, a small boys missing two fingers, a girl with a broken hip totally covered in plaster and a boy with a patch over one eye. Soon Bob's having a great time, so much so, I'm feeling a bit in the way.

I decide to leave him to it. I ring mum and arrange to go to town to sort out my amplifier. I'm eager to get playing my electric guitar, before I lose my resolve and change my mind slipping back to my acoustic rut. Mum says she doesn't want to spend hours in a music shop, so when I arrive home she hands me a bulky brown envelope. Mum says she'd like to go to bingo with Graham. I start to ask how Graham is going to manage, but change my mind.

Town is full of manic people hitting the Boxing Day sales, on the way Mum is explaining about her lucky pen to Graham. I think Grahams going to need more than a lucky pen, if he's going to mark off the correct numbers. I drop Mum and Graham off outside the Bingo hall, and park the van in a side street and head for the large shopping centre.

I take the lift to the music store, the large shop has a department with racks of sheet music, a keyboards and pianos area and at the back the wall is covered with an array of guitars, in the middle are two small glass rooms where you can go to try out various instruments before buying. In one of these a spotty youth in a Nirvana T-shirt is playing frantically on a bass guitar. His tie around his head, he seems to be concentrating more on his image in the glass than playing any chord correctly. I'm drawn to the room next door. A man in his fifties with long grey hair in a pony tail is playing lead guitar, I stand in the entrance leaning on the door frame. He starts a drum machine with a reggae beat and starts playing Bob Marley's *Three Little Birds* strumming guitar while singing along in a deep effortless voice. He plays a verse and chorus before making a few adjustments, and he's switched to The Eagles *Take it Easy*. He looks up aware someone is watching him.

"Hi" he says strumming a chord as he speaks, switching the amplifier off killing the drum beat dead.

"Can I help you sir?" I explain I'm after an amplifier. He guides me to various models plugging in the guitar and playing a couple of chords. Instilling the particular qualities of each one. He offers me a bass guitar to try with each amp. He accompanies me on a few numbers and we get talking. I'm trying to impress him by recognizing the songs as quick as possible and coming in with my bass lines. I haven't played bass since my *'Gordon and the Gobbers'* punk band days. I tell him about my residency at the *House of Gloom,* he seems quite excited by this. He explain how he has a band which plays at corporate events and wedding receptions. He's getting a little fed up with a couple of members who keep turning up late and are generally unprofessional. He then introduced himself,

"I'm Charlie, Charlie Mullens," he places his hand on his chest and nods raising his eyes like I should know him immediately.

"Oh... Charlie Mullens," I say still trying desperately to place who he was, I ask him more questions trying to extract more clues without offending my new found friend. He drops a few more bands and names he's worked with, then it dawns on me who he is. Charlie Mullens of seventies progressive rock band *Pink Revelations.* They produced several concept albums in the early seventies. None of which I owned due to the fact I was in the 'single/ Bob Dylan camp' at the time. The most successful and best known album was, *A Lamb Lies Down on the Dark Side of the Moon.* (A title made for gate-fold sleeves if ever there was one.) Never released on CD I guess they couldn't fit the title on!

We start playing a version of the Rolling Stones *Satisfaction* and have drawn a small crowd, the spotty youth, a gang of mall girls brought up on manufactured pop impressed that we can actually play, but not by our set list. A rather official looking man in an overly-tight suit taps his watch and has an annoyed look on his face aimed at Charlie, it's the shop manager reminding Charlie that he is supposed to be demonstrating the goods with the purpose of selling them. Charlie stops abruptly, whispering in my ear about the manager as he directs me to the amps. He points out the one he considers the best, or as he puts it the best one suited for the music he plays. It seems I've been asked to join the band, but I can't quite remember when. I end up with a Marshall 100w amp, probably a lot larger and higher spec, than I would have gone for and certainly more expensive.

Charlie made several promises about how it would pay for itself in the first few months. I get out Mum's envelope and count the money out, I then take out my credit card (which took a real battering over Christmas) and pay the difference.

Soon we've done all the paper work and I'm struggling out of the shop with a huge box. I just about make it down the lift to the van, the sooner I get a roadie the better. I drive to the flat and climb the stairs. I phone the hospital and ask to speak to Bob. He was annoyed to be dragged away from his friends. He seems very happy so I decided not to visit him as he tells me Mum has just left. Excitedly I remove the amp from the box, the flat is now full of bits of polystyrene and a large empty box. I glance at the instructions but decide to dispense with them and set it up on my own. An hour later I find the instructions and start again, twenty minutes and I'm plugged in and ready to start. I'm engrossed in my new toy and have been playing for about half an hour before my mobile rings. Its mum wondering where I am. I look at my watch its eight o'clock. I tell her all about my new purchase and new mate (sadly Mum recalls seeing *Charlie and the Pink Revelations* at the Nashville club in London around 1974). She tells me she's made a turkey curry, it looks like our turkey might make it to the new year as we haven't had any soup yet. I turn the amp off and put my guitar away in its case giving it a loving glance before shutting the lid and slipping it under my bed for safe keeping.

I think to myself this time tomorrow I would have seen Hazel again. I haven't seen her for a few days, but with everything that has happened it seems a lot longer. So much has changed that I have reassessed my whole life. Not that Bob isn't important, he is the biggest thing in my life, but perhaps I need to think of me a little more, after all if I'm happy then surely that's better for Bob.

It's a cold and frosty night, the van windscreen has iced over. I write on the top of the windscreen, Hazel & Nathan. I then clear a small hole to see through on the short trip to Mums. I get in, put the heater on full to clear the screen so by the time I get there our names have melted and are illegible. I'm in such a positive frame of mind I fail to think of this as any kind of omen. I try to impress some of my enthusiasm for my new amplifier into Mum and Graham, but to little effect. Graham is more interested in telling me that he won twenty-five quid at bingo. I give up and go to the microwave to find my curry. I put my dinner on a tray and get a bottled beer from the fridge. I go and sit in the lounge to watch telly. Then I remember our team has been playing, this just goes to prove how preoccupied I've been as I hadn't given it a thought all day. I flick on the teletext and find we won 1-0 and have climbed four places to tenth, the day just gets better and better. Mum and Graham are watching *Who Wants to be a Millionaire*. This puts the dampers on my perfect day Chris Tarrant is tormenting some balding, bespectacled man into risking £93,000. He ops for answer b. then Chris tells us it's time to go to a break, oohs and aars from the audience. I'd really like to be trying out my new amplifier some more. As Bob is on the mend I'll move back to the flat tomorrow. Chris is back on, more tension and waffle before he informs the hapless victim,

"You've just lost £93,000."

I think no he hasn't, he never had it anyway, he started with nothing and has won £32,000.

"Did I tell you I won £25" Graham tells me again,

"Yes, you did mention it," I say, Mum and I exchange smiles. *Millionaire* finishes and Mum turns the TV over to watch a romantic film. I'm not in the mood and I can't get into it, I'm nervous and excited about my possible reconciliation with Hazel. I take my tray out to the kitchen and stick my empty plate in the dishwasher. It's full up, but needs a complete reshuffle to work properly. I can't face it now and decide to leave it so I take a bath. I grab mums CD radio I plug it in the bedroom and pass the lead under the bathroom door. I select Bruce Springsteen *Darkness on the Edge of Town*. I get myself a whisky and ask Mum and Graham if they want a drink. Right let me check; music, drink and plenty of bubbles, I'm ready for my bath now. I slip in under the bubbles then I rise to the surface, blowing like a whale. I lean across and switch on the CD player, trying to keep the mixture of water and electricity to a minimum. Then I lie and relax, the opening bars of *Badlands* blast out. In my head I work out possible numbers for my new electric gig. When I'm seeing Hazel tomorrow I'll have a word with Colin about my musical change of direction.

I think about my meeting with Hazel. I've got it all planned like a military operation.

1. I go and see Bob at Ten
2. Leave the hospital around eleven-thirty
3. Back to flat shower, shave and generally make myself irresistible
4. Arrive at *House of Gloom* just before one

5. Hazel arrives, big hugs, I've missed you, sorry, let's stay together etc.
6. Tell her about Bob, (she's fine about me keeping him a secret and can't wait to meet him)
7. Live happily ever after

The water has cooled I turn the hot tap on with my big toe. I feel the warm water slowly creeping up my body.

* * * * * * * *

Hazel pushed her suit case shut then she dragged it to the floor. It's been the longest few days of her life. Whatever possessed her into coming, she knew it was over, her and Clive were history. They had just had a civilized conversation. Quite reassuring really Clive had accepted it was over. Clive had also said it shouldn't mean her having to change jobs. He said he would arrange for a transfer so they don't have to work together, which suited her fine. Strange, she thought he would be more cut up, or maybe she hoped he would. Now Hazel could go home and start the rest of her life, she hoped Nathan would be part of that. She needed to phone Joan, she needed to talk to her, see if she could stay there while she got her head together. She opened the bedroom door and padded across the floor, the tiles cold on her bare feet. She started to go down the stairs to use the phone. Half way down Clive's voice stopped her, she turned to go back, but something caught her attention, one name really,

"But Joan it's all over,"

"I don't care it's you I love, you I want to be with," Hazel sat on the stairs, the blood draining from her face.

"I'll be back tomorrow, I need to see you," Clive went on. Tears are now running down Hazel's face. For a long time she heard nothing, Joan must be talking.

"But...but" Clive said followed by a shorter pause.

"No.. you can't end it now, I wont let you" Clive's voice is raised now.

"You're going to regret this, I promise you," Clive shouts as he slams the phone down.

"Shit!" Clive says on his way to the kitchen. Hazel turns and heads back to her room, she can hear the clink of a bottle on a glass followed by a violent smash of the bottle against the wall. This made Hazel jump and quicken her step. She reached her room, closed the door leaning against it and breathing fast. Well that was that, betrayed by her best friend. Now truly she was alone.

Hazel went to the suitcase and pulled up the handle she opens the bedroom door slowly. Holding her shoes in one hand her case in the other she crept down the stairs letting the case drop gently one step at a time. When Hazel reached the bottom she glanced out at the garden, Clive was sitting by the pool with his back to her. The wooden front door was large and heavy, she decided to slip out the sliding window next to it. She waited until she was clear of the house before putting her shoes back on. She then made her way to the lodge house at the front of the complex. She knew there was a phone there and she ordered a taxi for the airport. She was glad the driver didn't want to practice any more of his broken English on her, after his initial conversation he left her to her thoughts. Tomorrow she would see Nathan and sort things out, but she was far from hopeful (mainly because he was a man.). Hazel needed to confront him about that women she had seen going into his flat that night. She was tired of confrontation, she felt bitter, betrayed by everyone dear to her. All right she had cheated on Clive, but surely Clive's betrayal was worse, with her best friend. Oh! it was a mess. Hazel cried again, she never imagined she would miss Nathan so. That she would find someone who made her laugh. That she would actually enjoy watching a football match, she had even got into the habit of checking the paper for his teams results, (how sad was that). He had rekindled her interest in music, (even Bob Dylan). Hazel wished she could have just have kept it a bit of fun. Instead, she had fallen in love. She signed deeply.

"Lady you OK?" The taxi driver said looking in his rear view mirror.

"Fine" Hazel said her voice breaking mopping her eyes with a tissue from her bag.

"You, sad to leave here ...yes"

"Yes" Hazel said forcing a smile.

* * * * * * * *

"You mean he can really go home," I said incredulously, the doctor made notes on Bob's chart as I spoke, I couldn't believe it, less than a week ago Bob had been critically ill, now he was coming home. I had been visiting Bob for an hour, I was waiting for the Doctor to do his rounds before I could shoot off and get ready to see Hazel, now I was torn between the relief that Bob was coming home and the worry of being late for Hazel. The Doctor spoke to Bob.

"Obviously you need to take care, nothing strenuous and no skate-boarding, but I can see no reason for keeping you here any longer." He then turned to me,

"I'll contact your GP, he'll pop in to see him in a few days," Bob had jumped off the bed, his large football shirt looking a bit creased and dirty, I think he slept in it. He started clearing out his bedside cupboard, laying out his Christmas presents on his bed. The doctor smiled as he put Bob's clipboard back on the end of the bed. I thought to myself, right it's just gone half past eleven, all is not lost I can still get Bob home and settled in time.

"Thanks Doc, for everything" I say taking his hand and shaking it vigorously with both hands.

"No problem, don't forget he's a boy. He's going to have accidents, hopefully not all as bad as this one." The other kids in the ward had gathered round excitedly, as Bob packs his stuff in a black bin bag I had acquired.

"It's not fair, you really going home Bob?" said the one-eyed boy.

"Yep," Bob said packing his *Hearsay* CD and the Pokemon video into the bag. Bob then gives out his sweets and comics Mum had brought him, to his new found friends, the one-eyed boy and broken-hip girl.

"I'd better phone mum, err carry on Bob I'll be right back," I run out of the ward to go outside and use my mobile. Nurse Sinnatamby is coming down the corridor,

"Hey, what's the rush?" she says as I ran past her.

"It's Bob, they said he can go home,"

"That's great news,"

I phone Mum and tell her the news, she's very excited. Then she points out that Bob has no warm clothes in hospital. I try to say that he can come home in his pyjamas, but Mum's having none of it. I'm wasting precious time arguing, besides I know I'm never going to win. So I go back and explain that I have to go home first to Bob. The ward gang have distracted him. Four of them are playing Game-boy all linked together.

I leave them to it, checking my watch as I run out.

11.52am. I jump in the van and set off, the roads are busy, the sales are still in full swing. I bang the steering wheel in frustration with my fist,

"Come on, come on."

12.07pm. Get to mum's house run inside find her stripping Bob's bed.

"What are you doing?"

"I wanted everything to be nice and fresh for when Bob gets back"

"That's great only I'm due to meet Hazel in less than an hour." She puts his sheets and duvet cover in the washing machine, slowly pours the washing liquid into the strange shaped washing ball, before promptly dropping it all over the floor. Mum starts to clean it up. I step forward exasperated and slip over, covering my jeans in the green gunk.

"Leave it Mum I'll sort it," I say probably raising my voice a little too loud, Mum gives me one of her looks. I slip off my jeans and add them to the wash. I go to pour the washing liquid into the drawer built-in to the washing machine.

"Oh you can't do that," says mum.

"What"

"You can't put it in there"

"What do mean that's what it's there for. Its only some smart advertising con that decided it would make more money if you shove in a ball first." Mum went off to Bob's room to get his clothes, muttering to herself. I shut the washing machine door and go to the bottom of the stairs and shout up,

"What number, Mum?"

"Oh! I don't know it'll all be different now" she says on the way down with a bag of Bob's clothes.

"Look... just tell us what number wash to put it on"

"4" Mum says reluctantly, shaking her head before adding,

"It won't work anyway," as she finally went out the door towards the van. I step back in the spillage, I run to the tumble drier and find some clean socks and pull out a still slightly damp clean pair of jeans. I decide I had better clean it up so I get the hand towel from the back of the door, place it over the mess and move it around with my foot.

12.18pm. I pull the door shut, Mum has reached the van and is sat inside, then Mrs Terry from the house opposite calls out,

"U-hoo Daisy, how's your Bob?" Before I can react Mum gets out again and walks towards her. I don't believe it, she was in the van, she was actually sat in the van, now she was walking away to talk to Mrs Terry. I get in the van and start the engine. I take deep breaths trying to compose myself. I push in a cassette tape. I forget it's the *Rolling Stones*, Mick sings *Time is on my Side*, Oh! thank you very much, I punch the eject button. I switch on the local radio station to get any traffic news.

12.23pm. Mum finishes conversation, starts to move away, then stops as Mrs Terry asks another question. I know this Mrs Terry she's not really interested in Bob at all, being one of those people who've always had it worse than you. I 'toot' the horn. She turns and runs (well an old person's type run, all arm movement with little speed, a fast walk really).

12.28pm. Right we're on the move now.

12.47pm. Get to hospital car park, full, drive twice round car park. Decide to let Mum get out go to get Bob dressed and ready. While I find parking spot, on fourth circuit I find a place. No change for ticket. Take a chance and leave it.

12.52pm. I get to Bob's ward, to my surprise they're ready, Bob has his coat on and is saying goodbye to his new-found friends. I collect up his black bag of presents. Nurse Sinnatamby comes in, I put down the bags and giving her a big hug and thank her for all her help. Embarrassed by this, she turns her attention to Bob kneeling down to talk to him and gently sweeping his blond fringe away to look in his eyes,

"Now Bob you take care"

"I will," Bob said wrapping his thin arms tightly around her neck. I check my watch, while getting this picture of Hazel, sat alone in the *House of Gloom* checking her expensive timepiece, while thinking to herself I'll give him five more minutes.

"Right we have to go," I say trying to encourage everyone to hurry up, but all to no avail.

1.07pm. All I have to hope is Hazel will wait, but then why should she, in her eyes, I had let her down again. We get in the van, I explain to Bob that I have to go out when we get back, but I tell him soon as we get home I'll set up his Playstation2, Bob is quite happy with this. Which is good because I already feel an utter shit for leaving him.

1.25pm. We get back home, I take the bags in and switch on Bob's Playstation2 which has been given extensive and rigorous testing over the last few days. I give Bob a quick kiss, run out of the door and jump back in the van. Mrs Terry has come out of her gate and is trying to intercept me, I almost run her over as I speed past.

1.29pm. I burst through *House of Gloom* lounge bar door. The bar is quite full, as most people are still off work. I scan the bar for any flash of red hair. Graham is sat in his usual chair, I ignore him. Big Dave is sat in a cubical on his own. I move across the bar to him, still craning my neck in the vain hope of catching a glimpse of red hair in one of the cubicles. I'm panting and out of breath,

"Hey mate, you haven't seen Hazel have you, that girl I told you about, the one with red hair"

"Good looking, long curly hair" he said gesturing with his hands down the side of his head,

"Yes, yes" I interrupt.

Big Dave is gesturing with his hands in front of his chest.

"Yes, Yes," I say leaning across the table to him now.

"Yep, I've seen her, left about ten minutes ago." Big Dave says with little regard for the relevance of this devastating news. I flop down in the seat opposite dejectedly. I put my head in my hands. It's all over. Dave gets up. He puts a hand on my shoulder,

"Drink?" I nod without speaking. I remove my phone from my jacket pocket. Select phone book form my menu. I press H, Hazel's name and number comes up, I press call,

'The mobile you have called may be switched off' I put the phone back in my pocket. Well I could go round the flat but I don't suppose Clive would be too pleased to see me, not after the golf club incident. I could park down the lane, walk up to the flats and hang around in the hope Hazel would come out. It wasn't a brilliant plan, but then the last one hadn't gone too well. It was all I could think of for now.

Big Dave returned with a pint and set it down in front of me. I study it intently in silence, I watch the tiny bubbles make their small journey up the glass before disappearing into the air. A short and pointless existence. I sigh, lift up the glass and drink half of it in one go.

"I hear your Bob's not been too good," Dave says in his typical understated why.

"Yea, but he's on the mend now, just brought him home,"

"Oh that good" Dave leans forwards,

"Only I heard he was in some kind of a coma"

"That's right," I say

"Poor kid, did you spend all the time playing Bob Dylan to him, to try and bring him round," I smile as I take another swig of beer. Knowing where this is going.

"No"

"Only if you played that shit to me all the time, you'd put me in a coma." Big Dave slumps on the table in mock sleep. I finish my pint and get up.

"Come on lets drink ourselves into a coma," I say picking up the two empty glasses. I move to the bar and ask Colin for two more pints.

"We were all sorry to hear about Bob," he says, one eye on pouring a pint and one on me. Colin is wearing a large jumper with a Rudolph the red nose reindeer on it. It's an obvious target for ridicule but I ignore it, it's just too easy.

"Graham tells us he's on the mend now," Colin says as he sets the two pints down on the bar. Graham stops chatting to Denis, his best mate. Denis is really an old country bumpkin. He starts each sentence with '*is it me*' and finishes with '*it was never like that in our day*.' He wears a well-worn Barbour coat, with deep poachers' pockets on the inside. From this he pulls various dead animals when requested by customers in the *House of Gloom*, sometimes rabbits and sometimes pheasants. This means Graham will turn up tomorrow with some dead bird for me to pluck. Graham moves in his chair at the sound of my voice,

"Is that you Nat?" Graham says in my general direction, I move towards him.

"Yes Graham, I'm here" I bend down and pat Quinn.

"That girl was here earlier, the one with the long curly hair, the nice smelling one" I leave Quinn alone and stand up.

"Did you talk to her"

"Yes, she asked me if I had seen you, I told her you were busy, what with Bob and all"

"You told her about Bob"

"Well yes, I said he had been in an accident. She seemed very interested in him, asked about his Mum too, I told her about Sasha, the girl with the scary hair, did I do the wrong thing."

"No... not you mate."

Oh well maybe it's for the best, all I have to do now is try and see Hazel explain to her why I denied and kept secret the fact I had a son. What could be simpler? I collect the beers from the bar.

"I'll catch you later mate, I'm over here with Dave," Graham returned to talking to Denis. As I go past Denis I stop and ask him

"Chance of any Venison?" Denis goes to put his hand in his coat I step back apprehensively. He takes his hand away laughing. He sucks in a breath through his ancient stained teeth, fingers his grey moustache before saying,

"Very expensive at the moment,"

"Oh" I say, a little disappointed because I know it's Mums favourite. Then having set me up and with the skill of a trained hunter he goes for the kill.

"Well its dead deer!"

Denis collapses in laughter, nudging Graham and seeking approval from those around him.

"Do you get it, dead deer," Graham is frantically trying to save his whisky from Denis's elbow. I shake my head and leave them to it, but I know in a few days time, at some unearthly time of night Denis will be knocking on my door with a lovely piece of venison.

I return to Big Dave sliding his pint across to him. We talk for a while, about women and how they're nothing but trouble. He tells me he's been out with Gail, the women with the 'large cleavage' three times. He talks of her with great affection, in a way I have never known before. I tell him I really thought Hazel was the one and how I really messed things up. There's an awkward moment of silence as we contemplate what we may have just admitted to. I sip my beer and look over Dave's head at the wall behind him.

"What the fuck," I say as I stand up, Dave saves his pint from spillage while swivelling in his chair.

"Ah, you haven't seen that yet." On the wall is a poster, it has a photograph of a man of around fifty with red-tinted glasses and bleached blond hair. He is poised about to play a large electric organ. Diagonally across the photo are the words,

Appearing Live this Sunday "Oliver and his Magic Organ!"

I tear the poster off the wall and march with it up to the bar. Colin is concentrating on pouring a pint of Guinness. I thrust the poster under his nose obscuring his view, and making him spill beer all over "Oliver's Magic Organ."

"Ah... I meant to have a word with you about that," he says nervously,

"Jane can you take over here" Jane the new barmaid moved over and rather too vigorously pulls on the pump. Guinness flows over the side of the glass. Colin moves to the end of the bar while gesturing with his eyes at the ceiling.

"So what's all this about," I say stabbing at the poster with my finger.

"Well I heard about Bob, I just thought... things are going to be a bit difficult,"

"Well everything's fine now"

"Yes well I've booked him now, besides, I think its time for a change"

"Well I've changed too, I've gone electric!" I say sounding a bit anxious now.

"Look, Oliver's in for Sunday, we'll have to see how he goes down, now I've got people to serve," Colin said starting to turn away.

"You must give me another chance," I say reaching across and grabbing Colin's arm, Colin was taken aback by the desperation in my voice.

"Look, how about I let you play tomorrow," Colin said lifting the Guinness soaked poster, Oliver now has two red streaks running down his cheeks. He discards it throwing it under the bar.

"OK, Friday night, you won't regret it." I think to myself, Friday night that's got to be better than a Sunday. The only thing is I've got just over twenty-four hours to learn a new set and get a complete make-over.

"That's settled then," Colin says, before leaning towards me,

"So what do think of the new barmaid?" Colin asks his eyes glancing at her. I look across at Jane as she fills a pint glass with froth, while Denis stares down the front of her blouse.

"Well apart from not being able to pull a pint she's OK"

"Oh I know, she's useless but she's got a great pair of tits"

I walk away shaking my head he calls after me,

"Oh its £15 quid for a Friday night," I turn about to argue, but change my mind. I'm sure once I get going I'll be pulling in the punters, and I'll be able to renegotiate my fee. I return to Dave.

"All sorted mate" I say as I sit down. We spend a couple of hours putting the world to rights. It was good to relax in our safe little booth. It had been a long tense week. Some time in the afternoon I tell Dave about meeting Charlie and joining his band. I think I accidentally let it slip that he was after a new drummer too. But I'm kind of hoping he didn't notice.

At the end of the afternoon I leave the van in the pub car park and walk home. The wind is bitterly cold, it clears my head. I have a busy day tomorrow as I have to get my girlfriend back, prepare for the biggest gig of my life, and beat Bob at his new football game.

Nineteen

I been hangin' on threads
I been playin' it straight
Now, I've just got to cut loose
Before it gets late
So I'm going
I'm going
I'm gone

(Going, Going, Gone © 1973 Ram's Horn Music)

Hazel turned up the car stereo as she pulled away from the *House of Gloom* her wheels spinning leaving gravel and broken promises behind her. The bass was so loud the whole car was vibrating but she needed it loud, real loud, that way she didn't have to think. (It was Travis *The Man Who*). Hazel didn't want to acknowledge her life was in free fall. Now not only had Hazel seen Nathan going into his flat with another women, she now finds out he has a son. How can someone keep that from you? and why? It's like she never knew him at all. A huge chunk of his life was missing. In the space of twenty-four hours she had been let down by everyone.

Life was like that, well Hazel's was, and she learnt that from an early age. Her father died when she was twelve just when she was getting to know him. At that precious time when girls grow in confidence and start to move away from their mothers apron strings. Her father would take her to Cricket matches, Test matches stretching out over long sultry summer days. Not everyone's idea of a good time but she loved it.

They would have long conversations, mainly through the Thursdays and Fridays of the five day match before it became interesting, (in those days not only did test matches last the full five days but with Ian Botham involved, they did become interesting). Then when the match reached its climax her fathers attention would be drawn to the centre of the field. Hazel would then read her book or coyly glance up at the large black West Indian's, for Hazel had hardly seen a black man in her suburban upbringing. These towering and powerful bowlers seemed like gods to her. During lunch and tea her father would read his paper, always *The Times*.

He would fold it meticulously into convenient quarters to read. Passing on critical comment on the current affairs and political situation of the day. Most of which went completely over her head. Not till she got older, suddenly she found she had a sound basic grounding and useful knowledge of subjects, the Middle East, Northern Ireland and workings of the Stock Market. Later it struck her as strange that her father took *The Times* for years, but always complained about and criticized its editorial content. Almost like bickering with an old friend.

Then her father was gone; Hazel remembered that dreadful day she found him dead sat in his chair. Her mum followed her into the room, but before Hazel could react her mum shouted at her saying,

"Don't you dare cry." At the time she had felt disrespectful and uncaring in some way. As she sat there quietly holding her mother's hand until her mother calmly walked to the phone. But looking back at it she can picture it perfectly. Her father strangely noble, almost regal sitting upright in his chair his gold rim glasses still on his nose. *The Times* folded in quarters on his lap (at the obituaries). Almost certainly about to call, to point out an error in the paper. Hazel didn't have the hysterical crying and sobbing of a twelve-year-old, but rather the beautiful and peaceful last image of her beloved father logged in her memory.

She was left with just her Mum, the memory of her father faded as time went by, but his image and influence grew. Her Mum found it hard to compete with an always-sunny memory. A bit like always remembering the summers as longer and hotter than they actually were. Then when Hazel was eighteen and about to take her "A" levels, her Mum had her first stroke. Hazel couldn't remember the exams, it was all a blur. She was treading water going through the motions and really wasn't too surprised when she failed.

After her mother died, Hazel went for an interview with a computer firm (only in the warehouse). When Hazel got there she got on really well with the lady from personnel. She was impressed with Hazel's confidence and amicable nature, so much so that she offered her a sales position there and then. While Hazel's career moved along nicely on a smooth track her love life was far more rocky and bumpy. She seemed to attract a succession of rather hopeless men, who she always ended up supporting financially and emotionally.

Once again Hazel was on her own. For now, but soon there would be a baby, someone who would also be totally emotionally dependent on her.

The next track on the CD started, it was her favourite track, *Driftwood* she turned the volume up one more notch. What was she going to do now? Where could she go? Clive would be back tomorrow and Hazel had to be gone by then. She thought about everyone at work, Joan was out of the question. Then she thought of Kathy, from accounts. Kathy wasn't one of her best friends, but she got on with her well enough. They often went to the gym at lunch times together. Hazel remembered having a long talk after their last workout just before Christmas. Kathy told her she had just split up from her latest boyfriend. He had moved out of the flat they shared, Kathy had been complaining that she could never afford to stay there on her own. Hazel had tried to be sympathetic, but in truth she was having her own problems with Nathan by then.

Kathy would now be on one of her fitness and diet phases, for she was one of those girls, who you could tell the state of her latest relationship by her weight and appearance. As she went from that initial exciting first stage of a new relationship, to the more settled safe stage (maybe the new boyfriend had moved in, and made some sort of commitment). Kathy would start to relax, become comfortable let herself go, she would start to eat and pile on the pounds. Then the thick chunky jumpers and tracksuit would come out. Then as her man up and left and her relationship imploded. Kathy would have a few bad weeks before picking which particular diet (and other methods of losing weight), she would use to get back into shape. That along with a new fitness regime would produce the desired results. Then out would come the crop-tops and short skirts, thus attracting a new man, like a moth drawn to a light, before the whole sad cycle would begin again.

Hazel thought she could do with eating well and staying fit as she didn't want to put on too much weight with the baby. Hazel dipped her hand into her handbag on the passenger seat and pulled out her mobile searched Kathy and dialled the number. It rang barely twice.

"Paul...is that you?" (Paul was her ex-boyfriend's name).

"Err, no it's me Hazel," Hazel said slightly embarrassed. She moved quickly on and explained her situation, her voice breaking at times. Kathy punctuated her story with 'you poor thing,' 'No,' 'Men' and 'the little shit.' When Hazel finished, Kathy said she would pleased to help out. She said she would put a bottle in the fridge, they could get drunk and talk about what total bastards men are. Hazel smiled and said she would be there in a couple of hours. The phone went dead. Hazel pulled into Thames wharf, she left the CD playing and the doors open, by the time she had carried makeup, personal possessions and clothes (as well as all her old LP's) down to the car. At least three people had come to the front door to complain. Hazel had trouble getting everything into the tiny sports car, she decided to leave some of her clothes so she could get her LP's in. A lady from one of the downstairs flats came out to remonstrate about the noise. Hazel stopped her dead in her tracks by thrusting an armful of expensive designer clothes at her. She told her she no longer needed them and she was welcome to take them to some charity shop, the lady was completely side tracked by this and forgot about her noise complaint as she recognized one of the labels.

Hazel took three attempts to shut her overloaded boot, then she jumped in and raced away from her glamorous life. Leaving the bemused looking neighbour standing in the foyer with around a thousand pounds worth of designer cloths in her arms.

* * * * * * * *

It was just gone nine on Friday morning and all was quiet at Thames Wharf. I had been there half an hour and had seen no one, most of the flats looked empty. I guess most people were away for Christmas. It was a grey and frosty December day, the year was finishing fast, and it looked likely I was going to end it as I had the last five, alone.

I was getting cold again so I started the van engine again and put the heater on. I breathed on my hands. The windscreen is misting up. I found my chamois from the inside door pocket. Suddenly I see someone through the hole I've cleared, a tall and formidable lady coming out the main door. She had a large bundle of clothes on hangers. I jump out of the van and stroll over to her. She looks a bit concerned at the strange man coming towards her,

"I'm sorry to bother you, but have you seen," I hesitate for a second, I can't think of Hazel's surname.

"Err... Hazel," then it came to me.

"Hazel Williams," the lady became a little defensive and holds the clothes a little tighter to her bosom, in a futile effort to hide them. She spoke over her shoulder as she made her way to the garage block.

"Packed all her stuff into that flash sports car and left," I took a few steps forward and grabbed hold of one of the dresses to stop her.

"Hey, all I know is she's gone," the lady said nervously. I looked down at the dress I was holding, it was the one Hazel wore the first time we slept together, that wonderful night (when England won their World Cup qualifier). The neighbour must have seen the recognition in my eyes. She pulled free and opened the garage, then pressing a key-fob she opened the car boot, lying the clothes in.

"Look, she just asked me to take them to a charity shop," the black dress was still flapping outside the car. I pulled my wallet out,

"I'll give you twenty quid for that dress," I said handing the note to her. She thought for a second, then pulled it out, screwed it in to a ball before handing it to me,

"Here," she said taking the twenty. As I turned to walk back to the van, she called after me,

"It's not even your size." I got back in the van as the lady shut the boot on her new found wardrobe. I held the dress up with both hands and breathed in. I could smell Hazel's perfume. I sat there, the van engine still running. So why had Hazel left? Clive and her must have split up. All I had to do was find her, explain about Bob, smooth things over and POW!

But right now my main priority was to practice for my big electric gig tonight. I laid the dress gently on the seat next to me. I don't know what made me buy it. Or what I was going to do with it. But right now it was all I had of hers. I pulled out of the drive just as a taxi came in. I had to brake sharply to avoid it. As I went past I could see Clive turning in the back seat. I could see a quizzical look on his face. He was obviously wondering what that golf club destroying "**Screw-it**" white-van man was doing showing his face around here again.

I get back to the flat and set about getting ready for my gig. I decided to carry the amplifier down into the warehouse to get the full effect in the wide open space. I had to go in and turn the alarm off first, before setting up, about twenty minutes later I was ready. I switched on the amplifier, a buzz filled the room. Then I strum a cord dramatically with wind-milling arms. The noise resonated around the warehouse, the silence shattered by the brilliant sound. It went on forever, it shook the racks of nails and screws, it rattled the windows. It truly was a beautiful note.

Time was getting on. I decided to start with a Dylan number, *Like a Rolling Stone*, that way it wouldn't be such a shock to my army of fans. (Well Sky,Tom and Sue). I had bought several songbooks, covering the Sixties, Seventies, Eighties and even the Nineties. I learn a couple of Dire Straits numbers and one from the Police, but in the end I only got one song from the nineties the Travis number *Driftwood*. It was nearly four when I was done, I hadn't seen Bob all day.

I loaded up the van with all my gear and went round to Mums. Bob was asleep on the sofa. I was concerned at first, asking Mum how long he had been asleep, but he had only been asleep for twenty minutes. He had been catching up on the films Mum had recorded for him over the Christmas period. I had a quick cup of tea and a piece of cake with Mum. I looked nervously at Dad's photo on the telly, I took a large mouthful of cake and gestured at the picture with my head.

"I hope Dad won't mind, about me playing electric guitar," Mum stood up and took the photo from the telly and cleaned the imaginary dust off with her sleeve.

"Oh you don't mind, do you Bill," she said holding the photograph at arms length before placing him gently back on the telly. Mum collected up the cups and plates and went to the kitchen to put them in the dishwasher. I got up to leave looking one last time at Dad. I muttered under my breath,

"I'll play *Like a Rolling Stone*"

"What did you say son," Mum said as I came into the kitchen,

"Nothing" I said kissing Mum on the cheek, Mum moved to put another plate in the dishwasher. I open the back door Mum calls after me,

"Have a good JIG son," I turn to correct her and see a wicked grin on her face.

The *House of Gloom* is very busy, even at the early hour of seven thirty when I arrive. I go straight through to the back room. The stage, well... really it is a proper stage now. Gone are the old crates and dodgy planks of wood, replaced by two smart steps leading up to a solid stage complete with a lighting rig hanging from the ceiling. This has no less than four different coloured spotlights, operated by foot buttons at the front of stage floor. I practice switching from one to the other, before leaving the single pale blue spotlight illuminating the mike stand. I lean my guitar case against the wall and go out to the van to collect my amplifier. I'm struggling back through the door when someone is on my stage,

"One, Two, One, Two...Hello Wembley," Big Dave making mock sound check announcements through the mike.

"Hey stop pissing about and give me a lift here," Dave dives off the stage and makes out he's fighting his way through adoring fans towards me.

"I'm sorry no autographs," he says raising his hands as he reaches me. He grabs hold of the other side of the box, we make it to the stage .

"Jesus! man what you got in here," we put the amplifier down and I try to explain to Dave why it's the best amp for me (as explained by Charlie). I know he thinks it looks like something the Rolling Stones would tour with. I then open my guitar case, Big Dave is totally blown away. He insists on trying various classic guitar styles and moves, these includes, The Chuck Berry Duck walk, The Jimi Hendrix playing with his teeth but I draw the line when he wants to ram the guitar into my new amp, in your best Pete Townshend style.

I take it off him and plug the guitar in and fiddle with the levels and sound controls. Dave becomes a bit impatient and starts to wonder back towards the main bar. Suddenly I start to play the first few chords of *Romeo and Juliet* by Dire Straits, then I start singing the opening verse. Dave stands opened mouth in the middle of the room. I sing one chorus and finish with a big dramatic flourish. Dave whistles loudly and shouts,

"More, more," he walks to the stage jumps up and starts to look through my set list taped to the mike stand.

"Bloody hell you've got something from the nineties in here," he takes my hand and shakes in mock enthusiasm.

"Welcome to the twenty-first century, thank fuck you've finally dragged yourself out of the sixties."

Dave goes to the bar shaking his head and muttering to himself, he has to get himself a drink to deal with his shock. I finish setting up just as Dave comes back with a pint for me. We stand and discuss the reasons for my total "Road to Damascus" musical transformation. We finish our drinks, I take Dave's glass and move towards the bar. He stops me by grabbing hold of my sleeve,

"Err...look, I know what it took, I mean going electric, ditching the Dylan stuff, what with your Dad and all," Dave knew how I felt about my Dad, he was very fond of him and cried openly at his funeral. Something I have never discussed with him, this huge, masculine man breaking down in tears. When Dave and I were teenagers back in the seventies, my Dad seemed the height of coolness. Him being a guitar playing, long-haired hippie with fairly liberal views, turning a blind eye to my friends smoking joints and drinking in our house. Unlike the majority of other Dads who at the time were playing Rolf Harris's stylophone, watching Charlie's Angels and driving Ford Capri's. I think Dave knew my playing only Dylan had started as part of my grieving process, but then it just dragged on and became my kind of tribute. Don't get me wrong, Dylan will always be a big part of my life. But what with everything that's happened. It's time to shake up my life and I was starting tonight. Dave pattered me reassuringly on the arm.

"Thanks mate," I said turning to the bar Dave followed me, slightly embarrassed by his show of affection,

"So definitely no Sex Pistols then," he says as I enter the bar.

Word has got round of my new Friday night spot and my normal folk fans are in. Sky, Tom and Sue, Tom is wearing a cheese cloth shirt with an outlandish waistcoat, (green with white Christmas trees on it). Sky is on the other end of the bar sipping a pint of cider. Graham is sat in his normal chair, Colin is just getting him a whisky.

"Hi Graham"

"Nat, can I get you a drink?" One of my many New Year resolutions is not to get caught by Graham.

"No thanks mate, I'm with Big Dave?"

"Oh fair enough," He says handing over a perfectly normal looking twenty pound note to Colin. I track it's short journey to the note checker and then ultimately safely into the till. Colin winks at me as he hands the change to Graham, he then takes my empty glasses fills them and far too happily takes my money. Graham asks me what time we were going to the big match next week. Football has rather been relegated to the back of my mind, what with Bob's accident and my musical metamorphosis. We had three games over the Christmas period, two away, we won both. The other one was the game I missed on Boxing day visiting Bob. Now the talk is of a possible play-off place. Then there's the F.A. Cup match against Liverpool, a side we have never played in a competitive match before. I had been trying to play down the importance and stature of the game in front of Bob, because I didn't know if he could come as I still had to get the all clear from the Doctor. I tell Graham I'll be round at one to pick him up. I turn back to Dave and hand him his pint,

"Please let me do something tonight," Dave says somewhat desperately,

Then I have a brain-wave, something that I'm sure even Dave couldn't make a mess of.

"I'll tell you what you can introduce me," Dave looks really pleased with this idea. I think to myself how could he possibly make a mess of that. We stand and sink a few more pints while Dave keeps looking at his watch and asking,

"Is it time yet?", finally around nine o'clock, I say its time, Dave races through to the back room. There must be nearly forty people in, plus around fifteen still in the main bar, including the rugby club crowd. By the time I'm halfway across the room, Dave is already on stage standing by the mike. I make a move to go up the steps, Dave rushes to the edge of the stage,

"You can't just come up, I've got to build you up a bit!"
I step back into the darkness and indulge him. Dave talks animatedly into the mike nothing happens, silence, then he switches it on. A terrible screech of feedback, then

"One, two, one, two," everyone stops talking, the room falls silent.

"Ladies and Gentlemen, it is my great pleasure to introduce to you, direct from the urban wastelands, the true sound of the suburbs," Dave's voice is getting louder and louder. I look round nervously and catch Tom looking aghast.

"So strap your legs round my engines, cause baby we were born to run" I step forward thinking he had run out of steam and clichés. But no such luck,

"I have seen the future of rock and roll, and he is here tonight, so are you ready to rock?" At this point Dave punches the air with a single clenched fist before looking out at the stunned crowd, expecting a big response. But no, total silence, people stopped their drinks halfway to their mouths statuesque. I half expected some tumbleweed to blow through the middle of the room. Defeated by the wave of apathy hitting him, Dave mumbles,

"I give you Nat," before slipping off stage in the direction of the bar.

I turn off the main lights plunging the room into darkness. I place my guitar round my neck, then I hit the yellow stage light as I play the first chord. I burst straight into *Like a Rolling Stone*. My theory being I would break them in gently by starting with a Dylan number. The reaction is fairly lukewarm. One or two people wander through from the main bar. The last note is accompanied by restrained applause. I start the next number *Roxanne*, Sky looks shocked, the blood draining from her face and she sits down. As the song goes on Tom and Sue look embarrassed, sitting on a table to my left. Tom tapping his glass of barley wine nervously with his fingers, feeling out of place with his folksy new waistcoat and open-toed sandals. I finished with a flourish, coming to the front of the stage and raising my arm to play the last note I'm really starting to relax and enjoy myself. As the applause fades to silence there is an impassioned shout from the back,

"Judas!" it's Sky, she storms out. A few people laugh, I go straight into the next number. *The River* by Bruce Springsteen, Dave comes running in from the bar I can see him giving me the thumbs up. The rest of the night goes very well. By the time I'm completing my last number the back room is full. The main bar has emptied, even the rugby club crowd is lined up along the back bar. Also at one point I catch a glimpse of someone, lit only by the small amount of light coming from the main bar. He's a familiar face a man with long grey hair in a pony tail. My last number is Travis's *Driftwood* the most up-to-date number I've learnt. As the last note fades away, I hit the light switch and plunge the stage into darkness. The room erupts, clapping, whistling, people standing up, Dave rushes up to the mike,

"Ladies and Gentlemen put your hands together for... Nathan." Tom and Sue have wandered up to talk to me, everyone else is making there way to the bar or putting on their coats to go home. Tom tells me he is a little sad over my change of direction. This is Tom being angry, but he's such a nice and ineffectual man it's difficult to tell. I feel a little sorry for them, even guilty in a way. They are the sort of old couple who still holds hands and whisper sweet-nothings in each other's ears.

I see Charlie coming forward from the back of the hall. He tells me he was very impressed. He then asked if I had given any more thought to his offer. Dave is hanging around behind me listening intently to our conversation.

"Who's this then?"

"This is Charlie, the man I told you about," Dave's eyes start to light up, enthusiastically he shakes Charlie's hand,

"They call me Big Dave, drummer extraordinaire," he says playing a drum solo in mid-air as if this might get him the job. Charlie looks at me for help.

"Well it's up to you, but he is a good drummer," I say before adding,

"Of course he's totally immature and mad, but then, show me a drummer who's not" Charlie nods, and then smiles as if he's recalling a number of incidents involving drummers he's worked with.

We arrange to meet up on Sunday at the warehouse, for Dave's audition and a possible rehearsal. Charlie says goodbye, and turns to leave, Tom comes up and stops him, asking for his autograph. Dave gives me a quizzical look. I explain in a low voice it's Charlie Mullens of seventies progressive rock band *Pink Revelations*. Suddenly Dave's face drops at this news,

"Oh no we're not playing all that progressive rock shit," I smile and wave at Charlie as he goes out the door, while saying through my teeth,

"No, I shouldn't think so, I don't think all fifteen minutes of *A Lamb Lies Down on the Dark Side of the Moon* would go down too well at a wedding."

I start to pack away my gear, while Dave beats out a rhythm on the top of my amp. Colin comes through and gives me fifteen pounds, he's a bit put off by the fact that the main bar had emptied while I was playing. But he is hoping word gets round the village and brings in a few more people next week. I was just pleased that there is to be a next week. I start carrying my stuff to the van. Dave helps me with the amplifier, as we reach the van something dawns on me,

"Dave"

"What's up man," he says beating out a rhythm on the side of the van.

"Do you actually own a drum kit at the moment?" Dave stops dead right in the middle of his extensive drum solo.

"Oh! fuck!"

Twenty

If not for you,
Winter would have no spring,
Couldn't hear the robin sing,
I just wouldn't have a clue,
Anyway it wouldn't ring true,
If not for you.

(If Not For You © 1970 Big Sky Music)

It's an hour to go before kick-off and the stadium is rapidly filling up. It's going to be the biggest crowd since we moved to the new stadium. The new ground stuck between a DIY superstore and a massive office complex all faceless blue glass buildings. It's taken a few years to get used to the new place. What with its smart seats instead of concrete terrace, which flooded every time it rained, its perfect view with no steel pillars in the way of the goals. But I still have a romantic view of the old town centre ground squeezed between the old terrace houses, like it had been dropped from outer-space. All my great memories are there, the promotions, the giant killing cup games and even relegation. We need to do something so I can have some great memories of the new ground, maybe, just maybe today's the day. Graham is sitting next to me and Bob is sitting the other side (I got the OK from the doctor yesterday).

I cast my mind back to the last week as I sit and watch our team warm up with strange fluorescent training equipment.

Sasha and Paul turned up on Saturday. Bob was really pleased to see them and Sasha got all emotional, but once she could see how well Bob was, she calmed down. It was difficult to think of all we had gone through in such a short time. Now she was having to leave him again.

They had a gift for Bob, it was a skateboard helmet and elbow pads. I was a little apprehensive at first, I had put the skateboard in the shed hoping he would forget about it and in time I could dispose of it. 'But you can't wrap them in cotton wool can you' as Mum would say. Sasha made Bob promise to come and visit them in Australia, you can bring your Dad if you like, she said looking at me. Sasha gave me her e-mail address so we could keep in touch. I've only ever sent one e-mail in my life, I was told I was sent a reply but I've no idea where to look for it. The Internet is a bit of a mystery to me, I always think the kind of people on the Internet are the sort of people you wouldn't talk to in a pub. But Bob said he would use the school computer he could even download photographs and send them. Then after a lot of hugging and kissing causing Bob much protesting, they were gone. I was glad Bob had got to know his Mum, but I was still unaware that indirectly she had caused the break up of Hazel and me. I know I had let Hazel down on a couple of occasions but it was hardly my fault, (well apart from the bit about not telling her about having a son.) if I could just talk to her I could explain every thing.

Dave turned up on Sunday to the rehearsal with a drum kit. I didn't like to ask where he got it from. But it had a bands name written on the bass drum. Dave had tried to hide it with a large poster of Gareth Gates. I ask him about it, he said, it gave his foot extra power knowing he was hitting him on each beat.

We started off learning a few old Beatles numbers, *I Want to Hold Your Hand* and *Please, Please Me*. Charlie turned out to be an accomplished blues guitarist playing both bass and lead. While I tackled most of the vocals and rhythm guitar. I had forgotten what a good drummer Dave was, if a little theatrical. Charlie seemed quite happy, if not entirely at home with some of Dave's choices of tracks. Charlie was into a lot of blues and early rock and roll. Dave was into New Wave and Punk. Strangely, Charlie informed us that New Wave was proving to be quite popular at weddings. Because the Punks of 76 had grown up and their kids that were now getting married to the Buzzcocks and the Stranglers. The kids of today stood at the side and looked bemused as their parents danced to New Wave. I had done the same at my first wedding aged eight amazed as the grown ups jived to late-fifties rock and roll. It was my Aunt Jenny's. She married Dave, a real rocker with greased back hair.

As we finished the last number Mum turns up with Bob, he was immediately drawn to the large drum kit. Dave sat him on it and gave him the drumsticks. He couldn't reach the bass pedal but managed to keep a good rhythm, I was quite proud of my boy. When there was a break in proceedings, Dave tried to teach him how to twist the drum sticks in his fingers. He called me over, his eye's wide and shining, a big smile on his face,

"Dad...when I grow up I'm going to be a drummer"

"That's good son, but you can't do both," I said as I ruffled his hair. Causing him to shake his head to clear his view of the cymbals he was just about to attack.

Charlie and Dave started to pack the gear away, Dave dismantled the drum kit while Bob protested. But he turned it into a great game playing on until the last cymbal had been removed. Bob, in fits of laughter as he tried to hit it, only succeeding in rapping Dave across the knuckles.

It was then that I got out my acoustic guitar and announced that I had written a song. I was strangely nervous as I tuned the guitar. I had always found it hard to write my own songs in the past. I suppose being exposed to so much Dylan at such a young age, everything I did seemed to come out a pale imitation. But out of my recent adversity I found the words just came out, I'm not saying it's anything like Dylan when he was getting divorced and writing *Blood on the Track*s or Clapton's writing *Tears in Heaven* after his son died. But I liked it and it was the best song I'd ever written. It's a slow soulful blues song and goes like this,

LOSING YOUR SMILE
Something precious should be kept locked away,
Safe and sound out of harm.
But when I thought I had lost you my beautiful boy,
The sun grew cold and the days shorter.
But you walked out of the darkness back into the light.
Now the sun has more warmth, and days are like endless summers.
    I've got those so glad I didn't lose your smile blues,
    Say it again, I've got those so glad I didn't lose your smile blues.

When I met you I knew you were the love of my life.
They say it's better to have loved and lost.
But the pain I'm feeling now your gone I ain't so sure.
Love conquers all, but this battles far from over,
Soon I will find you again and we will make peace.
A little part of me hopes that maybe you're sad too,
I know I shouldn't think it but,
    Perhaps you got the losing your smile blues too,

Say it again, you got them losing smile blues too.
When friends and family look at me, they think I'm just the same.
But a closer look at my face, the clues are all too clear,
they do not see my inner pain, nor the tracks of my tears,
In a room full of people, I'm a lone sailor on the ocean
All the while.
  I've got the losing smile blues.
  I say it again them old losing smile blues.

I really need to find you again
Cause we need to be as one,
Everywhere I go I see your red hair so fine
I see you all the time,
Someday soon I will surely be with you again,
perhaps then when we are together forever,
  We'll never get them losing smile blues,
  I say never get them, always smiling, losing smile blues .
  Losing, losing, losing, smile blues...

As I played, Charlie and Dave stopped putting stuff away and stand in silence. I looked across at Mum and could see her eyes shining with tears as she squeezed Bob to her. When I finished Dave broke the silence with an embarrassed cough before saying,

"Yea not bad, could do with speeding up a bit." Charlie was very impressed and it was decided we could slip it in at the end of the night, keeping it as an acoustic number. Dave thought this was a good idea as it would give him a chance to get to the bar first.

Monday morning I received a frantic phone call from Colin. Apparently "Oliver and his Organ" had gone down like, well, like a limp organ at an orgy. Which had put Colin in a spot as he had booked him to do tonights New Years Eve party. I wasn't sure if the world was quite ready for the full band. So Charlie and me did the gig between us. It turned out Dave had a Big record fair in Brighton on New Years Day, so was not too unhappy about not being included. I basically did much the same set as Friday but interspersed with Charlie doing his country, blues and some early rock and roll. Then at eleven the disco took over in the run up to the New Year. I did my song, most people were very impressed, especially those who knew me, like Graham who knew what I had been through.

I was just glad to be busy on New Year's eve. If the truth be known, I hate it. It's always a time to reflect another year over and what have I achieved. Well I'm alone again, as last year. I remember working out on New Years Eve when I was eighteen that I would be thirty-nine by the 2000 millennium celebrations. This seemed such an incredible age to me then, then in the blink of an eye it was here. Now we were beginning 2002.

I was out in the car park loading the van at the stroke of twelve. As people counted down to the New Year. I stood alone in the clear frosty night staring at the stars, as less than ten feet away people kissed, cheered and wished each other Happy New Year. I suddenly felt very alone and sorry for myself. After Bob's accident it was as if I should just be grateful he was all right. It was selfish to think about me, but as time moved on and the shock of nearly loosing Bob began to fade. I began to concentrate on me again. Well... more, Hazel and me. I needed to make every effort to find out what went wrong and put it right.

So on Wednesday the 2nd of January, my first day back at work, I set off to find Hazel's office block. It's set in one of these faceless business parks, all square buildings exactly the same. (the kind of industrial park where they don't actually make anything). There's no lorries delivering or taking away the finished product to sell, no chimneys belching black smoke. All call centres and customer help lines. Where it's trendy to have the name of the company so small you have to walk right up to every building to see it. Which makes locating it hard. I remember it's called "Computer aid" or something very close, but every company feels the need to incorporate the word "computer" in their name. Eventually I find it "computer care". I park the van and get the parcel addressed to Hazel Williams. It containing six boxes of brass screws. I go through the   revolving door, into the large foyer. Its has large pot plants and a modern stainless steel fountain. A middle-aged women is sat behind a raised desk in front of a switchboard. She has her hair in a tight bun and far too much make up.

I approached the desk.

The receptionist spoke in a robotic style, while leafing through the latest copy of OK magazine.

"Computer Care, I'm sorry he's on the phone, do you wish to hold?" I lifted my parcel into her line of vision, and tried to talk. She held up a single long manicured finger, without lifting her head. I waited patiently.

"*Computer Care*, putting you through," suddenly there was a lull in the incessant calls. I jump in.

"Parcel for Hazel Williams," the lady looked up, with a look like I was something she had trodden in.

"Over there" she said gesturing with her head at a table at the end of the desk. This was not part of the plan.

"Ah! no, I need a signature," she produced a pen, her eyes still transfixed on her magazine. Showing an article called 'when celebrities pop out' showing various people bursting out of their bikinis, all taken from miles away with telephoto lenses.

"It needs to be delivered in person," with an exaggerated sigh she pushed a button on the switch board. She spoke for sometime into her mouth piece. Then informed me in her dull monotone voice.

"She's in a meeting all day, then she moves to a new office tomorrow." New office, what new office I had to think on my feet.

"Oh well I'll deliver it tomorrow at the new office, where is it?"

"I'm sorry, I'm not at liberty to tell you that. Your only choice is to leave it here." So I left it there. I know its crazy, but I had this idea that when she opened the parcel. Of two inch by size ten brass screws in our own "SCREW IT" boxes she would guess they came from me. That way at least she would know I was trying to find her.

* * * * * * * *

Several floors above me around the same time Hazel's meeting was drawing to a close. Hazel was still sat at the conference table, trying to digest what she had just been told. She was to lead a team (including Joan) to cover a new contract. At the Blue Park, the massive new office complex near the football ground. It was what she wanted, her own team and a six month contract, just enough time before she would start maternity leave. For she had decided to have the baby, well I don't think she ever had any other intention. She was just kidding herself, this was all she wanted. She would raise the baby alone, she had no close family to judge or criticize her. The closest thing to family was Joan, so she had to make her peace with Joan. From the way she had acted so far this morning it was obvious that Joan had no idea that she knew about her and Clive. She called Joan back, Joan stopped in the door way turned, closed the door and sat down opposite her at the large conference table. There was an awkward pause, then Hazel stood up,

"How could you Joan," Joan nervously fumbled with her handbag looking for her cigarettes. She found them, selected one and with a shaking hand attempted to light it.

"I never meant to hurt you," her voice breaking, this was her worse nightmare as Joan was just getting her life back together. She was seeing her grandchildren, just popping in anytime now, with no fear of meeting her! She had finished with Clive, but he still needed her at work, she had too much experience and was too good at her job to let go, the same could be said of Hazel. That's why the new contract had been ideal Clive could move both Hazel and Joan across town, while he broke in his new personal assistant.

Joan opened her heart to Hazel though tears told her everything. This was the new Joan, all her old protective walls broken down. The new soft Joan, the Joan who plays with her grandchildren. Hazel was a bit taken aback, this was a side of Joan she had not seen. She had always given her good advice, helped her make those tough decisions, like who to make redundant and who to take on. Hazel took a deep breath, she got up and moved round the table and placed a hand on her shoulder. She knew she needed Joan, not only at work but as a friend. The Clive thing, well he always got what he wanted. She had spoken to him only the once since she had left. She told him she knew about him and Joan. There was no pleading for her to come back, he was more worried about work.. It was then he told her they had got the big new contract. Hazel had know it was in the pipeline, but she couldn't believe they would get it. She turn to Joan,

"Its going to be all right Joan," Hazel said as someone started to open the door. Hazel and Joan shouted in total unison,

"Not now" the door closed before it had barely opened two inches. Clive stood the other side of the door, was that Hazel and Joan together. He stood there listening on the other side of the door, wondering if he should call security. But no, he could only hear calm voices through the closed door. He walked away, he knew they would be forever out of reach now.

Hazel told Joan of her plans to have the baby on her own. She had worked out her maternity leave then when she went back to work well, she would have plenty of time to sort that out. Joan then composed herself put on a little make up. The two ladies left to do lunch. If I had still been in the car park I guess I would have seen them. I could have spoken to Hazel. But by that time I was in the new Blue park delivering boxes of nails to a nearly completed office block.

So I tried to console myself with the fact that I had this big game to look forward to. I was sitting with twenty thousand people and still feeling so lonely. Suddenly the theme from *2001* blasts out over the stadium's PA system braking my thoughts of the last week. The excitement in the crowd builds up. I can see the teams gathering in the tunnel. I take Bob's hand and give it a squeeze, he slides forward on his seat preparing to stand up. Then the intro to Robbie William's *Let Me Entertain You*. This is the signal for the teams to come out and for us to stand up. Blue and white balloons fill the sky, Bob jumps up and pats one.The stadium is a mass of colour and noise. Our captain runs to the stand then races up the touch line as we chant his name, this is all part of his routine. Then someone catches my eye. As the crowd begins to settle down and return to their seats. I can see a small boy in Liverpool kit making his way to the centre circle. He's the team mascot for the day.

It's Sam. I'm shouting to Bob but he can't hear me, so I lift him up. Sam has tubes coming from his nose, his mum wheels an oxygen tank along side him. By now Sam has made his way to the centre circle with considerable help from his Mum. A Liverpool player comes up to him and places a ball at his feet (it's only Michael Owen). Sam manages to kick the ball weakly to Michael, then he hands the ball to his Mum to hold. The vast majority of the crowd are oblivious to all this. He makes his way back to the far stand with his Mum and Michael. Michael pats him on the head and rejoins his team mates. The fans on the far side obviously aware of how ill he is applaud loudly. Sam waves to the crowd, I smile to myself as he disappears out of view.

The game, we lost 3-1. But I was glad for Sam's sake that they won. Shit I'm sorry I don't mean that. I've supported this club all my life; I could never think that. But it's history now. We can concentrate on the league now. God! I hate when people say that. So no happy memories to put in the scrapbook in my mind.

Twenty One

"No reason to get excited" the thief, he kindly spoke,
There are many here among us who feel that life is but a joke.
But you and I, we've been through that, and this is not our fate.
So let us not talk falsely now, the hour is getting late.

(All Along the Watchtower © 1968 renewed 1996 Dwarf Music)

January slipped into February and the days got slightly longer. I threw myself into the band, Charlie was well known and had arranged several bookings through word of mouth. The only draw back with weddings were the late nights that meant Bob couldn't stay over at the weekends sometimes. But we were earning good money, two or three hundred pounds for a big wedding. I was seriously thinking of giving up work and trying to manage with a part time job. I had started giving guitar lessons at Bob's school, word had got round the village and this had led to me giving some private lessons. So far the band hadn't interfered with football, I had been lucky with bookings falling on away games, but when we did have home games it meant a mad rush from the game to get to the evening reception. My team was going well, we had gone on an unbeaten run after the cup game. Perhaps we were concentrating on the league now. Anyway we were into a play-off place. All this helped me keep my mind off other things, the only other thing that really mattered was Hazel. I had called at her old office a couple more times. I sat in the car park in the vain hope that she might just turn up. The last time the horrible receptionist walked past she spotted me just sitting in my van, she gave me a funny look. she then went to talk to the security man on the gate. I pulled away as he made his way over, I'm sure she must think I'm some kind of stalker. After that I went round to Thames Wharf in the vain hope I might find some information. I parked the van down the road and walked up hiding in the bushes (God! perhaps I was turning into a stalker)

Clive did turn up with a young girl, very young, she must be his niece, I don't know why they drew the curtains in the middle of the day. After that I gave up, resigning myself to the fact that I might never see her again.

The reception tonight was your standard over the top do. The same old mix of grandparents, bored looking teenagers and tired fretful toddlers. Our live band at least impressed the teenagers, having been brought up on a diet of boy bands and manufactured pop idols. I never quite understood how they got away with calling themselves a band. A band to me was a group of people who could play instruments, and would actually breakup due to musical differences! Who were allowed to have spots, be slightly over weight, take illegal substances on a regular basis, drink too much and maybe even write their own songs.

We had been booked to play the night reception, it was held in an old mill in the next village to mine, which was good as I didn't have to rush from the match. I was in a good mood, we had won again this afternoon assuring our place in the end of season play-offs. We were an hour into our set, playing a number requested by the groom *Everything You Do Is Magic* by the Police. The bride and groom were dancing with their two young children. This seemed a bit of a big do for a couple that had obviously been living together for sometime. But why should I care, I would get two hundred quid for the night. After this track we were due to have a fifteen minute break. We finish the number, people drift off the dance floor back to their tables. We put on a CD to play through the amps in our absence and make our way to the bar. Charlie, Dave and I gathered in the corner of the bar. Then a lady comes up to me, I'm pretty sure it was the bride's mother. I had seen her dancing with what must be her grandchildren earlier.

"Nathan" I was surprised that she knew my name.

"Could I speak to you alone" Charlie and Dave exchanged looks.

"Is there a problem," Charlie said stepping forward, as he dealt with all the bookings. He had taken the mantle of band leader, which didn't bother me I was quite happy not to have the responsibility.

"No, No its nothing to do with the band," she turned back to me,

"This way," she said pointing at the door to the gardens. I glance at Dave and Charlie raising my eyebrows as I go past. We walked down a corridor. The working of the mill could be seen through a glass panel, a mass of running and foaming water. At the end of the corridor were the toilets, (which were a welcome relief after all, that rushing water). I pause outside the men's,

"Do you mind?" I say placing a hand on the door.

"No, I'll meet you outside," she said pushing the last door open. I did what I had to do and made my way outside. Spotlights lit up the garden and mill pool. The night was clear but still quite chilly for the end of March. A giggle drew my attention down the garden. A couple was just disappearing into the unlit part of the garden, it looked like the best man and one of the maids-of-honour. The woman ignored this and turned to me.

"Its Nathan, right, you played at the *Horse and Groom*, all that folk stuff."

"Yes," I said still a little bemused, I had no idea who this woman was or what she wanted. Unless she was after booking me, no can't be that.

"You're a friend of Hazels." At this I become more interested.

"Yes, I was, why what's happened? How is she?"

"She's fine, I'm Joan, Hazel dragged me along to hear you one night"

Joan went on to tell me how Hazel was and what she was doing now, she also explained how Hazel had followed me the night she was stood up, because of Sasha visit. Only to see me going in my flat with another women. I had to think

"What women, I can't think"

"Hazel said She had long hair, in like... dreadlocks"

"Oh! Sasha" I said looking pleased with myself, but this didn't seem to please Joan.

"Oh she's my son's mum" yeah right now that sounded better, talking about digging a hole. I quickly try to rectify things.

"Arh no, well strictly speaking she is Bob's mum but there's nothing in it, I haven't seen her for over five years. She's been in Australia. I said sounding more and more desperate and echoing as I disappeared down the hole I had dug!

"She only came to see Bob." I bite my bottom lip while looking at my watch, my time was running out, I was due back on stage.

"Look please, I need to see you later, I can explain everything," she smiled and gave me a gentle push,

"Go... go...after all, it's me that's paying for you, I want to get my moneys worth, I'll see you in the bar after," so I went back inside, Charlie and Dave were ready to go. I jumped up and slipped my guitar strap over my head.

"You OK" Charlie said.

"Never better" I say, then I nod at Dave. He counts in,

"One ...two... three," hitting his drumsticks together we break into the Stones *Satisfaction*.

Joan was true to her word and met me in the bar after our set. Her daughter and new son-in-law had left for their honeymoon in Majorca, with their two kids in tow twenty minutes earlier. After that the guests had started saying their good-byes and drifting away while waiting for the mini-bus booked to take people back to town. So hardly anyone was left as I sang my new song. Only one person listened intently and that was Joan, relaxing after her busy and emotionally draining day. Perched on a barstool while smoking a cigarette.

We completed our set and I made my apologies to the others, leaving them to pack up the gear. Joan had got me a drink and we sat at the bar. She asked me what I intended to do. I explained how I had made every effort to try and make contact with Hazel. That I was truly upset when we broke up and didn't really know why. Joan told me about Hazel's split with Clive, that she was living with a friend now. She told me about the new contract and the fact that they had moved office. She told me where, I couldn't believe it, the big new office complex next to the football ground. I go past it most days in the course of my work. Joan told me Hazel was upset I had emitted to tell her I had a son. I tried in vain to explain why I did this to her (I don't think Joan understood this, but then as I tried to convince her I couldn't understand it myself). I told her I thought it would scare her off and as time went on it became harder and harder to tell her.

There was a pause as she explored the inside of her handbag trying to find her lighter. I gazed into my whisky glass rotating the ice slowly. She lit a cigarette and blew smoke up towards the wooden beams.

"Look," Joan said, biting her top lip, searching for the right words to tell me something.

"What is it?" I asked leaning forward. Joan took another drag on her cigarette and gazed at the end.

"There's no easy way of telling you this, but if you really want to get back with Hazel you need to know this," I drained my glass, ice cubes and all.

"I do, I do," I say with a mouth full of ice .

"Well... Hazel's having your baby!" I choke, spitting an ice cube across the table Joan catches it and places it quickly in the ashtray.

"I don't know if it makes any difference, but if it does, then I'll say nothing to Hazel and let you get on with your life," I take a swig from my empty glass, God! I could do with another drink. I glance up at the bar; it's deserted, tea towels have been placed on the beer pumps.

"Do you mind if we go outside,"

"No," Joan says gathering her bag and standing up. Once outside I light a joint. The spotlights have been switched off so we stay near the mill on the bridge over the stream. We're both silent. I go to offer Joan the joint. She smiles but raises her hand in refusal.

I take a last puff inhaling deeply before letting the sweet smelling smoke out into the cool night air. I flick the tab into the jet black water below, it glides on the surface towards the roaring white water of the mill wheel. There is no escape. Like me drawn to Hazel, there was no fighting it, a conclusion was inevitable

"So," Joan says turning to face me.

"I love Hazel,I'm crazy about her, I want to be with her and our baby," Joan looked at me intently,

"I believe you, but if you let Hazel down," her voice trailed off, I knew what she meant. Joan went on,

"Look, I'll see Hazel tomorrow, tell her what you've told me," Joan says reaching inside her bag and bringing out a pen.

"Can you make it to Hazel's office on Monday say around one at the restaurant at the front," I recall the restaurant is a stylish round building in front of the main office block.

"Yeah, should be no problem"

"Give me your mobile number, I'll talk to her tell her everything you've told me, test the waters to see if she wants to try again. If she does I'll get her there and you can surprise her," Joan said smiling at her plan,

"I'll text you, but if you don't hear from me, you must promise never to try and contact her," I nodded my head, but deep down I couldn't promise never to try to see Hazel again or my child. I gave her my number and she wrote it on her cigarette box,

"Thanks for playing, I'm glad you've dropped the folk stuff." At that Joan turned to leave, I caught hold of her arm gently,

"Please, do your best"

"I will," she said as she disappeared through the door, for some reason I really believed she would.

* * * * * * * *

Bob is sat at the small table in the flat, he is doing yet another drawing to go on my fridge. The telly is on with the sound turned down, GMTV is on. Bob has decided to draw the Millennium stadium in Cardiff. I've been explaining that if we keep playing the way we are we would be in the play-off finals. So I describe in detail the layout and unique design of the stadium. How it has a slide-off roof (I explain this is so God is able see us play).

I've taken Bob out of school so we can go and see Hazel. He asked if it was a Baker day, I told him no, this was purely a Nathan day. I received a text from Joan early this morning,

Good news Nat, she 4gives U,
I will get her to canteen @ 1.
Rest up to U.
Joan.

I'm standing in the kitchen drinking coffee and eating toast, with lemon curd on - my favourite. I glance briefly at the silent television screen, someone catches my eye, I know I've seen her but can't for the life of me think where. Then the camera pulls back, I leap forward frantically search for the remote control. It's the girl with the piercings from the shop next door. I can't find the remote, so I move to the telly, I have no idea what you touch on the telly to turn the volume up. I press a flap at the front it drops down revealing various buttons. I press them all, the sound, colour and contrast all change. Then an orange coloured presenter in dark contrast speaks,

"So if you have a lottery ticket lying around, purchased from this shop for the mid-week draw around last November, check it out, it could be worth 3.5 million" I looked straight at the fridge, straight at Hazel's lottery ticket, the ticket that has sat on my fridge all these months. It almost seams to leap off the fridge in a cartoon-like state. The presenter goes on, "But don't leave it too long you've only got till mid-night tonight" I didn't check the numbers, I knew. I removed it and sat down in shock. Bob was a little bemused by my behaviour, but he had just completed his drawing and was glad of the extra space on my fridge, he busied himself rearranging his magnetic letters to hold his latest masterpiece up. A beautiful picture of a red stadium, a square roof open, with large impossibly out of scale blue and white footballers.

Then it hits me, this changes everything. I'm off to meet Hazel to convince her she needs to be with me. Not because I can offer her an expensive life style, luxury flat and flashy cars. Solely because I love her and I believe she loves me. How can I hand her the lottery ticket. Surely there is absolutely no way it will cross her mind that I'm trying to get back together purely for love not money.

Who would have thought one small ticket could have such an influence on two peoples lives. I mean without it, Hazel and I would never be together. I mean I might have, just might have plucked up enough courage to walk out of the shop and approach her. I might have fought back nerves, I may have dug deep in the recesses of my mind (or back issues of *Fighting Fit at Forty* for suitable chat-up lines). Then delivered it, Hazel may have been completely vulnerable, susceptible and stupid enough to have fallen for it. So there you have it, there is a minor, small if only atom size chance that we may have got together without the simple twist of fate of the flying lottery ticket. I need to think, I need to go to my thinking place,

"Right then Bob," Bob looks up from his drawing,

"I think we'll go and see Grampa." He knew what this meant and eagerly clambered down from his chair. He went to the kitchen and opened the cupboard under the sink. He removed a red bucket containing a scrubbing brush and a garden trowel.

We pull up at the church gates, behind the tall church spire the sky is black and heavy with rain. We make our way through the church on the crunchy gravel path. Bob is carrying the bucket, we stop at the outside tap, provided so people can water the flowers in the first few painful weeks before the wreathes and grieving fades.

Behind the main graveyard is a sort of overflow graveyard separated by a three foot high flint wall. A peaceful sanctuary surrounded by tall trees on one side and beautiful country views on the other. I help Bob turn on the tap, he tries to carry the full bucket but it's too heavy. I take it and he carries the trowel and scrubbing brush. Bob runs ahead through the gap in the wall turning right. He moves along the wall, I can just see the top of his head, he is checking the slate memorial plaques set in the wall.

The eighth one along belongs to my Dad, at the base of the wall a small box is buried containing his ashes. A hopelessly small, inappropriate box, but I know this isn't my Dad, not his spirit and certainly not his legacy. It's in me, who I am, how I think and see things, how I care, the passion within me. I've started to see it most in my son's eyes.

Bob busies himself with the scrubbing brush, cleaning the moss and algae off the slate. Tracing the gold letters with his tiny fingers.

Bill Peterson 1939-1995
May you build a ladder to the stars
And climb on every rung
Forever young

I work on the small flower bed below the wall, digging out weeds with the small trowel. Soon we've completed our task and stand back in silence to view our work. I suggest to Bob that he go to the bottom of the field to pick some of the daffodils I have seen there. So we can place them in the vase, (the others we can take to give to Hazel). So Bob wanders down the field with his empty bucket in his hand. As I watch him go I see the black cloud is nearly upon us. I pull the crumpled lottery ticket from my pocket, I bend down and touch the cold slate,

"What am I going to do Dad? if I tell her I'll lose her, if I don't possibly the same"

At this exact moment the loudest clap of thunder cracks right overhead, making me jump, I drop the lottery ticket, the wind gusts furiously. Then Bob screams, without a thought I turn running towards him. I can see the line of torrential rain moving across the fields like a wall of glass ready to engulf him. I reach him, pick him up in one movement and run. He's shaking, tears running down his face. The rain is falling so hard it stings my face, I pull Bob in close to my chest. I run through the graveyard, half way down the gravel path Bob feels safe enough to pull his head clear, over my shoulder he waves saying,

"Bye Grampa, don't get too wet"

I reach the van, put the heater fan on full as it's fighting to clear the windscreen of the condensation, because of our soaking clothes.

It's at this point I realize I've dropped the lottery ticket.

I wait while I try to settle Bob down, after a painfully long time, eventually he is relatively calm. I explain I've dropped something and have to go back, I wrap Bob in my coat, leave the engine on, slowly warming the cab. The rain is still beating down on the windscreen. I run through the graveyard again, by the time I'm back at dad's grave, my shirt has stuck to my back and my jeans are heavy with water, I'm soaked through. I search the ground frantically for the lost ticket, the ground is strewn with small cards from flowers, fondest memories and gone but not forgotten. But to no avail. I widen my search area, even to the point of going to the low wall right at the bottom of the field. I pull myself up and look over it, but it's no good.

I trudge back up the field my eye's still fixed to the ground for anything that looks remotely like a £3.5 million lottery ticket. Eventually I stand exhausted in front of Dad's stone, I run my fingers through my wet hair. I resign myself to the fact, that any worries and misconceptions that Hazel may have as to my motive of getting back together has now been removed. I only hope she didn't happen to catch the report about a certain unclaimed lottery ticket that morning.

I hold Bob's hand tightly as we stand at the side of the busy dual carriageway. I look at the huge blue office block, its a large horseshoe shaped building around ten stories high. In the middle is the circular building, the restaurant. It was raised above the ground and has a small verandah circling the outside with tables and chairs set out. The sun was shining but the wind still had a last a bite of winter in it, certainly not alfresco weather, despite this there was still three or four hardy souls trying to be continental. Clutching their prawn cocktails and side salad to their plates.

Bob is in his school uniform, black shoes, white socks, grey shorts and a bright red sweatshirt with the school name on the front. He looks very smart, how could anyone not fail to fall immediately in love with him and want to restart their relationship with his lying dad.

Bob and I went off to do my deliveries at breakneck speed this morning before parking in the football stadium car park and walking down. I tried to explain to Bob what we were doing here, but in truth I didn't really know myself. We had been standing here for five minutes watching a steady stream of people moving from the main building the short distance to the near packed restaurant. The stream had been increasing the nearer it got to one o'clock. Suddenly a large group came out of the revolving doors,

I catch a glimpse of red hair blowing in the spring wind. Then a lorry blocks my view and by the time it had passes us the group have reached the door and disappeared.

I led Bob to the pelican crossing, let him press the button and impatiently I wait for the green man to flash. We crossed the road and climbed the steps to the front of the canteen. We start to work our way round the outside verandah. It was difficult to see in clearly, due to the tinted glass and low bright sunshine. I reached the first window and put my face close to the glass cupping my hands to cut out the light. Bob looked up at me and copied me,

"What does she look like Dad," Bob said

"She's got lots of red hair, she's beautiful, very beautiful," I said staring dreamily into the distance.

"Right," Bob said moving on to the next window a small boy with a mission now. We moved from window to window carefully scrutinizing the occupants of each booth, much to their consternation. We had worked our way round to the back, I was beginning to think I had been mistaken. Then suddenly Bob caught sight of her he started tugging my jacket frantically while keeping his face tight to the window. I gave him the "thumbs up".

Joan was sat nearest the window Hazel was next to her, while opposite sat two distinguished looking businessmen in expensive suits. They were all deep in conversation.

Now there was the small matter to trying to attract her attention. I looked down at Bob he was pulling his ugly face by putting his fingers in his mouth pulling it as wide as he could and rolling his eyes. Due to his height his head only just appeared above the table. I looked at him and smiled, and started to do the same. Then Joan glanced out of the window and jumped back in shock. She then elbowed Hazel raising her eyebrows in our direction. Hazel looked from me to Bob, she then mouthed "Go away" while gesturing with her hand. I pointed at her and mouthed the words "I love you". By now the two businessmen had been distracted by the goings on. Joan was now pushing Hazel encouraging her to leave the booth. I could see her stand up and making her apologies to the now amused businessmen. Bob and I made our way to the front of the building. The automatic door swished open and Hazel stepped through the doorway, the spring sunshine lighting up her face and the breeze scattering her hair, she had never looked lovelier.

"What are you doing here?" Hazel said trying to sound annoyed.

"We've come to see you," I said, she looked from me to Bob and seemed to grow calmer.

"This must be your mysterious son," Hazel said crouching down so she was face to face with Bob I put my hand reassuringly on his shoulder, he looked up at me, wondering if things were going well. The wind had blown Bob's blond hair in his eyes, Hazel moved a hand slowly towards him, and Bob pulled away momentarily thinking she was going to ruffle it. But with one ever so gentle finger she removed the hair from his eyes. Bob decided this was the time to give her one of his much-practised sweetest smiles Hazel stood up again and looked at me.

"He's very handsome, Joan's told me all about his accident and everything, I still don't understand why you kept him secret, why would you think it was such a big deal?"

"I don't really know myself, it just started and as it went on it just got harder and harder to tell you, thing got very complicated," I tried to change the subject,

"Anyway, how are you?" I said looking at Hazel's small but perfectly formed bump. Hazel pulled her coat together,

"Fine, fine" she said, a little fluster. I had so many questions I wanted to fire at her. So many things I had thought of since Joan had told me on Saturday. So many plans and dreams if thing worked out. I could give up work to look after the baby, just doing my gigs at weekends. We could move back with mum, we would be a proper family, I had it all worked out. But I knew now wasn't the time. She obviously had made her own plans and up until twenty-four hour ago that didn't include me.

People were trying to go in and out the door, every time we move the automatic doors hissed open, letting a blast of cold wind into the canteen. Much to the annoyance of the diners inside. So we moved down the steps out of the way.

"Well do you want to see me again," I said, Hazel smiled and looked down at Bob,

"Only if you promise to bring your chaperone," she glanced behind her at the canteen, a small crowd had gathered around the doorway, I could see Joan and the two businessmen, along with several people pressed up against the glass,

"Look I really have to go," having just found her again I didn't want to let her go so soon,

"I...I really, I want to see you're all right," I moved towards her, she met me halfway we held each other close. Bob covered his eyes and made a noise ....ugh!

Hazel and me were oblivious to this as we kissed. The crowd behind us cheered. The wind gusted again her hair blew haphazardly around her face, bits of litter swirled around us Hazel smiled perhaps remembering a windy November night. We broke apart and she spoke to Bob,

"I'll see you again Bob, look after your Dad make sure he doesn't do anything stupid,"

Then she turned, went up the steps stopping briefly at the top to wave. Then she went through the door and hugged Joan. I stood with a silly grin on my face, then Bob tugged my jacket,

"Did it go Okay Dad? Do you think she liked me?"

"Oh! Yes son who couldn't like you, come on I think someone deserves a McDonalds," I said ruffling his hair, I knew he loved it when I did that.

We had only just started our ice cream, when Hazel texted me.

Twenty Two

Oh, can't you see that you were born to stand by my side
And I was born to be with you, you were born to be my bride,
You're the other half of what I am, you're the missing piece
And I love you more than ever with that love that doesn't cease.

(Wedding Song © 1973 Ram's Horn Music)

The Registry Office was full of close friends and family. The Registrar instructed everyone to stand. I glanced behind me, Hazel stood there in a cream low cut dress and large rimmed hat with lace over the front. She held baby Rachel in her arms, she was six weeks old. I can't remember her birth weight exactly, men never can, but it was a lot more than Bob's. He had wanted to call his sister Kylie but we managed to convince him it wasn't such a good idea. I had to break the chain of silly names.

I felt a bead of sweat run down the side of my head, it was a warm October day, we were having a bit of an Indian summer. I took a deep breath. The music started, I looked at Graham, he was really smart, and I had done a good job in choosing his suit and tie. Quinn laid at his feet a large cream ribbon round his neck. Mum appeared in the doorway and everyone turned to look. I looked at Bob standing next to her, he was having trouble with his shirt and bow tie, running his finger round the inside of his collar trying to stop it rubbing his neck. In his other hand he held a red satin cushion with two gold rings secured by ribbons.

Oh! you thought it was Hazel and me? Well it's still very much on the cards, but it's not very rock and roll is it, well that's what I tell people.

It's Mum and Graham getting married. I was as surprised as you were, I had no idea, I mean I knew they were seeing a lot of each other, lots of trips to bingo. But I didn't think love was blossoming in between "two little ducks" and "legs eleven". Mum had a talk to me about Dad, I understood, she said how he would always be her prince charming, the love of her life. But this was more about friendship, growing old together and looking after each other.

Hazel and me, we moved into Mum's house, now Mum was getting married and moving in with Graham. The plan was going well, as soon as Hazel finished her maternity leave I would leave work and look after Rachel. Hazel had always planned to go back to work, I would still do my gigs at the weekend and a few guitar lesson around the village.

The band, it was still going well, we were getting more and more gigs. We have even made a CD, which we sell at our gigs. My song is on there, (track 12) it's also been included on a compilation CD made up of local bands. Dave did tell me that he heard my song played on Radio Two the other day, but I think it was just one of his wind-ups. We were doing the reception tonight at the *House of Gloom*, free of charge of course, but I planned to get a round of drinks for the band out of Graham.

Football; we reach the division two play-off final. I took Bob to Cardiff as promised. But we lost; supporting a team is like that. Your life may be going great, then football goes and kicks you in the bollocks. I was probably happier than at any time in my life. But we couldn't just win to put the icing on the cake oh no. The same thing happened the year Dad was dying and Bob had just been born so ill. We won the Division Two championship, all this tragedy was going on at home, yet my team were playing the best football ever.

In our home program after the big Liverpool game I read that a few days after his big game Sam had died. I felt sad, very sad, especially having to explain this to Bob. But in a way I was glad he fulfilled his lifelong wish, however short that life was. Most people slip into old age having never achieved their greatest ambition. I remember when I spoke to him he had total belief he would achieve his.

Oh I nearly forgot, Sky, she only went and won the lottery, only just claimed it in time. Left the ticket in a winter coat and only found it when she saw the bit on breakfast telly. Anyway she gave half to some local donkey sanctuary and then went off to live in a hippie commune in Ibiza. She's paid for Tom and Sue to come out and see her a couple of times. According to them she's never mentioned me, I guess Sky never forgave me for going electric.

* * * * * * * *

Anyway the service all goes very well, Bob doesn't drop the rings,

Quinn didn't bark and no one cried, apart from Rachel and me. At the end Mum led Graham outside. I went to move, but I became aware that everyone else was standing still and seemed to be focused on me. Then the Registrar spoke,

"Please remain where you are for the next wedding," I turned to Hazel mouthing 'what's going on,' she lifted the lace from her face revealing a wicked grin. Behind her, Mum came back in and gently took baby Rachel from her. Bob standing next to her, beaming from ear to ear, his cushion replenished with two new gold rings. Behind him were Dave and Charlie. Dave was even wearing a suit, slightly too small but still a suit.

The Registrar continued,

"Please stand," I stood up still puzzled by what was going on, Hazel stood next to me, took my hand and gently squeezed it.

The Registrar spoke again,

"We are gathered here today for the wedding of Nathan King Cole Peterson and Hazel Williams."

THE START

Order Form

I wish to order .... copies/copy of Just the Ticket at £5.00 ea

Name ....

Address...

....

....

Post Code ....

Tel No. ....

Email ....

I enclose a cheque/PO for £ .... + £1.50p&p

Please make cheque payable to D.S. Terry

If you require a signed copy (for future investment/sale on ebay)
please write message here

....

....

....

Please feel free to visit my Web site:
www.justtheticket.org.uk

Email: terry@25southbanks.freeserve.co.uk